AMISH
SWEET SHOP

BOOKS BY EMMA MILLER

Plain Murder
Plain Killing
Plain Dead
Plain Missing
Plain Confession

BOOKS BY LAURA BRADFORD

Portrait of a Sister
Death in Advertising
30 Second Death
And Death Goes to . . .

BOOKS BY MARY ELLIS

Living in Harmony
Sunset in Old Savannah
Love Comes to Paradise
A Little Bit of Charm
A Plain Man

The
AMISH
SWEET SHOP

EMMA MILLER
LAURA BRADFORD
MARY ELLIS

KENSINGTON BOOKS
www.kensingtonbooks.com

KENSINGTON BOOKS are published by

Kensington Publishing Corp.
119 West 40th Street
New York, NY 10018

All Kensington titles, imprints, and distributed lines are available at special quantity discounts for bulk purchases for sales promotion, premiums, fund-raising, and educational or institutional use.

Special book excerpts or customized printings can also be created to fit specific needs. For details, write or phone the office of the Kensington Sales Manager: Kensington Publishing Corp., 119 West 40th Street, New York, NY 10018. Attn. Sales Department. Phone: 1-800-221-2647.

ISBN-13: 978-1-4967-1860-0
ISBN-10: 1-4967-1860-7
First Kensington Trade Paperback Printing: January 2019

ISBN-13: 978-1-4967-1862-4 (ebook)
ISBN-10: 1-4967-1862-3 (ebook)
Kensington Electronic Edition: January 2019

10 9 8 7 6 5 4 3 2 1

Printed in the United States of America

Contents

The Sweetest Courtship

EMMA MILLER

Chapter 1

"Jacob, you really needn't look so sour." Clara glanced at her only son and then tugged on her black prayer *kapp,* adjusting it until it was just right.

"I'm not sour." He frowned as he poured sugar into the kettle on the old iron wood stove he'd converted to propane gas. No one would say Beechy's Sweets wasn't modern.

The entire kitchen in the back of the candy shop smelled of chocolate, a rich, earthy aroma as pleasing as Clara had ever smelled in her fifty-eight years of life. It was a scent that she associated with contentment, if not happiness, because while her life had not turned out as she had thought it would, it was still a good life, a blessed life. And her greatest blessing was her son, her only child, her only tangible evidence of the beloved husband she once had.

"I'm not sour," Jacob repeated, reaching for a long-handled wooden paddle he'd fashioned in his own wood shop for just this task. "I just think you're wasting your time with these interviews. I don't need any help here." He stirred the kettle with greater vigor than necessary. "We do this together, *Mam*. You and I."

Clara harrumphed. "We won't be doing it together, you and I, while I'm in Indiana with Sadie and the little one. I could be gone three weeks, longer if there are complications."

Her mouth twitched into a smile at the thought of her upcoming trip. Her niece was expecting her first baby soon and when Clara's youngest sister said she wouldn't be able to help after the baby was born, not with nine little ones still at home, Clara jumped at the opportunity to go. She loved babies and she loved an adventure and traveling alone to Indiana would certainly be one.

"You can't run the cash register, wait on customers, and make the fudge," Clara pointed out, smoothing her apron as she checked the clock on the wall. She hoped the first applicant of the day would be prompt, otherwise Jacob would be ready to cross the young woman off the list without even giving her an opportunity to interview. "This is our finest year yet, with so many orders for Valentine's Day." She smiled at him. "You make the best fudge in Lancaster County. Everyone says so. Your secret recipe is the key, I tell them."

Jacob continued to stir the bubbling fudge. Most candy makers used a thermometer, but not her son. He went by the feel of the mixture of butter, cocoa, and sugar as he brought it to a boil. One minute too long, or too short, and the whole pot of fudge would be headed for Sam Troyer's pigs.

"Which is why I don't need any help," Jacob continued, his frown not budging. "You hire a girl to work here and the secret won't be a secret much longer, will it?"

Clara studied her Jacob for a moment, a bittersweet smile on her lips. He looked so much like his father, God rest her Matthew's soul. Jacob was a handsome man of thirty-six, tall and slender with dark hair and a smile, when he dared share it, that could bring light to a room.

Clara's Matthew had only been a few years older than Jacob was now when he'd passed suddenly. She and Jacob had tried running the farm alone after that, but there was too much work, not enough time and with economic bad times, well . . . they'd found themselves at risk of losing the house and their sixty acres. It had been Jacob, barely into his twenties at the time, who had come up with the idea of selling the candy Clara made for friends on special occasions. Mostly they made fudge, a recipe Jacob had tinkered with over time. First, they had prepared it in their kitchen in their farmhouse, selling it at farmer's markets and such. In a year's time, they were bringing in more income from the candy than their farm. Then, five years ago, they'd taken a chance, sold a portion of their land to the Amish farmer next door, and bought a little house on Main Street in Bluebird. Bluebird was barely a town, more just a crossroad in the midst of thousands of acres of farmland and woodland, but tourists bound for Lancaster passed through it every day. The sales they made in their little store, plus the orders Jacob received from several shops in Lancaster on Englisher holidays, were enough to keep Clara and Jacob comfortable. She and her son had taken a tragedy and made sweets out of lemons. And it was a good life. Her one wish, however, before she died, was to see her son wed and God willing, with children of his own. Grandchildren to keep Clara in her dotage.

The bell on the front door jingled and Clara reached for the notebook where she was keeping notes on all the job applicants. "*Ach,* our first interview of the morning." She threw up her hands in excitement and then pushed through the swinging doors that led from the kitchen into the shop.

"We don't need to hire anyone," Jacob shouted after her.

Clara let the doors swing shut behind her, hoping her son's

voice hadn't carried. "Good morning," she greeted. "You're right on time." Five minutes early, in fact, she noted. She liked this young lady already. "Rose Bontrager, I'm guessing? I'm Clara."

The young woman who was gazing through the glass at the candy counter turned to Clara. "*Ya*, Rose, that's me." She smiled a smile that Clara thought might be one of the prettiest, most genuine she'd even seen.

Rose slipped out of her heavy wool cloak. "It's so warm and cozy in here. It feels wonderful. And the smell." She inhaled deeply. "Amazing. It's so nice to meet you, Clara." She tugged on one string of her black bonnet. "My cousin Mary told me you were hiring."

"*Ya*, Mary Byler married to John Junior Byler, right? A nice girl. Junior cuts our meadow when it gets too high."

"She thought I might be suited to the job," Rose explained.

The two women stood there in the middle of the candy shop looking at each other for a long moment, sizing each other up, and then Clara made a clicking sound between her teeth. "I suppose we'll see about that, won't we?"

Rose gave a nervous laugh, glanced at the floor, and then at Clara again. "I'm sorry, I'm just a little nervous. New to town. And I've never interviewed for a job before."

"No need to be nervous. You can hang your cloak and bonnet there," she told Rose, pointing to the pegs on the wall Jacob had added for just that purpose.

Clara watched Rose hang her outer garments. Rose was small and slender, but not so slender as to seem weak or sickly. And pretty, very pretty, but not so pretty so as to be at risk for suffering from *hochmut*. A woman too prideful of her looks could be difficult to live with. Better that she has a sweet disposition. Though Jacob did like a pretty face.

"Come, sit with me," Clara invited, waving her to a little table Jacob had brought from the barn at home. He'd whitewashed it and added darling little mismatched chairs that he'd painted to match. Above the table, on the wall, Clara had added a pastoral painting of an Amish farmyard surrounded by the rolling hills of Lancaster County planted in alfalfa hay. The nook was a place for customers to sit and have a taste of their sweets, or just relax for a moment on their way to or from Lancaster. "Tell me a little bit about yourself, Rose."

The young woman, who looked to be about thirty, slid into the chair across from Clara and folded her hands.

Rose had told the truth when she said she was nervous about the interview, but she pushed on because she wanted this job. She wanted this opportunity and she was a woman who always tried to do her best, whether it was making a batch of applesauce or trying to impress one of the most respected elders in the town where her cousin resided. "Well . . . I worked in an orchard once. My uncle got me the job. I can run a cash register. I'm good with numbers," she said, trying not to feel flustered. It wasn't really the Amish way to talk about one's self. "And . . . and I'm good with Englishers. A lot of your customers must be Englishers."

"No, no, no. Tell about *yourself*, Rose." Clara stared intently at her from behind round, wire-frame eyeglasses. "How old will you be come your next birthday?"

Rose pressed her lips together, trying not to smile. An odd question for a job interview, but just as her cousin had promised, she had liked Clara Beechy the first moment she set eyes on her. The older woman was short and sturdy and chubby, with a twinkle in her nutmeg eyes that immediately made Rose feel comfortable.

She'd almost chickened out this morning and not come for the interview. While she had that little bit of experience working in an orchard years ago, an Amish woman of her age didn't usually seek a job outside her home. Of course, that was because she should have had a husband and children to attend to.

It had been her cousin's suggestion that she apply for the job, to get out of the house and meet others because not only Englishers came to Beechy's Sweets, but Amish, too.

Rose met Clara's gaze. "I . . . I'll be thirty-one come May Day."

"Perfect!" Clara declared, opening a little calico-covered notebook and removing a pen from behind her ear. "Parents both living, *ya*?" She glanced up. "Both healthy?"

Another odd question. But now that Rose was here, she realized how much she wanted this job. The little shop was darling. It looked as homey and welcoming as her mother's kitchen back home in Delaware. And it smelled of earthy chocolate, sweet vanilla, and . . . happiness. She made eye contact with Clara. "Both living, *ya*. And healthy. My father still works his farm. A hundred and forty acres. With the help of my eldest brother. *Mam* is in good health. She cares for *Dat*'s mother, and I have two little brothers and a little sister unmarried and still at home."

"And how many children did she have?" Clara looked up, her pen poised over her notebook. "I mean . . . how many siblings do you have? All healthy as well?"

Rose laughed, unable to help herself, and picked a bit of fuzz from her sleeve. She'd changed her dress twice, first putting on the blue, then the green, then the blue again. Then she debated whether or not to wear an apron. In the end, she'd left the starched white apron hanging on her bedroom door. Surely Clara and her son were looking for a modern woman, a backward girl wouldn't be able to deal with Englisher customers, would she? "I have six brothers and five sisters. *Ya*, all healthy."

Clara was scribbling something in her notebook. "You cook I assume? Well?" She glanced up. "What's your best dish? When asked to bring a dessert to a potluck?"

Rose pressed her lips together to hold back a chuckle. She wanted to ask Clara if they'd be hosting a lot of potlucks during business hours, but her cousin had told her that Clara could be a little eccentric. At least for Old Order Amish. "An apple-layered streusel with dried cranberries and a cinnamon crumb topping. I'll make you one if you like, so you can try it."

"And if I want something simpler? Something quick?" Clara pressed.

Rose thought for a moment. "Well . . . a *schleck boi* is always good in a pinch."

"*Ya.* A custard pie is good for a snack when a man comes in from the barn in need of a cup of coffee." Clara's mouth twitched. She didn't smile, but her eyes were twinkling. "And a main dish?"

Rose surrendered to a hint of a smile. "Something with ham. My father has always raised hogs, so I'm good with pork." She thought for a moment. "Probably *schnitz un gnepp.* My *grossmama* taught me to make it."

"Perfect!" Clara again turned to her notebook, scribbling excitedly. "Jacob does love a good ham with dried apples and dumplings." She glanced up. "He's my son; it's his shop, really. I just help where I can."

Rose raised her eyebrows, not sure what to say. While she didn't have any experience with job interviews, she was pretty certain being able to make a dish the owner enjoyed wasn't a requirement of an employee. "Does he?" She glanced over his shoulder. "Will I have a chance to meet Jacob. To say hello."

Clara frowned. "Not today if I can help it. He's in a mood. You know men." She lowered her voice until it was barely more than a whisper and peered at Rose through her spectacles. "He doesn't understand why we need to hire someone, but he'll learn soon enough. You understand the circumstances, *ya?* Your cousin told you that I'll be out of town?"

The large fluorescent ceiling light in the middle of the shop suddenly flickered and Rose glanced up.

"Bulbs need to be replaced. Jacob just hasn't gotten to it." Clara gave a wave of dismissal.

"Um . . ." Rose returned her attention to Clara as the light flickered again. "*Ya*, Mary said you'd be gone a few weeks. But that there would be time to train me first. And that you'd possibly want to keep someone on after you return."

Clara scooted closer to the table, though her round belly barely fit beneath the table. "I understand you're not walking out with anyone." She was whispering again. "But that you hope to find a husband here in Bluebird. *Ya?*"

Rose felt her cheeks grow warm and she looked down at her hands on her lap. Why would Clara be asking such a thing? Was Clara worried she would marry and then Clara would have to train another clerk? "Lord willing."

Clara nodded and met Rose's gaze. "I'm sorry for your loss. But you seem well."

Rose smiled bittersweetly. "Ours is not to question God's ways," she said, not wanting to speak any further of the loss of her husband and child.

"Certainly not." Clara closed her notebook, slipping her pen behind her ear. "Well, I think we're done here."

"We are?" The little bell over the door rang and Rose looked up. Two English women were coming in the door. She glanced back at Clara, unsure of how the interview had gone. "I've taken too much of your time. I should go so you can see to your customers," she said as she got to her feet. "It was so nice to—"

"I'm sorry. Can't you stay?" Clara rested a hand on her ample hip. She was wearing a navy dress, white apron, black hose, and black shoes. "I understood you were available immediately."

"Can I *stay?*" Rose asked, hoping Clara meant what she thought she meant.

Clara nodded in the direction of the two Englisher women, both in jogging suits, one hot pink, the other lime green, with puffy down vests overtop. They had to be sisters they looked so alike. "To work," she told the surprised Rose as she got out of her chair. "No time like the present to start learning."

"So . . . I have the job?" Rose grinned.

"Didn't I just say that? Grab an apron hanging from the hook behind the counter. Everything's self-explanatory. Prices are marked. We just got a new digital scale. I'll be here if you need help."

The woman in the pink jumpsuit approached Rose. "Excuse me, miss. Is your fudge fresh today?" she asked, squinting from behind pink jeweled glasses. She had a big pink fuzzy scarf wrapped around her neck. "I like my fudge fresh."

"Freshly made every day," Rose assured her. "Let me grab my apron, and why don't I get you a little sample to see for yourself." She glanced in Clara's direction and Clara winked at her. Smiling, Rose hurried to grab the apron with the Beechy's Sweets logo on it and get to work.

Watching Rose make conversation with the customers, Clara reached for her notebook on the table. It wouldn't do to leave it out and risk Jacob seeing it. Or Rose, for that matter. There was no need for them to know that the job applicants she'd interviewed for the last three days weren't just interviewing for a job behind the Beechy's Sweets counter, but also for that of a bride.

Clara smiled to herself, pleased with her own creativity at solving two problems at once. Jacob needed help in the shop, whether he could admit it or not. At thirty-six years old, it was also clear he needed a little help in the marriage department. The past was the past and it was time he was wed and gave her grandchildren before she was too old to enjoy them.

Clara had to give herself a pat on the back for coming up with this idea. Of course, in the end, all would be left to God's will, but there was nothing wrong with giving young folks a push in a certain direction. The moment she'd set eyes on Rose, she knew she was the one for Jacob. And now not only would Clara have someone in the shop to help them, but she'd get a chance to get to know her daughter-in-law-to-be.

Clara glanced in Rose's direction. Rose was busy ringing up

the Englisher in the pink outfit. And not only had Rose sold her two pounds of fudge, but some taffy, too. And Rose had had no trouble figuring out the fancy scale or the cash register.

She chuckled to herself as she headed for the door to the kitchen to tell her son that she'd hired a shopgirl. If this went as well as she hoped, Clara thought she just might go into the matchmaking business.

Rose glided beside her cousin on a borrowed push scooter and laughed at Mary's retelling of a neighbor's encounter with a goat in her kitchen. The cold morning exhilarated Rose as well as the anticipation of her second day at Beechy's Sweets. Having Clara hire her on the spot had surprised her, but not any more than the strange questions the older woman had asked during the interview.

Rose had ended up working all day and the hours had slipped by like sugar through her fingers. She found that not only was she capable of dealing with customers, both English and Amish, but she enjoyed it. And Clara had been as good as her word, available anytime she had a question. The only unsettling thing of the day was the fact that the proprietor, whom she technically worked for, never stepped into the front of the shop, even to say hello. When Rose had told that to Mary, her cousin had laughed and said that sounded like Jacob Beechy. She said he had a reputation for, while being a godly man, having a less than pleasant disposition. That didn't prevent the occasional young woman from trying to catch his eye, Mary said, but so far, no woman had done so. She'd hinted that he'd once had a sweetheart, but had said she didn't know the story firsthand, and she worked hard at not being a gossip. Rose had asked Junior what his opinion of Jacob Beechy was over dinner. He'd just muttered something about it being better for people to make up their own minds when it came to summing up a man and asked her to pass the corn muffins.

"How long until Clara goes to Indiana?" Mary asked.

Mary had offered to accompany Rose into work this morning. Rose had assured her she could find the place on her own again, but her cousin had whispered that her mother-in-law had offered to watch the new baby for an hour or so, and Mary was eager to have a few moments without her four children and the bustle of her farmhouse kitchen. Worried about the cold, Mary's husband had suggested he drive them to town in the buggy. The two women had, however, been eager to be off and alone for a few minutes, so they had taken scooters the two miles into Bluebird. Mary would drop Rose off at the sweet shop and then go to the market to get a couple of things before heading home to a day of cleaning and cooking and childcare.

"Clara leaves in three weeks. The Monday after Valentine's Day. Between now and then, they have several big orders to fill for shops in Lancaster. The last one has to be delivered on Valentine's Day. Clara said he's a shrewd business man, Jacob. Fair of course," she added, glancing at her cousin. They were dressed identically in heavy black wool cloaks and their black bonnets over their prayer *kapps*. Both wore gloves and pretty scarves Mary's mother-in-law had knitted for them for Christmas. Rose's was blue, to match her eyes and Mary's green, to match hers.

Rose had settled easily into Mary and her husband's household. It had been so kind for them to invite her to stay with them indefinitely. A change of scenery, a good way to start a new life, now that she was ready, her mother had insisted. An opportunity to find a husband, she meant. Only Rose wasn't offended by the idea. It was time. Past time. It was every Amish woman's dream and duty to be married with a family. God had brought peace to her heart over the last year and she really was ready.

So here she was, in little Bluebird, Pennsylvania. She had a job and her cousin was already plotting to introduce her to several eligible bachelors.

"You want me to send Junior to pick you up after work? It will be dark." Mary looked at the sky. "With maybe more snow on the ground."

"I'll be fine." Rose laughed. "We have snow in Delaware, too."

"Not like this."

"*Ne.*" Rose gazed out over the field as they approached the edge of town. "Not like this. Not so pretty." She shivered as the wind tugged at her wool cloak. "Not so cold."

"Call if you change your mind, *ya?*"

"Call?" Rose frowned, slowing her pace. She was used to a push scooter at home, but not going so far. And there were no hills in Delaware. Kent County was as flat as her applesauce pancakes.

"*Ya.* The store has a phone, I know. How else would they take these big orders from the fancy candy stores in Lancaster that Clara was telling you about?"

"*Ya,* they have a phone. I answered it yesterday. Even took an order." She fell in behind Mary as she heard an automobile approaching from behind them. "I meant how would I call *you?*"

"Junior has a cell phone." Mary hopped off her scooter and began to push it up the last hill that led into town.

Rose did the same. "A cell phone?" she murmured, unable to hide her surprise.

Old Order Amish had no phones, at least not where she came from. Of course, Amish businesses had them, and sometimes teenaged boys sneaked them, but not families. Not for personal use. The Amish were meant to be detached from the Englisher world and that meant no telephone or electric lines. Of course, the rules had been easier to decipher in the past, back in the days before cell phones, when all phones had actual physical lines.

"For emergencies." Mary waved at a man in a red truck that

passed them. "I keep it in the kitchen drawer." She waited for Rose to catch up, and they walked their scooters side by side. "You can give the number to Clara. In case she needs to call you for something. I wrote it down and put it in your lunch box in your bag." She indicated the backpack Rose was wearing, something else Rose didn't have in her parents' home. Inside was a lunch box with several slices of thick sourdough bread, a hunk of yellow cheese, and a thermos of hot peppermint tea.

"Don't look so shocked," Mary teased. "We don't use it to call the weather channel recording to get the forecast."

Rose didn't even know there was such a thing.

They stepped up onto the sidewalk at the edge of the quaint, picturesque town that Rose thought could have come right out of a picture book. Only three blocks in each direction, there were quaint little bungalows, two-story homes, and quite a few stores for a community so small. Within Bluebird, there was a quilt shop, several gift shops, a market selling bulk groceries, an ice cream shop, a hardware store, and a couple of other places Rose had yet to explore. And of course, Beechy's Sweets.

On the second block, the two came to a stop in front of Beechy's storefront. Mary gazed up, dabbing at her nose with a man's red handkerchief she'd plucked from beneath her wool cloak. "You want I should come in with you? Jacob might be there alone."

"I'm going to be alone with him when Clara's gone," Rose countered, suddenly feeling nervous at the mention of the store owner. Between what Mary had said about him at dinner the previous night and what her husband *hadn't* said, Rose was worried about meeting him now. "Times have changed. We all agreed it was all right for a single woman my age to work with a single man Jacob's age. You mother-in-law said herself that there was plenty of coming and going of others in the shop for it to be respectable."

Mary stared at the front door. "I didn't mean *that*. I mean what if he's in one of his moods? I told you he has a reputation for being stern."

"I'll be fine," Rose insisted. "Besides, Clara will be here. And I have to meet him at some point, don't I? Go to the market, Mary. I'll be home in time to help with supper."

She watched Mary step back on her scooter and head in the direction of the grocery store, then walked up the freshly shoveled sidewalk to the door. She knew she was a few minutes early, but that would give her a chance to get some more bags out of the storage closet in the back and get them arranged by size before they opened for business.

At the door, she stood for a moment in indecision, wondering what to do with her scooter. The snow was coming harder now; it didn't seem smart to leave it outside. Maybe Clara would have a place in the back where she could park it. She walked up to the door where a "Closed" sign hung, the window shade still turned down, and turned the knob. It was locked. She glanced over her shoulder at the street. She'd seen fresh buggy tracks going up the little driveway into the back, so she knew Clara had to be there.

She turned back to the door and knocked.

A brusque male voice from just the other side of the door startled her. "Not open yet!"

Chapter 2

Jacob stood on the stepladder shaking his head as he plucked a finishing nail from his pocket. Could the Englisher at the door not read the sign? They weren't open for another twenty minutes.

Holding the nail in place in the molding above the door, he pulled the hammer from where it hung on his leather belt and tapped it lightly to align it before striking it home. He'd come in early this morning to repair the piece of molding that was at risk for falling and striking a customer in the head. The little house they'd converted into a shop was in the perfect location on the main street in town, but it had been in terrible shape when they'd bought it. Even after the major renovation he and his cousin had done, it seemed as if there was always something left to be repaired or re-repaired. He and his mother kept a running list, a list that never seemed to get any shorter.

She hadn't seemed well this morning, his mother, and he was concerned. She'd come downstairs late. She'd made oatmeal for their breakfast after he milked their cow and fed the livestock, but there had been no scrapple or eggs to go with it. It was her arthritis, she'd explained, opening and closing her hands to demonstrate. She'd still been in her nightgown, nightcap, and flannel robe, something he rarely saw. When he'd suggested she stay home for the morning and rest, she'd jumped at the offer. Then she insisted he take the buggy and she'd catch a ride into town late morning with their neighbors, as she did some days when she had work to do in the house.

Another tap came at the door, this one more of a bang. It startled Jacob as he took a final swing at the nail and he missed and hit his thumb. "*Ow!*" he hollered, shaking his injured hand.

"Hello? Are you all right?" came a feminine voice from the other side of the door.

Jacob climbed down the stepladder, pushing his injured thumb into his mouth as he slid his hammer back into place on his belt. "I said we're not open!" He knew he should be thankful for the Englisher customers that provided the finances to allow him to care for his mother and the farm his father had left him. And he truly was, most days. But the fact was, some Englishers didn't have any manners.

He jerked the old roller shade on the door's window back to peer at the intruder. "Can you not read—"

Jacob halted mid-sentence as his gaze met a young Amish woman's. Bright blue eyes framed in thick lashes. The prettiest eyes he thought he'd ever seen. The pertest of noses.

She studied him from beneath the brim of her traditional Old Order black bonnet, a concerned look on her face. Her brows furrowed. "Are you all right, Jacob?"

He stared at her through the glass, feeling a little light-headed. Maybe he'd come down the ladder too fast. Who was this girl who knew his name?

"Jacob?" she repeated.

Then he realized that while he couldn't identify the face, he recognized the voice. From the previous day. It was the girl his mother had insisted on employing to help him out in the shop, help he didn't need. Only she wasn't a *girl*, she was a woman.

The new employee had worked several hours out front after his mother hired her on the spot. Jacob had been so annoyed with his mother that he'd finished up the batch of fudge he was making and then gone home to muck stalls, cut wood, and catch up on some other chores that needed his attention at the farm. He'd not returned to the shop until five-thirty and the girl... *woman* was gone by then. What was her name? Rhonda? No... something with an *R*, but an unusual one for an Amish woman.

"Will you let me in? It's cold out here." She looked peeved, now. It was snowing harder than when he'd arrived this morning and flakes swirled around her black bonnet, striking her rosy cheeks and freckled nose.

"And why would I let you in?" he asked. "No customers until ten. It says so right on the sign." He tapped on the window where the hours were posted in the corner.

Jacob didn't know why he pretended he didn't know who she was. Maybe to see what mettle she was made of. If she had even a chance of being able to work for him, which was doubtful, she needed to be bright... and thick-skinned. There were a lot of people, Amish and English, who believed him to be abrupt, harsh even. Jacob just thought he was honest. And not wasteful of people's time. He wasn't about small talk, he was a man of honest communication and hard work.

The woman with the pretty blue eyes pursed her lips. And then he remembered her name: Rose. "Because I work here and if I don't get the bags from their case before you open, your customers will be carrying their fudge and taffy out of your shop in their hands!"

Jacob didn't know why that struck him as funny, but it did, and he had to press his lips together to keep from grinning. Her quick retort had earned her entrance. His thumb still smarting, he turned the deadbolt on the door. She grabbed the knob and turned it, pushing in. The bell attached to the door rang as she stepped onto the homemade mat that said *Welkom.*

Jacob stepped back and watched as she dragged her scooter in behind her, leaving a trail of snow across the wide-planked pine floor he'd just refinished a few months ago.

"What are you doing?" he asked.

She set the scooter down on its side and whipped off her black bonnet, also dotted with snow. "Which part? The coming to work or the taking off my bonnet and cloak so I can do my work?

"You're making a mess with that thing." He pointed to the scooter.

She shook out her bonnet. "A little snow in Pennsylvania troubles you?" She shook her cloak next, adding more snowflakes to the floor that turned into little drops of water.

"Why did you bring the scooter in," he demanded, pointing again.

"I couldn't well leave it in the snow. I'll put it in the back. And then mop up." She walked to the pegboard to hang her cloak and bonnet. "I should probably have a key to let myself into the back."

He drew himself up indignantly. "I'm not giving you a key to my business."

"Then I'll keep bringing my scooter in the front door, *ya?*"

He shook his head. Annoyed and against his will . . . enchanted. Though not a word heard often among the Amish, it was the only word he could think of. Like one of the fairy tales his mother used to read to him when he was a little boy. Not exactly what an Amish woman was supposed to read to her child, and certainly not her little boy, but Clara had always been an odd duck. Everyone in Bluebird had always said so. And a more faithful woman one would never meet; she was always the first to help when a friend, family member, or even stranger was in need.

"Look at the time." Rose glanced up at the clock on the wall, seeming unruffled. "I'd best get this parked and you'd better get that ladder put away." She stood the scooter up. "Is Clara in the back?"

"Um . . ." He was so taken aback by her response to him . . . or lack of response to his *tone*, as his mother liked to call it, that he didn't reply at once. "N . . . *ne*."

"No?" She raised her eyebrows, then frowned. "She said she'd meet me here first thing. She was going to show me how to pack up individual mail orders and ship them."

"I usually ship the mail orders."

"She said they were getting out later than they should."

"She said *what?*" Obviously, this woman had no idea how much work went into running a shop like this. "I—There's a lot to do, this time of year." He pushed his thumb into his mouth and tasted blood. Apparently, he'd hit it harder than he first realized. "Not just making the candy, but ordering the bulk supplies."

"She was going to show me how to do that, too." She flashed a smile. "Is she coming in later?"

"Yes, she just . . . she was feeling a little under the weather. Arthritis in her hands." Though the more he thought about it, the more he wondered just how *under the weather* she was. It wasn't like her to shirk responsibilities, yet she'd seemed eager to send him off alone this morning.

"I'm sorry to hear that. I have a good recipe for a poultice wrap. I'll make it up for her tonight." She nodded at him. "You all right? Your thumb."

"It's fine. I hit it with the hammer. Fixing the molding over the door." He dropped his hand to his side. The thing was really smarting now, throbbing to the rhythm of his heart beat. "I'm handy with a hammer." He had no idea why he'd said such a ridiculous thing. She made him feel like he was back in the one-room schoolhouse he'd attended down the road. That year he'd been smitten with Mary Joe Yoder. Seventh grade. He'd said ridiculous things to her for weeks.

Again, Rose raised her brows, but she didn't say anything. Instead, she wheeled her scooter toward the door that led into the back, leaving a slick track of water behind her. "I'll get the mop and turn on the kettle. Make us both some tea."

It was on the tip of Jacob's tongue to tell her he didn't drink tea. Amish men his age didn't drink tea, only boys and old men. But the truth was, he *did* like a good cup of strong tea, especially with a piece of peanut butter fudge. He made an excellent peanut butter fudge.

She glanced over her shoulder at him. "You probably should move that ladder away from the door." She nodded in the direction of the clock. "We open in ten minutes."

Jacob took a step forward, intending to respond, but his mind was blank. Instead, he went to fold the ladder, nursing his thumb.

"You and Jacob have a good morning?" Clara asked.

Rose and Clara sat at the little table under the painting of a blue Pennsylvania sky, a farmhouse, and rolling fields. Painted by a neighbor, Clara had told her. Rose didn't know any Amish painters. He'd passed the winter before at the age of ninety-three, Clara had explained.

"What did Jacob say about our morning?" Rose took a bite of the savory beef stew Clara had brought from home. That, with the homemade bread and cheese Rose had contributed, made a hearty lunch on such a cold, snowy day.

Clara's mouth pursed and then she smiled as she reached for the pepper shaker between them. "Other than try to hide his bandaged thumb?" She chuckled. "Not much."

Both Clara and Rose had invited Jacob to share lunch with them out front. There was plenty of room for a third at the wooden kitchen table and an extra chair in the back. The snow continued to fall, so they'd only had two customers since eleven. But instead of joining them, muttering something about billing, Jacob had taken a big ladle of stew from the pot on the back of the stove in his tea mug. He'd then retreated to one of the rooms in the back of the shop that served as his office.

"But he thinks you're pretty. And smart," Clara said quickly.

Rose frowned. "I don't think he wants me here."

"What man likes change?" Clara took fresh butter with her knife from a plate and slathered it onto her bread. Then she added a slice of the soft cheese. "He'll appreciate you once he sees how much of a help you can be. He keeps talking about streamlining the business. He says our retail sales are good enough, but there's a big business in wholesale. That's why these orders for Valentine's Day are so important to him." She took a bite of the bread and cheese, smacking her lips with pleasure. "Truth is, he's worried. There's talk of one of those big mart stores opening nearby. A place like that, he says, could shut the doors of every business in Bluebird. If we don't make changes."

Rose nibbled on a piece of bread with the soft cheese. She and Mary had made it over the weekend and it was their best batch yet. She wanted to ask Clara if Jacob had really said he thought she was pretty, but she didn't. It wasn't the Amish way to dwell on looks; what was in a man's or woman's heart was what was important. Still, they were humans, made in God's eyes. And she couldn't deny Jacob was handsome . . . and had nice forearms. She'd seen them when she stepped into the kitchen earlier and he'd been stirring a pot of caramel with a big wooden paddle, his sleeves rolled up to his elbows. For just a moment, she imagined what he would look like stirring a pot in her own kitchen. Which was silly. He wasn't her type.

His type being grumpy.

"So back to what I was saying, it takes Jacob a little while to warm up to folks," Clara explained. "Women. He's had a hard time with women. Single women," she added.

"Because they don't like him?" It came out of Rose's mouth before she could stop it.

But Clara didn't seem offended. In fact, she chuckled, her cheeks growing rosy. "We all have our pasts that make presents."

Rose nodded in agreement. She knew she wasn't the girl who had married her Chester eight years ago. How could she be after all that had happened? "So, it's his past is it?"

"Partly at least. He was in love with a girl. Adel," Clara said softly. "They were going to be wed."

Rose glanced up at Clara. "She broke it off?"

Clara shook her head. "She died."

"Oh my." Rose pressed her hand to her chest, her heart instantly going out to Jacob. She knew loss, the sort that could take over your life if you let it. "I'm so sorry. How long ago?"

"Eight years."

"*Eight years?*" Rose repeated, more than a little surprised. It wasn't the Amish way to hold on to grief. Better to give it to God and move on, her mother often told her. "And he's not . . . met anyone else?"

"*Ne.* My son guards his heart, I think." Clara glanced up slyly. "But if he met the right woman . . . a woman like you, maybe . . ."

"Me?" Rose wiped her mouth with the blue cloth napkin Clara had brought from home. "I don't think I . . ." She knew she blushed. "I don't think I'm his sort."

Clara leaned across the table, lowering her voice. "And what sort is that? Pretty, a hard worker? A woman who doesn't put up with his nonsense?"

Rose pressed her lips together, pushing back from the table. She didn't quite know what to make of this conversation, though it didn't make her uncomfortable, per se. Mostly because she didn't know an Amish mother with a single child of married age, male or female, who didn't like to put in a good word for him or her.

"I suppose we should get to work. I have a lot to learn in the next few weeks." Rose stood, picked up her bowl, and looked down at Clara. "If you're done, I'll wash up the dishes. It'll only take me a few minutes and then I'll cut that fresh fudge. It should be cool by now."

"Thank you, dear." Clara used the heel of her bread to sop up the last bit of gravy from the stew in her bowl and slid it across the table. "You're attentive to your elders. Jacob admires that in a—"

The ring of the old-fashioned dial telephone on the wall drowned out Clara's last words.

"I'll get it." Rose set the dishes down and hurried through the swinging half door, to the phone behind the counter. "*Goot* afternoon, Beechy's Sweets," she said, just as Clara had instructed. "Rose speaking."

"*Goot* afternoon," a friendly female voice said in *Deitsch*, the language most Amish spoke amongst themselves. "Is Clara there?"

"*Ya*, just a minute." Rose held out the phone receiver to Clara. "For you."

"*Ach*, wonder who that could be." Clara got up, wiping her mouth with the napkin. "Englisher or Amish?"

"Amish."

Behind the counter, Rose handed the phone to Clara, then she went back to the table to clean up. She'd get the dishes done and then cut the fudge. Maybe she'd even get to taste a little sample. Jacob's disposition might not be the sweetest, but his fudge was the best Rose thought she'd ever eaten. The new batch was maple walnut and she couldn't wait to try it.

"Oh my," Clara said as Rose carried the dishes through the

half doors between the shop and behind the counter, and then stepped out of the front room, into the kitchen.

"*Ya, ya,* I suppose I could . . ." Clara went on.

Rose carried the dishes to the large stainless steel sink meant only for cleaning. Jacob had pointed it out that morning, as if he didn't think she would understand why in a commercial kitchen, one sink would be for cleaning while another for food prep. As if she wouldn't be able to read the little signs he had printed neatly on index cards. If it was just him and Clara working in the kitchen, she wondered what the need for the signs would be, but she didn't ask.

Rose was just finishing up the lunch dishes when Jacob walked into the kitchen, carrying his bowl and plate. He'd taken a slice of her bread and a large piece of cheese into the back with him. "I'll take that," she said cheerfully. Before he could protest, she took them from his hands.

"Th . . . thank you. The cheese was . . . it was *goot.* Tangy for soft cheese."

She smiled at him. Knowing he had lost the woman he loved. Knowing he had once loved a woman made her suddenly look differently at him. "My cousin and I just made it last weekend. I'll bring more tomorrow."

"Jacob! Rose!" Clara called, bursting into the kitchen. "I have news! I . . ." She seemed flustered and excited at the same time. "That was Lizbet, Sadie's sister. Sadie's gone into labor." She fluttered her hands. "I have to call Wilma and see if she can take me to the train station. Baby's early but she's gone to a hospital and Lizbet says that Sadie's husband Joe says everything's going to be just fine. Sadie's in no danger. The baby might just be a little small." She clapped her hands together. "So that means I'll be on my way and you two . . ." She looked from Rose to Jacob. "Will be on your own."

Jacob took a step toward his mother, his face suddenly stormy. "Absolutely not. You can't leave her here with me. Not with all the orders we have to fill in the next two weeks." He gestured toward Rose. "She . . . she doesn't know the first thing about candy making," he sputtered. "Or . . . or running a store."

"Well, I'm going to Indiana on the evening train." Clara clasped her hands together, grinning. "So I suppose, the two of you best figure it out together."

The following morning Jacob stood in the dark candy shop staring at the clock. She'd be there in five minutes. Rose. Half the night he'd lain in bed trying to figure out what to do with her. He'd tried to convince his mother to stay another day or two, at least to train Rose. After all, she was the one who thought he needed a shopgirl; she was the one who had hired her. But his mother had been uncharacteristically stubborn. Usually he could convince her to see things his way. But not yesterday. She had bordered on obstinate. She went home, packed a bag, and had their favorite driver pick her up and take her to the Amtrak station in Lancaster. She hadn't even made him supper before she went. And the last thing she'd said as she left the house was that she loved him and that she hoped he saw an opportunity when God presented it to him.

He had no idea what she was talking about. And didn't have time to figure it out. The previous morning, before the call from Indiana, he'd accepted yet another wholesale order for chocolate fudge and peanut butter. Twenty-five pounds each. It would be a stretch to deliver them in the week leading up to Valentine's Day, with all the orders he'd accepted already. The last order had been impulsive. Prideful. And now he regretted it. Now that he knew his mother wouldn't be here to help him with it.

It was something about the upheaval in the shop that had him unsettled. Usually he was so clearheaded. Always God- and task-minded. But Rose . . . no . . . his mother *hiring* Rose, had set him off-kilter. Kept him from thinking clearly. Yesterday he'd actually added too much butter to a kettle of caramel fudge he was working on. He intended to layer it with chocolate fudge. Instead, the batch went into the bucket for his neighbor's pigs.

Jacob glanced at the clock. Two minutes. She'd be arriving in two minutes full of smiles and suggestions. The previous day she'd convinced Clara that if they stacked the boxes they used for the candy on end instead of flat, they would be easier to grab quickly when filling large orders. His mother hadn't consulted him, hadn't even given the idea some thought. And now all of his white boxes with the words Beechy's Sweets and their phone number and address stamped on them were put together, arranged by size, under the wooden counter.

Jacob glanced at the door. Last night, when he couldn't sleep, he'd considered the idea of telling Rose when she arrived that he wouldn't be needing her any longer. He told himself he could pay her an additional week's wages and send her on her way. That was more than fair, and it would give her a whole week to look for another job. He didn't know why she was working anyway. Very few Amish women worked outside the home. At her age, she should have been married by now, with children. What was she doing working in a candy shop?

A sound coming from the back of the shop startled Jacob and he turned in the direction it had come from. It was the back door he'd heard, the one that led out to the lean-to where he stalled the horse during the day. He was certain he'd heard it open. But who could be letting himself in the back door? It couldn't be thieves; they'd never had a theft in Bluebird for as long as he could remember.

But that was definitely the door and the sound of—

As he walked out of the kitchen and into the hallway, he spotted a push scooter lying in the entryway. Then Rose in her black cape and bonnet appeared. She was wearing a large backpack and also carrying a lunch pail covered with stiff fabric. "Good morning," she said, sounding far too cheerful to suit him.

He stopped short. "How did you get in? We always keep the back door locked."

She set down the pail and held up something shiny. "Which is why Clara gave me a key." She dropped it inside the pocket of her apron, removed her backpack and then her cloak. Next came her bonnet. She hung them on the peg rack beside the door right beside his heavy denim coat and wide-brimmed wool hat.

"I brought coffee. Ground this morning fresh. Clara said we were almost out." She patted her starched prayer *kapp* to be sure it was in place. "She said you liked your coffee freshly ground." Another smile.

She was a pretty thing, he'd give her that. Not flashy like some of the younger single Amish women he knew. She was dressed neatly in a clean, rose-colored dress with a white apron, black stockings, and sturdy black shoes. Rose for a rose, he thought.

Then he felt silly and looked away. "We've got a lot to do today. I made a list."

"I love a list."

Her cheerfulness grated on his nerves. "We've got to start making boxes for the Valentine's Day shipments. We're going to need hundreds. That's time-consuming. And the roses that go on the truffles need to be premade." He pressed his fingers to his forehead. His hair was shaggy. He should have had his mother cut it for him before she left. "I need an inventory of the pantry, too. Not sure I have enough sugar. And we'll have more customers coming in. It's always busy leading up to the Englisher holidays."

She was gathering up her belongings. "Just write it all down."

He watched her. She didn't seem intimidated by him, not

like most young Amish women. He wondered what was different? Himself or her?

She walked past him, the backpack on her shoulder, the lunch pail in her hand. "If I have any questions, I'll ask." She headed down the hallway, then looked back. "You better get to work, Jacob. Not just stand there lollygagging."

"*Lollygagging?*" He meant it to come out stern, but his voice sounded a little playful. Like hers.

She smiled. The prettiest smile. "I'll start the coffee, open up for business, and then bring you some coffee and a cinnamon bun. Fresh made this morning."

Before he could tell her that he tried to avoid sweets, she was gone. The key to his back door in his shop in her apron pocket. What had his mother been thinking when she'd given this girl the key to his shop?

He glanced at her scooter. She'd brought it right inside. As if this were her place.

Chapter 3

Late in the afternoon, an hour before closing, Rose glanced up at the ceiling light that was flickering again. She returned her attention to her work. It had been quiet all afternoon with only a few customers coming in, which was a good thing because in the morning they'd been overrun. At one point, she'd actually had to call Jacob to join her behind the counter. He hadn't been happy about the prospect, saying he was too busy. Something about mixing up more of the peanut butter that he made for his sweets. But Rose hadn't taken no for an answer and she'd had him cut and box fudge while she rang up customers. The crowd had just died down when Clara called to check in. She told Rose she was having a wonderful time and the baby was adorable. Then she'd spoken to Jacob.

He'd taken the phone through the swinging door into the kitchen, stretching the curly phone wire so far that Rose thought for certain he'd pulled it right out of the wall. He'd then proceeded to talk in a quiet voice, but not so quiet that Rose couldn't hear him. He was talking about her, saying it wasn't going to work. From his response to Clara, Rose suspected the older woman hadn't agreed with her son and he hadn't liked it one bit. But men rarely did like it when a woman knew best and said so. After the call, he'd hung the phone up loudly and gone into the back. Rose hadn't seen him since.

It had crossed her mind more than once in the last few hours that maybe she should quit. Or rather just make the agreement with him that they weren't suited to work together. But she was never one to give up, or give in. And there was something about Jacob that, despite his grumbling, she liked. She'd realized this earlier in the day when they'd had a conversation over a cup of tea. Maybe it was his work ethic. Or his devotion to his mother. Or maybe it was his forearms. She smiled, then chastised herself for inappropriate thoughts. She was a widowed woman. Had once been a mother. She knew better. Hard work was one of the best ways to rid oneself of such thoughts, that and a preacher's long sermon, but for today she just had the work.

She was seated on the wooden stool, making boxes at the counter. The tiny white boxes she was making would hold just four chocolate truffles, or four pieces of fudge. Fudge was Jacob's specialty, as Anna Lapp who'd come in to the shop had explained. Best fudge in Lancaster County and every woman in it wanted his secret recipe. Rose had been tempted to ask Anna some questions about Jacob. Had he really never walked out with a girl since he lost his betrothed? He was such a handsome man, she found that difficult to believe. She could also see the opposite argument. He wasn't exactly easy to get along with.

Rose reached for her marker. The boxes had seemed plain to her, even after she'd stamped the shop's name and address on, so she'd dug up a red Sharpie from the little kitchen in the back and added a couple of hearts and curlicues. She glanced at the growing pile of boxes stacked one inside the other. They weren't very Amish looking. When decoration was added to something, a carving in a bed or a dresser, the design was usually plain and based on nature: pine branches, a cluster of walnuts, or maybe a simple scroll. No hearts, and certainly not red ones. But in only two short days, Rose was getting to know their Englisher customers and she was certain they would like the boxes, still plain, but just a little fanciful.

The overhead lighting flickered again and made a buzzing sort of sound. There were long fluorescent bulbs inside it. One or more needed to be changed. She knew it because her husband had had the same kind of overhead lights in his woodshop. She'd never changed a bulb herself; they were long, unwieldy glass tubes. But she'd watched Karl do it on more than one occasion, first bouncing their son on her knee, then trying to corral him so he wouldn't get into his father's tools. Their light had run on a generator. The Beechys used electricity here at the candy shop. A necessary evil Clara had explained to her. But fully approved by their bishop.

Rose set down her marker and got up off the stool, studying the overhead light. She had seen the light bulbs in a box in the broom closet off the kitchen. And there was a ladder near the back door. She wasn't very tall, but with the ladder it wouldn't matter, not even with the high, ten-foot ceilings of the old house. She only hesitated a moment and then headed into the kitchen. Jacob wasn't there, but there was a fresh batch of peanut butter caramel fudge cooling on the wooden counter. She snitched a bit of crumb as she went by. The man could make fudge, she'd give him that: creamy, sweet, and full of flavor.

In the back, she retrieved the box of light bulbs first, which was almost as tall as she was. But not heavy, just cumbersome. It wasn't until, on her second trip to the back, with the ladder, which *was* heavy, that Jacob pushed himself, in his office chair, out into the hall behind her.

"Where are you going with that?" he called, his disapproval discernable in his voice.

"The shop," she answered, lugging the ladder into the kitchen.

She was almost to the swinging doors before he appeared behind her.

"Give me that."

"I've got it," Rose answered cheerfully, trying to manage the door and the step ladder that was taller than she was.

Jacob reached around her, his hands brushing hers as he took the ladder from her. "What are you doing with a ladder?" he demanded.

She followed him into the shop and pointed at the flickering light overhead. It was almost dark outside now and the problem even more obvious. "I'm going to change the light bulbs." She looked at him frowning at her and smiled. "Could be a fire hazard."

He exhaled impatiently, carried the ladder into the customer area, and plopped it down under the light fixture in the middle of the room. "You can't climb this ladder and try to do that," he grumbled, opening it. "You'll break your neck."

She rested her hands on her hips, watching him climb the ladder. "I've used a ladder before. I can manage. And it needs to be done."

He shook his head. "Why didn't you ask me?"

She hesitated before she spoke. "Because you're not exactly . . ."

"Not exactly *what?*" He stopped halfway up the ladder and looked down at her.

"Approachable," she said softly. He met her gaze and there was something beyond the antagonism in his voice that suggested a vulnerability. In his heart. She was quite certain of it. "Admit it, Jacob. You don't want me here."

He exhaled, holding her gaze a moment longer before he looked up at the light fixture again. "It's not that I don't want you here, Rose."

It was the first time he'd called her by name.

"It's just that . . ." He exhaled again. "I work better alone."

"Which isn't always what's best, is it? Because we're not

meant to be alone in this world. We're meant to lean on each other. To help each other."

"You sound like my mother."

She looked up at him. "Is that a bad thing?"

He looked down again and a smile came over him. Just a small one, but a smile nonetheless. "No, it's not. Clara Beechy is the kindest, wisest woman . . . *person* I've ever known." He suddenly looked embarrassed and clambered the rest of the way up the ladder. "This could have waited for another day," he grumbled. "I've got things to do. The distributor sent the wrong cocoa and I have to order more before five."

She watched as, at the top of the ladder, he stretched to reach the far side where the cover to the recessed light released. She cringed as he leaned over. "You should probably move the ladder over and little to—"

He leaned farther, going up on the toe of one boot.

"Jacob—" She took a step to grab the ladder as she saw it come up off one leg.

When bad things happen, people say it seems like everything moves in slow motion, but it had never been that way for Rose. When her parents and the bishop came to the door to tell her that Karl and her son were dead, it had been over in an instant, in one heart-stopping flash. And the same happened as she saw the ladder tip.

"Jacob!"

He tried to shift his weight back to right the ladder, but it was too late. And it was over before Rose could reach him.

Jacob hit the wood floor hard, the ladder crashing down on top of him. If he made a sound as he hit, she didn't hear it. Rose dropped to her knees beside him. He'd banged his head hard; she'd seen it bounce as he hit the floor.

"Jacob?" she whispered. She reached out to brush his hair from his forehead so she could get a better look. It was a sandy blond and straight and thick and it smelled clean. He was going to have a nice-sized egg on the side of his head where he hit it. She could feel it already rising. But what if he'd hurt himself seriously? What if it was a brain injury? she wondered, trying not to panic. She quickly said a silent prayer.

His eyes were closed.

"Jacob?" she said again, her voice trembling. She reached out to touch his chest between his leather suspenders. The green shirt rose and fell beneath her hand. And he was warm. Very warm. "Jacob!" she said a little louder.

"I'm just going to lie here," he replied quietly. He still hadn't opened his eyes. "Embarrassment. I think I'll just lie here, and die of embarrassment."

Rose was so relieved that she laughed.

His eyes flew open and she laughed again. Then she reached to brush the hair from his face again. When she realized the emotion she was feeling wasn't just relief, but also tenderness, she pulled her hand back as if burned by melted chocolate. While Jacob's bishop may have agreed to allow a single woman to work for a single man, stroking his hair while he was lying on the shop floor would definitely not be endorsed.

"I'm sorry." She tried not to laugh again, but couldn't help herself. She was just so thankful he was all right, at least mentally. She'd had a neighbor back in Delaware who had fallen from a ladder and had never spoken again, never fed himself again. "Are you hurt badly?"

He closed his eyes and then opened them again. "The ladder. Could you possibly get it off me?"

"Oh!" She jumped up and grabbed the ladder and dragged it, scrapping it across the pretty plank floor.

He sat up and caught his breath. Then he started to try to stand and sat down hard again.

Rose immediately dropped to her knees in front of him. He looked as if he was going to pass out, he was so pale. "Just sit there for a second. Breathe. You hit your head pretty hard."

They were eye level and he met her gaze. His eyes were brown with streaks of green. Nice eyes. And nice teeth; unlike many Amish men she knew, he took care of them. His breath was slightly minty.

"Would you like some help getting up?" she asked.

He frowned. "I would not." He started to get up again and this time cried out in pain, grabbing his knee. Tiny dots of perspiration beaded up on his forehead.

Without waiting for his permission to help him this time, Rose grasped his arm, shifting some of his weight to her shoulder, and he slowly rose on the good leg. The moment he tried to put pressure on the injured one, though, he moaned and lowered his head.

"I think it's my knee," he said, pain in his voice.

She looked down at his knee and up at Jacob. Arm and arm like this, she felt strangely unsettled. It had been a very long time since she'd touched a man so intimately. "You need to go to the hospital and get an X-ray. It might be broken."

"Rose." He swallowed hard, biting back his pain. "It's not broken."

"I can't believe I broke my knee." Jacob groaned, lowering himself into the easy chair in his parlor, cozy now that Rose had stoked the woodstove. Not only had she warmed up the house, but it now smelled of soup bubbling on the stove and biscuits she was reheating in the oven.

He was still embarrassed, hours after the incident. He couldn't believe he had fallen off a ladder, right in front of Rose. Especially after he'd just lectured her about it not being safe for her. And now, hours later, she was still right here. Still with him. He couldn't decide if he was relieved she'd been here to help him into his house or mortified. Of course, the place was as neat as a pin, even in his mother's absence. It wasn't that. It was just that he wasn't keen on someone seeing him so vulnerable. He wasn't keen on Rose seeing him this way.

"Don't be so hard on yourself. Accidents happen." Rose took from him the crutches that had been given to him in the emergency room. "It could have been so much worse. I told you about my neighbor. And my uncle Abel fell out of his wagon while unloading grain and broke a leg *and* an arm. You could have been killed if you'd hit your head harder."

Jacob frowned. He was hungry and tired and not only did his knee hurt like the dickens, but so did his head. No concussion, thankfully. But now that they were home from the hospital, the reality of his situation was sinking in. His kneecap was broken, and the doctor had made it very clear that it would be six to eight weeks before Jacob could put weight on it. And if he *did* try to walk on it too soon, he'd need surgery and that would lay him up for months.

Six to eight weeks? How was he going to get the orders made in time for Valentine's Day? That was only two weeks away now. He could suddenly imagine that big store going up a few miles away; he could see his customers passing through Bluebird, on their way to get their reduced-price chocolates made from machines in far-away countries. He could imagine boarding up Beechy's Sweets forever.

"I'm going to get you that soup before I go." Rose rested the crutches within his reach and pushed a footstool closer to him. "Elevate it. I'll get some more ice for the ice bag."

"The driver's outside waiting to take you home." Jacob used both hands to lift his leg and prop it on the stool. "You should go."

"And what? You're going to hop into the kitchen, get your soup, and then hop it back in here?" She rested her hand on her hip. It was a motion he'd seen her do several times now. Mostly when she was frustrated with him.

But he couldn't be annoyed with her. She'd been so good

through the whole thing. Not every woman could handle an emergency the way she had. Certainly not a single woman without the experience of running a household. There had been no hysterics, which was interesting because his Adel would burst into tears if she dropped a cup of coffee. But not Rose. Rose had been calm and reassuring, concerned, without being stifling in her attention. After he fell, she'd helped him to a chair and then started making calls from the list of Mennonite and English drivers his mother kept by the phone. And she hadn't given up until she'd found someone who could take them to the hospital in Lancaster and then home. Once she'd secured a driver, she'd locked up the shop and gone with him to the emergency room, even though he'd told her time and time again that he could go alone. And now here she was in his home, getting him soup before she left him.

"John Junior brought your buggy home from the shop, put up your horse, milked your cow, and fed up for the night. He'll be back tomorrow morning to milk and feed. By tomorrow night, he'll have some folks organized to help you out until you're able."

Jacob stared at the leg brace on his knee; it fit over his work pants but went from mid-calf to mid-thigh. "I can take care of my animals myself."

"Probably. But not for a few days. And this will give you a chance to let people return kindnesses. Junior said you milked cows for Joe Yoder for two weeks when their little one was in the hospital at Christmastime. And when Eli and Sarah Mast had the fire last fall, they stayed here with you a month until their house was suitable for living. With *three* children." She was waggling her finger at him. She was bossy for a single Amish woman. An employee.

"They were little children," he protested. "Hardly heard or saw them, me being at the shop most days.

"We're not going to argue about this, Jacob. Not tonight. You need to eat and get to bed. It's a good thing your bedroom is downstairs. Stairs and crutches don't mix well. Now tomorrow morning, I'll be by. I don't have my own buggy and horse. We'll have to use yours, but I can hitch up just fine. Junior will bring me when he comes to milk. You and I'll get to the shop and figure out where we go from there."

He looked up at her. She was a small woman, not thin, not heavy. Sturdy, but in a good way. And pretty, even prettier than he had realized. The light from the kerosene lamp she'd lit created a hallo around her head, making her look something like an *engel* he'd seen portrayed in picture books.

He had to shake the thought from his head. "Where we go from *there? From where?*" he asked, trying to bite back his anger.

He wasn't angry at her. He was angry at himself for being so reckless. Maybe if he hadn't been so busy looking at Rose, trying to be clever, maybe he wouldn't have fallen. "I can tell you where we go from here. Tomorrow I call my customers and cancel the big orders. There's no way I can make fudge at the stove, leaning on those crutches. I won't be able to lift the kettle. And you heard the doctor; he said that for the first week I really shouldn't be on my feet any more than necessary." He shook his head. "I suppose I should call *Mam,* but even if she comes home, there isn't any way—"

"We're not calling Clara," Rose interrupted. "She's not coming home. We're not ruining her trip over this little hiccup." She frowned and pointed at him again. "And you're not cancelling the orders."

"*Hiccup?* You think this is a *hiccup?*" He pushed his hair off his forehead. She'd taken his hat from him when they'd come inside and hung it on a peg in the kitchen. "Rose, this isn't a hiccup, it's a disaster."

"It's not a *disaster*. Your husband and little boy being killed in a buggy accident is a disaster," she said, her voice softening. "*This* is just a hiccup. We're going to figure it out."

He studied her face in the pale light. He couldn't tell if she was talking about another family incident because almost every Amish man and woman knew of someone killed in a buggy accident . . . or about herself. For some reason, he'd assumed she was single because she'd never married. It hadn't occurred to him that she might be widowed. How could it not have occurred to him?

The realization that she could have suffered such a loss made him feel foolish for being upset over his injury. Over orders for fudge for an Englisher holiday. He wasn't an unkind man. How had he been so thoughtless? He wanted to ask Rose whose husband and son had died in a buggy accident, but he sensed this wasn't the time. He sensed he already knew the answer by the look on her face.

Instead of asking her about the buggy accident, gentling his tone, he said, "I appreciate your encouragement, but who's going to make the fudge?"

She smiled and turned away, striding out of the parlor. "I am, Jacob," she threw over her shoulder. "And you're going to teach me."

Chapter 4

Rose rode beside Jacob in the buggy, hoping she didn't look as nervous as she felt. Taking care of him the previous day hadn't been difficult. She was good in an emergency, and she was good at managing a crisis when she had tasks to perform. What she wasn't good with was conversation. Being alone with someone like this. With a man. With Jacob, sitting close in the buggy, with only her lunch pail between them on the buggy bench.

He had been in a bad mood when she arrived at his farm with Junior. But she didn't take his crankiness personally. She knew he was frustrated by his injury and probably a little embarrassed by his fall. After all, he *had* just given her a lecture about how she'd fall if she climbed the ladder.

She sneaked a glance at him. He looked handsome this morning in his denim coat and wide-brimmed wool hat. He had shaved; unmarried Amish men didn't have beards. And he smelled of Ivory soap, fresh and clean. She liked a man who didn't smell of the barn.

Rose had offered to drive the buggy, but after awkwardly managing to get in without bending his knee, he'd taken the reins from her without a response. And now they were almost to Bluebird. She'd meant what she said the previous evening when she told him she thought they could still make the fudge for the orders, but this morning she was having second thoughts. Not so much because she didn't think she could learn to make it, but because she wasn't sure she wanted to work so closely with Jacob. The previous day, while waiting for X-rays, he had been so nice that she'd thought maybe his interest in her went beyond the attention of an employer with an employee. But by his behavior this morning, she'd been mistaken; he clearly didn't like her.

She glanced at him to find he was watching her. She looked straight ahead.

Or maybe he did . . .

Jacob cleared his throat. "I, um . . . I've been thinking about what you said." He nodded as an Amish man in an orange hunter's beanie passed them in a wagon full of grain, going in the opposite direction. "About trying to fill the orders. See . . . it's important to . . ." He stopped and started. "There's talk of those big stores opening not far from Bluebird. It may be that people start buying there instead of at Beechy's and I'd lose my foot traffic. These wholesale orders might be what makes or breaks me by next year."

There was something in his tone of voice, a vulnerability that Rose appreciated. She liked the idea that he felt he could share his concerns with her. She took a breath. "I know you didn't want Clara to hire me, Jacob, but I think . . ." She glanced up at him. "I think maybe it was God's intention . . . for me to be here. To help you."

He tightened his grip on the reins and guided the horse up the snowy driveway that ran along the sweet shop, toward the single-stall barn in the back. It was a clear, cold day, but the sun was shining. "I don't know about that, but . . ." He exhaled. "I guess what I'm trying to say is that . . ." He looked at her. "I'm grateful you're here and I think maybe . . . just maybe we can get those orders made."

She smiled, clasping her gloved hands together. "I know we can do it. Of course, I don't know that I can work in the back and see to customers." She went on quickly before she lost her nerve. "So, I asked my cousin Mary's niece to come in today. She's a nice girl: modest, friendly, and she knows how to deal with Englishers because her family has a big vegetable stand, summers." The look on Jacob's face made Rose wonder if she'd overstepped her bounds. "Just to help midmorning to early afternoon," she added, trying to soften the blow. "Our busy time."

He stared at her. "You *hired* an employee?" He turned on the bench seat of the buggy so that his good knee brushed hers. "For *my* shop?"

"No, I . . ." She pressed her lips together, wondering if she had pushed him too far. But it was too late now. Taking a breath, she made herself meet his gaze. "*Ya, ya,* I did, Jacob, and when you see how many pounds of fudge we're going to make today while Lydie runs the cash register, you'll be glad I did."

"Rose, that's not how you stir it," Jacob directed from where he sat on a stool in the shop kitchen.

She had arrived on her own before him that morning and had already started a pot of peanut butter fudge. After resting for a few days, he'd felt stronger physically and had declined her offer to come hitch up for him. The funny thing was, he discovered he missed her smile at his back door this morning. And he didn't like the idea of her coming to town on her push scooter, not with the icy roads. A car could slide just a little and then what? When he'd found her here this morning, he'd made it clear that Monday morning, he would pick her up in his buggy. And he wouldn't take no for an answer. Her cousin's farm was only another mile from his. It wouldn't take any time at all to fetch her.

"It's not how *you* stir it." She turned on the little step stool she'd set in front of the stove, his big wooden paddle in her hand, and flashed him a smile. "Clockwise, counterclockwise, it really makes no difference to the sugar." Her brows suddenly furrowed with concern. "Or does it?"

"I wasn't talking about—" The look on her face registered and he realized she was teasing him. No one ever teased him. His mother sometimes, but no one in his church community, or his neighbors. Not even the couple of male friends he had. It was probably his own fault, at least partially. He'd gained a reputation for being serious, even stern at times and he'd let people go on believing that. It was easier. Then they didn't get too close. They didn't get close to him and then die on him.

"You're not funny," he told her, unable to resist a chuckle.

"No? Then what are you laughing about?" She kept stirring the fudge.

"It's going to burn," he warned. "You stirring it that way, without a pattern. A plan."

Her cheeks were rosy from the heat of the gas flame and bits of reddish-brown hair had fallen from her prayer *kapp* to frame her face in curls. "It's not going to burn." She reached across the stove to retrieve a tiny, half-pint jelly jar from the counter.

"What's that?" he asked her. He started to rise from the stool, but he had his leg elevated on another stool and the moment he tried to stand, he found himself off balance. He sat down before he fell down and made a fool of himself again. "Rose, what are you putting in my peanut butter fudge."

"Secret ingredient," she said, blocking his view as she removed the lid of the container. "It's just an experiment."

"No. Absolutely not. We don't experiment with my recipes. We don't change the recipes ten days before Valentine's Day."

"This isn't going to be sent to the shops in Lancaster. It's a recipe for here. A small batch for me to practice with," she told him as she dropped lumps of something from the container into the kettle of fudge. "It probably won't even make it out front. That's what you said."

"We don't change the recipe," he repeated. He tried to look stern, pointing at the jar. "What's in there?"

She pursed her lips, clearly put out with him, but not angry. She never got angry with him, not even when he tested her patience. "I'm not going to tell you." She screwed the lid back on the jar and returned her attention to the bubbling pot of fudge. "Is the pan ready? Another minute and—"

"Rose! Do we have pink salt water taffy?" Lydie hollered, pushing open the swinging doors between the shop and the kitchen. She was a plain girl, thin, long-faced, and always seemed to struggle to speak. At least around him, but she'd already lasted almost two days, which was two days longer than the two girls his mother had tried to hire the previous year.

It wasn't until Lydie entered the kitchen that she spotted Jacob and then her eyes got big. She looked to Rose. "Salt water taffy," she repeated. "Pink," she choked out.

"There's plenty of taffy in the bin on the table," Rose told her.

"Who wants salt water taffy in February?" Jacob leaned back against the butcher block counter, directing his comment to no one in particular.

"Those, those are mixed. She wants just pink. It's . . . it's for a baby shower. Whatever that is," Lydie said, keeping her gaze fixed on Rose.

"Look under the counter. If we have any, it will be in one of those plastic bins." Rose stirred with one hand while talking over her shoulder. "I think there's a couple of dozen pieces of the pink still there. It's double wrapped so it will be fresh."

"Under the counter," Lydie repeated, backing out of the kitchen. "Under the counter. Pink."

Jacob waited until she was gone. "Are you sure she's able to work the cash register?" He lowered his voice. He didn't want to hurt the girl's feelings, but he did have a livelihood to protect. "Can she count money? She seems . . . slow."

Rose made a face as if that were the silliest thing she'd ever heard. "Yes, she can count money and run the register. You just startled her." She turned off the flame beneath the pot. "She wasn't expecting you. And you scare her."

"I *scare* her?"

"When you use that voice," Rose pointed out calmly. She grabbed two hot mitts from a nearby drawer and lifted the pot of fudge.

He started to rise awkwardly. "You should let me—"

"Sit," she ordered. "You told me your knee was swollen last night."

He lowered himself back onto his stool. She was so pretty today he could barely take his eyes off her. He thought the heat from the stove and the tiny beads of perspiration at her temple actually made her even prettier. He liked a woman who was a hard worker. He liked a woman who enjoyed her work. "You take a man's dignity away, telling him he can't milk his own cow or carry a pot of hot fudge to the counter."

"Nonsense." She stepped off the step stool and carried the pot toward him. She was surprisingly strong for her size. "There will still be plenty of milkings and batches of fudge after your knee has healed properly."

He was ready with another one of his homemade walnut wood spatulas, this one shorter and made for spreading. He narrowed his gaze. "You know, I saw those little hearts you've been putting on the chocolate truffles." He pointed at her with the spatula. "You use white chocolate and color it with food coloring?"

"Mm-hmm." She tipped the pot and he pushed the hot peanut butter concoction into the buttered pan.

"I don't usually put hearts and such on my candy. It's not *Plain*. Not very Amish."

"Good thing we're not making the truffles for the Amish, then. They look nice in the little white boxes inside the mini cupcake papers, though, don't they?"

"Inside boxes with hearts and curly thingies drawn on them."

"You saw my boxes, too?" She looked up at him.

"I did." Scooping the last of the fudge out of the pot, he began to spread it. "And you're right, they do look nice," he admitted. "Very . . . English."

"And most of your customers are Englishers, so maybe they'll like them and buy more, *ya?*"

She carried the pot to the deep restaurant-grade stainless steel sink he'd bought at an auction. Their backs were to each other, which gave him the opportunity to ask the question he'd been wanting to ask since the night they came home from the hospital.

"Rose?"

"Hmmm?" She turned on the water spigot.

"Could I ask you a question?"

"Of course." He heard her pump dish soap into the dirty pot.

"Were you . . ." He exhaled, feeling uncomfortable. But the question had been on his mind; he'd lain in bed the previous night wondering. He turned on the stool so that he could face her. "*Mam* said you're thirty. That's old for a—I didn't mean that you're old." He exhaled again, frustrated that he couldn't figure out how to say what he wanted to say. "Rose, were you—" He pushed the fudge around the pan. If he didn't hurry, it was going to start to harden and he wouldn't get the shiny look on the top he liked. "Were you married?"

"I was," she said softly.

When she didn't say anymore, he considered letting the conversation go. But he couldn't. He didn't want to. "What you said . . . about a disaster, about a husband and son dying in a buggy accident." Ignoring the fudge, he watched her at the sink. She was wearing a blue dress today, cornflower blue, like the flowers in his mother's summer garden. Like the blue of Rose's eyes. "Is that what happened to you? To your family?"

She leaned over the sink, scrubbing hard with a plastic dish brush. "Two years ago. Someone driving a pickup swerved to miss a deer and hit the buggy and . . . they died. Our Isaac was five. His name was Karl, my husband."

"Rose . . ." Jacob felt a lump in his throat and a sort of melting in his chest, like sugar melting in a hot pan. He had the craziest urge to get off the stool, hobble over, and hug her. "I'm so, so sorry."

"*Ya* . . ." This time she was the one who exhaled. She turned off the water, lowering the pot upside down on the wooden dish rack on the counter. "So we've both had loss, you and I. I'm sorry, too. For you." She grabbed a dishtowel from a hook and turned to him, drying her hands. "Clara told me about your fiancée. That she had died. Could I ask what happened?"

He looked down at the pan of fudge. It wasn't going to look as good as most of his batches did. He'd let it go too long and it was already beginning to crystalize along the edges. "Adel was her name. She had epilepsy. We thought her medicine was controlling the seizures, but . . ." He hesitated, wondering how long it had been since he had talked about Adel. Years. "She had a seizure while sleeping and . . . died."

Rose was watching him and he saw tears gather in the corners of her eyes. For *his* loss.

And suddenly he felt humbled by Rose's pain, pain that he could only imagine, and by the smile she still managed. His Adel's death had been a blow, but they'd not even wed yet. There had been no children. He had loved her, but not the way a man loves a wife of many years, a wife who has given him children. He wasn't so naïve as not to realize that.

Jacob looked at Rose. He wanted to say something, but he didn't know what to say. Instead, he just watched her. Waited for her to meet his gaze, and when she did, he said nothing, because nothing he could say would take away the pain he had seen flicker there.

And then she offered the smallest hint of a smile. A smile that made his heart swell, a smile that reminded him of the bible verse that said God would heal the brokenhearted and bind their wounds. He'd always liked that verse from Psalms.

"I'll go check on Lydie," she said, hanging the hand towel back where it went. "See if she found that taffy."

Jacob watched her go and for the first time since he met Adel, he wanted to know a woman better. He wanted to know Rose better.

"*Mam,* why didn't you tell me about Rose's husband and child?"

Jacob tried to keep his voice down so Rose, out front in the shop, wouldn't hear him. When his mother called, he could have hobbled to his office in the back. But then he would have risked Rose hearing something of the conversation if she didn't hang up quickly enough after he picked up the other extension. Instead, he'd asked Rose to bring the phone to him in the kitchen, stretching the line to its full capacity. He was standing, his back to the wall, a crutch in one hand, the old avocado-green phone in the other. He'd gotten a good deal on the wall phone at a yard sale in nearby Bird in Hand. Englishers used fancy cordless phones now. A phone was necessary to run a business and their bishop had approved the installation, even though it connected the Beechy family to the outside world, but a fancy new cordless phone wasn't a luxury Jacob needed or wanted.

"The accident," he whispered when his mother didn't reply.

"She told you?"

His mother sounded excited on the other end of the phone. It was a good connection. The fact that he could hear her so well when she was six hundred miles away still fascinated him, even though he knew the Englishers had had the technology for years.

"So you've been talking?" she went on. "She's been talking to you? You've been talking together?"

"We *talk*." He tried not to sound defensive. "We're together every day." Of course, not the previous day, because it had been the Sabbath. He'd gone to church at his neighbor's home. The sermon had been about prayer, based on the scripture from John 17. Preacher Isiah went on a little too long; in Jacob's mind the man always stretched an hour sermon into two and a half hours, but he'd still had some good points.

"How could we not talk, *Mam?*" Jacob went on in a bluster. "I have to tell her how much sugar to add to the pot. When the butter's getting too brown. There's a lot of talking."

"I mean *talking,* talking," she said. "Talking about *personal* things."

The word *personal* made him feel slightly uncomfortable and yet . . . warm at the same time. It had been a long time since he had had that kind of conversation with a woman. If he was honest with himself, it was the first time he'd talked like that with anyone. Even Adel. But he had been so young then. Known so little about the world or himself.

"You should have told me her family died." Jacob wanted to say like his Adel, but he didn't because he and his mother never talked about her. He never talked about her with anyone. Until Rose.

And now he couldn't get his mind off Rose's tragedy. Ever since she told him, he'd been thinking about it. About her. She didn't seem like a woman whose loss had been so great, such a short time ago. She seemed happy. Grateful for what the good Lord had given her, not angry over what she had lost. He didn't understand how she could be that way, especially with her husband and child gone only two years. He still felt the pain of his Adel's death every single day. The hole she had left inside was still there, big and gaping.

Jacob admired Rose for her resilience. Her strength. And a part of him felt a little guilty. What right did he have to still mourn Adel so deeply when Rose had lost so much more than a fiancé? Not that one could measure loss exactly, or categorize it, but it had really made him rethink his own feelings. Behavior.

"You should have told me," he repeated.

"Wasn't my tale to tell," his mother replied. "That's good that she's telling you such things," she went on. "She's a nice girl, isn't she? Not just pretty. But a good person. And fun. My cousin Mordecai knows her bishop from Delaware. Said he had nothing but good to say about her. A faithful woman. Properly *Plain*. And an excellent cook, I hear. Mordecai and his family stopped by on their way to Wisconsin to see the new . . ."

Jacob closed his eyes, only half hearing his mother as she rambled on. It had been sleeting this morning. He'd managed to get his buggy hitched up himself, climbed in with help of a milking stool, and fetched Rose. If he'd left five minutes later, he would have missed her. He found her on the road on her push scooter, headed for town. She'd been wet and cold and he'd chastised her for setting off in such weather when he'd told her he would pick her up from now on. She'd only laughed it off and said she wouldn't melt or freeze. But as she was talking, she'd loaded her scooter into the back of the buggy and reached out to him for help climbing up to the seat. And at that instant when he'd taken her hand, he'd wished he hadn't been wearing leather gloves and she her woolen ones.

In the close quarters of the buggy, Rose had smelled of wet

wool and fresh *fastnachts*. Homemade donuts she'd brought to share with him for lunch. She'd packed sausage patties and biscuits, too. They'd shared tea and donuts in the little kitchen in the back, and she'd laughed at him when he'd split a donut in half and slid a piece of sausage between the two pieces. Jacob had been disappointed when she'd declared it was time to get to work and left him in the kitchen to finish his tea alone.

"So, Jacob, *is* it?" his mother asked, bringing him out of his thoughts.

"Is what—Sorry, *Mam*. What did you ask?"

"The fudge making. Is it going well? Dorcas Lapp wrote me to say she'd been in the shop the other day and the two of you were busy beavers, you and Rose. She said you hired another girl. Do you think you'll have the orders together in time to deliver them to the Englishers?"

"I can't say," he admitted. "Rose says we will. But you know how she is."

"How's that?"

"You know . . ." He searched for the right words. "Optimistic."

His mother laughed on the other end of the phone. He tried not to smile.

"And is that a bad thing?"

"*Ne* . . . yes. Can be if it's not realistic." He exhaled impatiently. He didn't like the emotions bubbling up inside him. He didn't like thinking so much about Rose and what she thought and what she said. He didn't like caring what she thought. "I'm trying to be realistic. I think I should at least cancel the one big order for Amish market. They don't just want fifteen pounds of fudge. There's truffles, too. Twenty dozen. Boxed," he added.

"I know you won't make the fudge until you're a week out,

but you could start making the truffles now. Once they're dipped, they'll stay fresh in the walk-in."

"That's what Rose said," he grumbled.

Again, his mother laughed. "How's the knee?"

"Fine."

"You staying off it?"

"I should go. Work to be done."

"*Ya, sohn,* you have a lot of truffles to make."

He wanted to tell her this was no joking matter. His was worried about his livelihood. About being able to take care of the farm, of her. And even his future. The previous night he'd dreamed he had a son. A little brown-haired boy with cornflower-blue eyes. He knew his mother's greatest wish was to have grandchildren. His hope for children had died with Adel. But his dream had been so vivid. And he'd woke missing the little boy he'd held on his knee.

"Put Rose on the phone."

"She has customers."

"*Ach,* let Lydie wait on them. That was smart of you to hire her."

"Take care of yourself, *Mam.* Don't let Sadie overwork you."

"Nonsense. Mostly I sit and rock that sweet baby. I'll call again later in the week," his mother said. "Take care of yourself. Now let me talk to Rose."

Jacob tucked the phone under his arm and leaned against the wall for a moment. Then he called loudly, "Rose!"

A moment later, she stuck her head through the doorway. She had what looked suspiciously like a smudge of fudge at the corner of her mouth. "*Ya?*"

"My mother. She wants to speak to you. I told her you were busy, but—"

"*Ne,* I'll take it. Lydie has everything under control. By the way, Mrs. Cranston, the lady down the street in the blue house, she said to tell you she loves the new peanut butter fudge recipe.

She came back for another pound. We'll have to make more."
She took the phone from him. "Clara!"

"What new peanut butter fudge recipe?" Jacob demanded.
"You weren't supposed to put that batch out."

"Everything is just fine." Rose turned and walked back into
the shop, leaving Jacob to stand there watching the doors swing
shut.

Chapter 5

Rose looked up from the box of truffles she was packing to see her cousins Mary and Hannah coming through the door, their black wool capes covered in a dusting of snow. Both were rosy-cheeked and laughing, carrying cloth bags of purchases on their arms.

"Rose!" Mary's sister greeted as she closed the door against the sharp wind. "Sorry it's taken me so long to stop by. We've been so busy at the hardware shop." She glanced around the candy shop. "How's it going? With you know who," she added softly, a hint of conspiracy in her tone.

Rose came off the stool behind the counter, her eyes widening as she looked at Mary. She wondered what Mary had told her sister. When Rose had admitted to Mary that she found Jacob attractive, she had assumed it had been in confidence, but then she'd not said it was a secret. And the truth was, women did like to talk romance; potential romance, romance lost, it didn't matter. Women had since the beginning of time, according to her grandmother Lena.

"I didn't say a thing," Mary defended, keeping her voice

down. "Only that the two of you were getting along. Well . . . at least that he hadn't fired you yet." Then she mouthed, *Where is he?*

"Office in the back," Rose answered, closing the lid on a twelve-piece truffle box. She added a little red foil heart sticker to seal it. She'd bought them from the general store down the street in the section where the town's Englishers bought Valentine's Day cards. No doubt Jacob wouldn't be pleased when he saw them, but she'd sold two boxes of truffles that morning to customers who made a point of saying they liked the foil heart stickers.

"Well . . . that Jacob is a handsome, eligible bachelor. Even if he is cranky," Hannah teased with a smile. "He owns a farm and this shop and he's well respected in the church," she added. "You could do worse than walking out with him, cousin."

"I'm not *walking out* with Jacob," Rose argued, feeling a little bit like she was in her early twenties again, talking with girlfriends about going to singings and riding home with a boy.

It was the way her Old Order community back in Delaware had dated. Young, unmarried women and men met for various activities sanctioned by the church, which gave them an opportunity to mingle, while still being well chaperoned. At the end of an evening, a boy had the option to ask a girl if she'd like to ride home with him. It was the way she had met Karl, who'd been visiting family in Chestnut Grove. They met at a taffy pull and married six months later.

Hannah walked over to the display table of brightly colored sweets in jars. "Red licorice," she exclaimed. "I do love red licorice. I may just have to have a few whips."

Mary stepped closer to the counter, removing her black bonnet. "Did you say anything to Jacob about the fundraiser Wednesday night at the schoolhouse?" she asked Rose, smoothing her white prayer *kapp.*

Rose frowned. "No, I didn't say anything to him about the fundraiser." She slid the boxes into the display case next to a tray of single truffles she'd hand dipped that morning while Lydie ran the cash register. Lydie had gone home early to go to a dentist appointment.

"It's a good cause. Maybe Jacob would like to come. Barbara and Eli's little Jesse will be having his surgery in another week. They say he'll be running again by summer."

Rose nodded. Little Jesse Fisher has been born with a heart defect and he was scheduled for surgery in a children's hospital in Philadelphia. The Amish didn't have medical insurance, so it was up to families and the community to pay the bills as needed.

"It *is* a good cause," Rose agreed. She'd actually considered inviting Jacob. She thought it might be good for him to get out in the community and do something social. With his mother out of town, he had to be lonely, there at the farmhouse by himself at night and on the weekend. But in the end, she hadn't invited him because a part of her was afraid he would say no. And then she would be disappointed.

"You should ask Jacob."

The swinging doors between the kitchen and the shop sprang open and Jacob hobbled in on his crutches. "Who should ask me what?" He nodded to Mary. "Good to see you, Mary." He looked to Hannah who was fishing licorice whips out of a jar. "Hannah, how are things at the hardware store?"

"Things are *goot*. And it's *goot* to see you on your feet," Hannah responded.

"Rose says you're getting along well." Mary nodded in his direction. "She says the crutches are barely holding you back. Everyone in Bluebird is saying a prayer, hoping your candy orders will make it to Lancaster in time for the silly Englisher holiday."

"Not holding me back one bit." Jacob glanced at Rose as if

to suggest she shouldn't have said anything to them about his concerns. "We've actually agreed to some additional orders." He steadied himself on his crutches. "What were you talking about? Who should ask me what?"

Mary glanced at Rose and Rose could feel herself blushing. She wondered if Jacob had been listening on the other side of the door and hoped she hadn't said anything inappropriate. For a man on crutches, he certainly could move quietly when he wanted to.

"We were talking about the fundraiser at our schoolhouse tomorrow night. It's supper and an auction to benefit the little Fisher boy's heart surgery," Mary explained.

Jacob halted beside Rose behind the counter. "Mm-hmm," he acknowledged.

"Everyone's invited. It's eight dollars at the door for as much chicken and dumplings a person can eat. Hannah and I were just going around collecting donations for the silent auction." She smiled prettily. "We were wondering if you'd like to make a donation."

He glanced at Rose. "Of course." He nodded in the direction of the two boxes of truffles she had just sealed with the foil hearts. "Rose can get a couple of things together for you. Englishers, too, or just Amish?"

"Both. The elders thought we might raise more money if we included all our neighbors." She chuckled. "And them Englishers, they do love chicken and dumplings."

He leaned on one crutch and stroked his smooth skin. He had shaved that morning and standing so close to him, she could smell his shaving soap. She suddenly felt nostalgic, and a little sad. It had been a long time since she'd smelled a man's shaving soap.

"Then we should donate a gift certificate, too, *ya*, Rose?"

Rose was surprised that he was consulting her. He spent a

good deal of his time telling her that he was in charge around here. "I . . . *ya,* that would be nice. A good thing to do."

"Two, I think," he said. "Twenty dollars each. And the chocolates. But you'll have to make the gift certificates up," he told Rose, turning to head back into the kitchen. "We don't have any of those fancy printed ones. There's paper in my office."

"That's so generous of you, Jacob," Mary called after him. "Thank you. The Fishers thank you. You should come to the fundraiser. Rose and I are making biscuits. I know you like her biscuits."

His back was to them. "Not much for social dinners," he said, his voice suddenly sounding gruff.

The three women were silent until he disappeared into the back and then Mary broke into a wide grin. "Very generous."

"Chocolates and gift certificates." Hannah carried her little brown paper sack of licorice whips to the counter. "Generous, indeed. Might even say *goot-maynich.*" She met Rose's gaze, a twinkle in her eyes.

"Kind, *ya,* a kind man always makes the best husband, you know," Mary injected.

Rose cut her eyes in the direction of the kitchen, then back at her cousins, a silent warning to hold their tongues.

The sisters just laughed. Hannah paid for her licorice and Rose promised to bring the boxes of candy and the gift certificates with her the following night. The women then said their goodbyes and headed out into the lightly falling snow. Rose was just settling down on her stool to begin packing more truffles, hopefully truffles they could hold back to have delivered with an order going out the following morning. She had the number of boxes the customer had ordered, but then Jacob had said the man would take an extra two dozen boxes, if they could manage. Jacob had seemed doubtful, but then he'd been surprised by how many truffles she'd been able to make in only a couple of hours.

She was just arranging the mini muffin papers in boxes when she heard the doors from the kitchen swing open again. Jacob entered the shop and then he just stood there behind her. She suddenly felt self-conscious. She wondered if he was upset, thinking she had somehow put him on the spot about the donations. When she finally turned to him, though, the look on his face wasn't one of anger. He was just standing there, watching at her.

Rose met his gaze and he didn't look away as he often did.

"You're going?" he asked.

"What?"

"To the fundraiser tomorrow night?"

She nodded. "*Ya,* like they said. We're making biscuits. A lot of biscuits," she added, feeling silly when the words came out of her mouth. Something had changed between her and Jacob over the last day or two and she couldn't quite put her finger on it. It wasn't anything he had said, just a . . . feeling that was awkward and exciting at the same time. Like a spark between them.

"Riding with Mary and her family, I suppose?"

She looked down at the candy box in front of her. "*Ya.* I'm sorry. I should have told you. I can work late tonight, but not tomorrow night." They both had put in a couple of extra hours the previous day and intended to stay again that evening after they locked the doors. After hours that night, they'd be making their first batches of fudge to ship and Rose thought she was more excited to get started than he was.

"Would you . . . could I . . ." He stopped and started again. "If I go, would you . . . like to ride home? With me?"

She almost blurted, "But I have a ride home." Then she realized what he was asking. He wasn't just offering a ride home. He was asking to *take her home* from an event, as in asking her home from a taffy pull or a singing of their earlier days. It was an Amish date of sorts that he was asking her on.

Rose looked up at him from where she sat. She thought of the kindness of his gift for the Fishers. Of the laughter they'd shared in the kitchen that morning when he'd spilled sugar trying to help her measure out twenty cups. She thought of the occasional smile she got out of him and realized she *would* like to ride home with him. Alone in his buggy.

Rose glanced down at the candy box in front of her again and then back at him. Suddenly she saw possibilities where she had not seen them a moment before. Her earlier suspicions had been accurate; he liked her. Otherwise, he wouldn't be asking to take her home. From what she heard from the women of the Amish community, Jacob Beechy didn't take girls home from church suppers.

She smiled, almost shyly at him. "I'd like that, Jacob."

He didn't answer. He just nodded. But then when he was in the kitchen again, she heard him whistling to himself.

"You look pretty tonight, Rose," Alma Stoltzfus remarked, taking in her blue dress and white apron and *kapp*. She accepted the basket of fresh biscuits from Rose in the makeshift kitchen area they'd set up at the schoolhouse. "I hear a young man is taking you home."

Rose gazed out over the tables that had been set up for the fundraiser supper. There had to be fifty people seated on the long benches that had been unloaded from a church wagon, which was usually used to transport chairs, benches, and tables from home to home where church was held every other Sunday. She could hear cars and buggies still pulling onto the schoolhouse yard. They'd had so many more folks show up for supper than expected that Mary had run home to bake a couple more batches of baking powder biscuits in her two ovens. For now, they were asking people to just take one at a time, but promised more were on their way.

Rose caught sight of Jacob sitting with a group of men and was surprised to realize that she was nervous about riding home with him after the supper. It was silly, really. She'd seen him every day since Clara hired her, all day, with the exception of the Sabbaths. She'd ridden to and from work with him in his buggy multiple times.

But somehow this was different. The previous night Mary, always the matchmaker, had suggested the possibility of romance, even marriage, between Rose and Jacob. But Rose wasn't ready to let her mind go there. Not yet. It wasn't that she wasn't ready to marry again. She was. She truly believed it was God's wish that she be a wife and a mother again. But it was her heart that wasn't ready to consider the possibility Jacob could become her husband. She had loved Karl. Could she really love again? Could these feelings of admiration and attraction become love? Because while she understood that men and women married for different reasons, she had to agree with the cute Englisher Valentine's Day cards she'd seen at the general store. For her, marriage wasn't just about commitment, it was about love.

"I hear it's Jacob Beechy." Alma leaned closer to Rose, peering at her through tiny, oval, wire-frame glasses. "Is it true?"

Rose felt as if she had been caught with her hand in her grandmother's cookie jar, staring at Jacob so brazenly. She returned her attention to the older woman, but before she could respond sensibly, Alma went on. "Peculiar man that Jacob. Nice looking. Hardworking. But peculiar. Keeps to himself. Can have a bit of a sourness to him." She gazed down at the basket of biscuits in her hands, then up at Rose. Alma barely stood five feet tall, but she seemed formidable. "But faithful. And his mother is a good woman. I like Clara. Of course, she's odd, too, so we shouldn't be surprised."

Rose offered a smile as she moved more biscuits from the

metal sheet pans they'd transported them in to keep them warm, into another basket.

A woman Alma's age who Rose didn't know walked up to them, a water pitcher in her hand.

"Letty, this is Rose," Alma introduced. "I was telling you about her. Came from Delaware to stay with Mary and Junior Troyer." She leaned closer. "She's walking out with Jacob Beechy."

Rose held up her finger. "I'm not—"

"He asked to take her home," Alma interrupted, paying Rose no mind. "Even with him on crutches. He must be mighty sweet on her. She's working for him, you know. At the sweetie shop. You heard Clara went to Wisconsin, *ya?*"

"Indiana," Rose said softly.

"*Ya.* That Clara, she has a good heart, helping her niece that way," Letty agreed, giving Rose a once over, then looking at Alma again. "Looks like a sturdy girl, even though she's small," she told her friend. "I suppose she might be able to make something of Clara's boy."

Once Rose might have been mortified to have the two older women standing beside her, talking about her as if she wasn't there. Talking about what should have been a private matter between her and Jacob. But one of the good things she had learned in the tragedy of losing her family was that the Amish community truly did care for its own. They weren't just about prayers and words; they were about action. And when someone poked their nose in business that might not be looked at as their own, their heart was in the right place. Rose had also learned that those older than she was, those who had experienced more of life's trials, really did usually have good advice. And they saw the world accurately.

Rose's gaze strayed to Jacob again and she was surprised to see him looking at her. She dared a half smile. He didn't smile back, but he held her gaze, making Rose feel warm and pleasant . . . even a little excited.

The two elders were still chattering away, but now the subject was a neighbor Rose didn't know. She reached for another basket to refill with biscuits and when she looked up again, Jacob was standing there.

"Alma. Letty." He nodded to both women who had stopped midsentence to stare at him.

He was only using one crutch tonight. Rose didn't know how wise that was; he had to be putting weight on it which he wasn't supposed to do. But she knew him well enough to know not to mention it in front of the other women.

"Have you eaten?" Jacob asked Rose.

"Um . . . *ne*. We'll . . . the women serving will sit down later. After everyone else has eaten."

"You'll be lucky if there's anything but chicken bones left by then." With his free hand, he took the basket of biscuits from Rose's hand and passed them to Alma. Both women stared up at him.

"It's all right if Rose takes a break from serving, isn't it?" he asked, stepping back to make way for her.

Alma's mouth worked up and down for a moment before she managed a "*Ya*."

Letty echoed her and then both women agreed again, "*Ya, ya*."

"She should take a break."

"Have something to eat. Working so hard. *Ya*."

"Practically a guest herself in Bluebird, still."

Rose cut her eyes at Jacob as she walked past him and then stepped aside to let him take the lead. They chose a spot at the end of a long table, separating themselves from a group of young men and women of dating age. Everyone was laughing, caught up in their own conversations and paid no mind to Jacob and Rose.

Rose sat down and Jacob took the seat across from her. He passed her a roll of silverware wrapped in a napkin from a Mason jar in the center of the table. Then he reached for a big bowl of stewed chicken and dumplings on the table and began ladling out a portion for her.

She laughed as he filled the bowl to the rim. "How much do you think I can eat?" she asked.

"You forget I've seen you eat. Two ham and cheese biscuits today at lunch and three oatmeal cookies." He put a biscuit on a side plate for her. Then grabbed a second and added it to the plate.

"We're only supposed to be taking one until Mary gets back with more," she warned under her breath as she unfolded her napkin and placed it on her lap.

He shrugged. "You made them. Folks will wait."

Suddenly Rose realized she was starving. And she didn't really even mind him teasing her about how much she ate. Her father had always said she was pint-sized, but she could eat a quart. "Aren't you eating?"

"Ate."

Their gazes met again and then she bowed her head to say a silent grace. When she opened her eyes, he was still watching her. "Stop," she murmured, dipping into the bowl of stewed chicken and dumplings with a spoon.

"Stop what?"

She was blushing again; she could feel it. He looked nice this evening. He'd gone home and changed his shirt and he'd shaved and combed his hair. "Looking at me like that," she said, a playfulness in her voice that surprised her. "People will be talking, Jacob."

He shrugged. "Let them talk, *Rose*."

The way he spoke her given name suggested an intimacy that had somehow found its way between them. They were sitting across the table from each other; there was nothing inappropriate about their behavior. They weren't doing anything the bishop wouldn't approve of, yet . . . Rose felt different about Jacob and she sensed he felt different about her.

She didn't know how to respond, so she took a bite. He watched her eat, seeming to enjoy her appetite. They'd broken bread together before, so she felt no awkwardness, and they soon fell into easy conversation. They talked mostly about the upcoming candy orders that had to be filled and about how they planned to work out their time so they could make the deadlines. Jacob even agreed to hire a boy he knew to load the orders into the van he hired to deliver them.

They laughed and talked and Rose ate two bowls of chicken and dumplings and both biscuits and Jacob had another biscuit and before she knew it, the fundraiser supper was over. The diners left with the secret auction items they had won, and no one remained but the crew of young men and women who had volunteered to clean up.

As Rose was rising from the table, Mary approached her, already dressed in her cloak and bonnet for the winter night. "Your twenty-dollar gift certificates each went for thirty dollars and someone paid twice the price as they would have paid in your store for your chocolates." She shook her head. "Englishers."

Jacob raised a shoulder and let it fall. "Everyone knows tonight was for a good cause. I'm just glad I could help."

"*Ya,* the whole evening was a great success. The Fishers are in Philadelphia with their little one, but they'll be thrilled when they hear. And thankful." Mary smiled. "Well, we're headed home. Jacob's bringing you, *ya?*"

"*Ya,*" Jacob answered for Rose as he stood and leaned on his crutch.

Mary looked him up and down, her black old-fashioned pocketbook hanging from her elbow. "You think that's wise, just the one crutch? You break the other knee there won't be much courting for you."

"Mary!" Rose murmured under her breath, embarrassed. "He's just bringing me home."

Mary raised her eyebrows at Rose and returned her attention to Jacob. "See that you have our Rose home in an hour, Jacob. Junior and I are responsible for her, you know, her being a single woman and staying with us."

He nodded.

"*Ya*, I should think I would be home in an hour." Rose stacked up her bowl and plate and silverware. "I'll help clean up here and it's not a five-minute ride to the house." She picked up the dirty dishes.

"You'll do no such thing." Mary took the stack of dishes from Rose's hands and set them on the table. "Your job is done. Let the clean-up crew do theirs. The point is for us to do this as a community. Here in Bluebird, we share the joys, we share the burdens." She tugged on the strings of her black wool bonnet. "Take a nice buggy ride and have her home in an hour, Jacob."

Mary walked away, and Rose just stood there for a moment. She'd been an independent married woman, then a widow for long enough that it seemed strange to have someone giving her a curfew. But it made a part of her feel good—to be cared for. And it was also a little exhilarating to be in the position of being courted again, if indeed that was what Jacob intended. She looked to him. "I'm ready if you are."

They said their farewells, got dressed in their winter outerwear, she in her cloak and bonnet, he in his black wide-brimmed dress hat and wool-lined denim coat and they walked out into the darkness. By the time they started down the dark road, snow was beginning to fall. They were both quiet, just listening to the steady *clip-clop* of the horse's feet and watching the snowflakes fall, but Jacob found that it was a comfortable silence. That was something he liked about Rose. While she was certainly a woman he could have a conversation with, she also knew how to just be silent and be content in solitude.

Jacob dared a sideways glance at Rose. There was just enough light coming from his buggy lamps for him to see her. She was looking straight ahead. He couldn't see her eyes because of the brim of her black bonnet, but she had a serene smile on her face. He cleared his throat and looked ahead again. The reins felt comfortable in his gloved hands. Riding in the darkness beside Rose felt comfortable to him and he wondered if this was the way it was supposed to be between a man and a woman. A couple. Not that he would assume they were a couple. He wasn't even sure she liked him. But she must, otherwise she wouldn't have agreed to ride home with him, would she?

He cleared his throat again. "Nice night," he said.

"*Ya*," she agreed. "I'm glad we took the long way home. I love the snow. It doesn't snow like this in Delaware. Not often enough, at least."

"Winters can be harsh here, though. Some winters, a lot of snow to shovel just to get to the barn."

She turned to him so that he could see her face. She was smiling slightly, her eyes sparkling. "I wouldn't mind, most days, I think." She chuckled. "And then there's always spring to look forward to."

"So . . . you'd consider moving to Bluebird?" The moment he said it, he wished he hadn't. It was too much. It was too soon. If he really was interested in courting her, he knew he shouldn't push her too hard too quickly. He needed to give her time to consider the idea. The possibility.

"*Ya*." She looked at him. "In the right circumstances, I think." She folded her hands in her lap. She was wearing hand-knitted gloves with the tips of the fingers missing. "I've stayed too long with my parents. Being with Mary and Junior, I've realized that."

"So . . . you'd like your own home again someday. A . . . husband?" he dared.

She laughed. "Of course." She looked at him again. "Wouldn't you like a wife, Jacob?"

He held her blue-eyed gaze for a long moment before he returned his attention to the snowy road. "*Ya*. I didn't think I did. After . . . Adel." He nodded slowly. "But I think I do, Rose."

She smiled again, and it made him smile.

Chapter 6

"Levi! Careful with those boxes," Jacob warned, hobbling down the hall after the teenager he'd hired to load the van with the candy orders. "They're fragile."

Rose followed Jacob, a case of carefully packed peanut butter fudge in her hands. "He's fine, Jacob. Levi, you're fine," she called to the patient young man. This was the third delivery Levi had assisted with in the last week. They were down to the wire now with only two more orders to be delivered in three days' time, on Valentine's Day, but Rose was sure they were going to make it. Despite his accident, Jacob was actually going to be able to fill his orders.

Rose followed the men out the door to the waiting van that backed up to the rear porch. It was a clear, cold, sunny day. There, Jacob stood and watched Levi go down the steps. Rose waited for the teen to stack his armload of boxes into the rear of the van and then she passed hers to him. "That's the last one," she told him. "But you can come back Saturday morning, *ya?*"

"*Ya,*" the young man answered as he closed the van doors.

"See you Saturday, Rose." He glanced quickly at Jacob. "See you later."

"*Ya. Danke,* Levi."

Jacob's tone was gruff, but Rose knew now that people mistook his tone for one of discontent not realizing that emotion was what made him sound brusque sometimes. It wasn't that Jacob was unfeeling, it was that sometimes maybe he felt too much. As an Amish man in a community where emotions weren't readily expressed, that had to be hard for him.

Jacob gave final instructions to the English driver, Tom, and then he and Rose stood on the porch and watched the van pull out of the stone-paved driveway.

Rose lifted her face to the warmth of the sun. "This feels good, doesn't it? The sun."

Jacob hooked his thumb in his pocket, leaning on his crutch, tipped his head back, and closed his eyes. "*Ya,* it does," he agreed after a moment.

"And it feels good to almost have these orders done. You're going to get those last batches of fudge finished and Saturday the final deliveries will be made. You did it, Jacob."

He opened his eyes, looked down at her, and reached out to gently tug on the sleeve of her green dress. "You did it, Rose," he said quietly.

"We did it together."

For a moment they just stood there looking at each other. In the week since the fundraiser, they had shared a whirlwind of late nights making fudge and truffles and quiet buggy rides; they'd even gone to visit neighbors together on visiting Sunday. While neither had actually come out and said it, Rose was pretty certain they were courting. At first, she had thought things might have been going too quickly, and had expressed as much to Mary. Her practical cousin, however, had pointed out that at her and Jacob's age, courting was done quietly and often swiftly in most Amish communities. After all, they weren't in their early twenties. They both knew what marriage entailed and they both knew how they felt about matters. About each other.

As Jacob held Rose's gaze, he lowered his hand and caught her fingers with his. They touched all the time, passing each other ingredients, getting in and out of the buggy, but this touch was different. And a little thrilling.

"I haven't thanked you, Rose."

"Jacob, thanks aren't—"

"Please," he interrupted. "Let me finish before I chicken out."

She smiled up at him. And was quiet.

"I never could have done this without you, not because it wasn't possible but because . . ." He seemed to search for the right words, but as he did so, he didn't break eye contact with her. "You were the one who convinced me I could do it. You had confidence in me when I didn't have it in myself. And . . . and you worked really hard and . . . and I want you to know that means a great deal to me."

"Well," she said, surprised by the emotion that tightened her throat, "I can truly say that I've enjoyed every moment of it. Well, almost every moment." She held onto his fingers. Holding hands was totally inappropriate. An unmarried man and woman of their age, they'd be the talk of the town if anyone saw them, but she didn't care. Feeling the warmth of his fingers made her realize how much she missed the comfort of human touch. Of a man who'd cared for her. And she truly did think Jacob cared for her. And she knew she cared for him.

She gave a little laugh. "I did not enjoy it when that customer cornered me, trying to find out what was different about your peanut butter fudge."

"I didn't know what you'd added to my recipe." He tried to sound terse, but he didn't fool her. "That was the only reason I told him to ask you."

She grinned. "It was just an experiment. If no one liked the fudge, I would have gone back to the old recipe."

"Well, everyone in Bluebird is talking about the confection I'm making. Some say they like the peanut butter better than the maple walnut now." He managed half a scowl, but he was still holding on to her hand. "You're going to have to tell me what you did. I'm going to have to ask for your recipe."

She smiled slyly. "And what if I don't want to tell you?"

He narrowed his gaze, looking down at her. "Then I'll have to figure out a way to get it out of you, won't I?" he teased.

"Rose! Rose!" Lydie called from behind them.

Rose pulled her hand from Jacob's just as Lydie pushed open the screen door to the porch. "A customer wants to know if she can get two pounds of the new peanut butter fudge by Friday." She gestured. "In a box with those hearts drawn on them. And that sticker."

Rose looked up at Jacob, and he burst into laughter.

"What?" Lydie's eyes grew wide as she looked from Rose to Jacob and back at Rose again. "What did I say?"

And then Rose laughed with him.

"It's not hardening as quickly as it should," Jacob worried aloud.

He was sitting on the stool at the counter in the kitchen, resting his knee. It was late Friday night, after eight. He needed to get home and care for his animals. He'd made arrangements for his neighbor's boy to milk that evening, but there were still his chickens, his old mare, and his mother's goats to be tended to. The goats didn't need to be milked; they were more his mother's pets than anything else, but he knew she'd want them fed and locked up in the barn for the night by a decent hour.

Rose came to stand beside him. In place of her prayer *kapp*, she was wearing a woolen scarf tied over her head. It kept her hair neater and her *kapp* safe, she'd explained to him when she came into the kitchen from the back after they closed the shop. Jacob liked her in the scarf. A woman in a scarf seemed homey to him. A sign that she was contented in her surroundings and with him, and he liked that. He liked that Rose felt comfortable in a head scarf, reserved for family and good friends, in front of him.

"It's going to set up just fine," Rose insisted, peering over his shoulder at the three-pound pan of fudge. "Give it a few minutes; it's still hot."

"I don't know if I have enough butter to make another batch this large if it doesn't turn out. It looks grainy." He glanced up at her. "Does it look grainy to you?"

She laughed and picked up a little crumble of fudge left on the wooden counter from the last batch they'd made. "It's going to be fine. It's *goot;* just give it a moment."

He sighed and stared at the pan of fudge as if his gaze could harden it to the perfect consistency. "We cut and box this and we're done."

"We sure are." She picked up several dirty utensils and carried them to the sink. "I don't know what we'll do with ourselves with the orders complete. I suppose I'll be back to making supper with Mary again."

He turned on his stool and watched Rose as she dropped the utensils into a tub of soapy water and reached for a scrub brush. She was wearing the blue dress again today. His favorite. And his big, heavy denim apron over it. He liked seeing her in his apron, even if it fell almost to her ankles. He liked seeing her in his kitchen and he couldn't help but imagine her in his kitchen at home.

Did he dare to dream he might be able to convince her that she belonged in his kitchen? In his home? With him? He was fairly certain she was attracted to him. Cared for him. It was the little things she said, the way she laughed when he told a joke that wasn't all that funny. The way she listened to him, genuinely interested in what he said. And the way her face had lit up the few times he dared take her hand. *Ya,* she definitely cared for him, the question was, how long did he let things go before he expressed his feelings for her? She was a catch for certain; if he didn't start courting her officially, he knew someone else in Bluebird would. James Yoder had said as much himself at the fundraiser supper. He'd asked a lot of questions about Rose and then seemed greatly disappointed when Jacob told him he'd be taking her home that night.

Jacob's feelings for Rose had come so suddenly, so unexpectedly that, at first, he hadn't been sure what to do with them. But he'd hung on to his feeling for Adel for so long that it had been a surprising relief to see them float away. God's work, he suspected. But still miraculous.

"Could I ask you about something?" Rose said, drawing him out of his thoughts. "We don't have to talk about it if you don't want, but I'm curious." She turned to him, a wet wooden spoon in her hand. She reached for a dishtowel and began to dry it. "I . . . Would you tell me about Adel? We've talked about Karl and I was just thinking . . ." She looked down at the floor and then up at him. "I'd like to know something about her. How you met?"

Jacob was startled to hear Rose speak Adel's name when only a moment before he'd been thinking of her. But suddenly it all made sense to him. For years his mother had insisted God had a plan for him, that God had chosen a woman for him to marry, to love. His mother had said it was up to Jacob to recognize her when he saw her. Was it God putting Rose in front of him now, this happenstance of having her come to work for him all the way from Delaware when he had had no intention of hiring someone?

Was Rose meant to be his wife?

Jacob brushed his hair from his brow, wishing again that he'd gotten a haircut. He didn't want Rose to think him unkempt. Some Amish men he knew let their hair grow long past their collars and didn't bathe as often as perhaps they should have, but his house had never been of one of shaggy hair, dirty hands, or boots that smelled of manure.

Jacob met Rose's gaze and he found his voice. "Adel and I met when she came to Bluebird with her sister, Bea. They were staying with family friends; her sister was betrothed to a young man who lived here. Bea and her family have since moved to Ohio." He paused, not because he was uncomfortable speaking about Adel, but because he suddenly realized it was so long ago that he had to concentrate to remember the details of her face. "We were courting. We had talked of marriage, though the banns hadn't been cried." Again, he hesitated, not because he didn't want to tell Rose, but out of respect for Adel. "I loved her," he said, emotion welling up in his throat. "And then she died."

Rose stood there in front of him, the spoon and towel in her hand. They were both quiet for a moment and then she said quietly, "And you never met anyone else after Adel? Anyone you could give your heart to?"

It took him a long time to speak, but it wasn't an uncomfortable silence. The kitchen was warm despite the wind blowing outside and it smelled of chocolate and vanilla. "*Ne.* Not until I met you," he dared.

She smiled at him. "You'll make me blush."

"You already are," he teased. He wanted to say something more. *Ne,* what he wanted to do was take her in his arms. Maybe even kiss her. But he respected her too much for that. There was time and a place for such things and among the Old Order Amish, it was marriage. If he wanted to kiss, he'd have to marry her. Of course, he'd have to get her to agree to it first.

"Let's finish cleaning up," he told her. "By the time we have the kitchen *ret* up and the boxes ready, I think this fudge will be ready to cut."

She grinned. "And then you can ship it off in the morning."

He rose off his stool. "I was thinking about riding with Tom over to Lancaster with these last cases." He took a breath. "And . . . I was wondering if you'd like to go with us. With me. And . . . have lunch."

She dropped the spoon into a utensil crock on the counter. "Lunch? What about the shop?"

He shrugged. "Lydie can handle things for a couple of hours." His words surprised even himself as he didn't totally believe that, but the truth was, he didn't care. For the first time in a very long time, the shop didn't matter all that much. What mattered was Rose. "I think we deserve a little time off, don't you?"

"Jacob Beechy." She reached for his hand. "Are you asking me on a date?"

He was the one who blushed this time. "I think I am, Rose Bontrager."

Rose was so excited the following morning about her very first trip to Lancaster that she was up long before sunrise. She bathed and dressed and helped her cousin make breakfast and feed the children. She refused to let Mary's teasing about her new beau get to her. Rose didn't really know where she and Jacob stood, relationship-wise, but she was looking forward to finding out.

Rose was dressed in her cloak and bonnet a good ten minutes before Jacob arrived in his buggy to take her to town to meet the Englisher van driver who would take them and the final shipment of Valentine's Day Beechy's Sweets to Lancaster. He also appeared to have taken extra care with his grooming; he was freshly shaved, and it looked as if he'd tried to cut his own hair. Not a bad attempt, actually, though Rose's fingers ached to give him one more snip just over his right ear.

At the shop, Jacob gave detailed instructions to Lydie, who hopped first on one foot and then the other in anticipation of being left to run the place on her own for a few hours. She even dared make eye contact with Jacob once. Levi loaded the van and went on his way, and then finally, Jacob and Rose were off with their driver, the last of the boxes of candy stacked neatly in the back of the van. Jacob rode up front with Tom and the two men talked while Rose was content to watch the wintery countryside go by.

Southeastern Pennsylvania had a very different landscape than where she had lived in Delaware. While Delaware was very flat, with woods and small fields that surrounded small farms, Lancaster county had rolling hills, and larger farms and fields.

Once they entered the town of Lancaster, Rose was surprised by how built up it was and how many cars there were driving alongside Amish wagons and buggies. There were even traffic lights! While it was exciting to be in the "big city," it was all a little overwhelming compared to the sleepy crossroad of Bluebird.

The van first stopped to drop off an order at Yoder's Candy Store on a busy street where cars honked their horns and the sidewalks were crowded with Saturday shoppers and tourists. There, Rose remained in the van, even though Jacob invited her to join him inside while he spoke with the owner. She peered out the window as families, both English and Amish, caught her eye. And Englisher husband and wife walked side by side, the mother carrying a sleeping infant in a denim baby carrier and the father balancing a little boy of about three on his shoulders. She also spotted an Amish husband and his wife. They had four children and each parent was hanging on to little mitten hands as they walked along the sidewalk talking and laughing. The scene made Rose a little teary. She missed being a wife and a mother. She missed the kind of laughter she saw between the strangers.

At the second stop, Lancaster Central Market, Rose agreed to go inside with Jacob. Mary had encouraged her to see the big building filled with food stalls, telling her she could buy anything from freshly squeezed orange juice to a side of ham there. Tom got a cart and wheeled the delivery into a huge red brick building with arched windows and doors. Inside, he proceeded to the little store that sold not only homemade chocolates and candy, but homemade potato chips as well. Once the business transaction was complete, Jacob made arrangements to meet Tom two hours later for their trip home and suddenly Rose found herself alone with him.

At first it seemed awkward, walking around with Jacob in a setting beyond the store or an Amish school or farmhouse, but they were soon laughing and talking as they walked from stall to stall. Jacob told her that Lancaster Central Market was the oldest market building in the whole United States and that there were Amish families who supported themselves selling their goods there. There were deli counters selling not just lunch meats by the pound, but also tall roast beef sandwiches on homemade breads, and potato and macaroni salads and every kind of slaw one could imagine. And the bakery! There were Dutch apple and cranberry pies, pear streusels, cream-filled Long Johns, and cakes that stood a foot high. A person could have eaten something different every day at the Lancaster Central Market for a year and not sampled every food that was available. And there was produce there, too, mostly tubers and fruits like apples that store well. Jacob explained that in the spring and summer there would be more produce stalls and Englishers came there to buy every fruit or vegetable that could be grown in the county. And folks, many Amish and Mennonite, didn't just sell perishable foods; there were stalls with jams and jellies and pickles and preserves and handmade quilts and wooden toys.

Looking at the food made them both hungry and they soon agreed it was time for lunch. They did, after all, need to get back to Bluebird where Lydie was running the store. Rose suggested they just grab something there at the market and find a place to eat, but Jacob said he wanted to sit down at a restaurant. Rose realized then that he might be tired after walking on his injured knee for so long and agreed to a restaurant meal. Eating out was something she rarely ever did at home and when she did, it was usually at a fast food burger place to suit her younger siblings.

Rose tied the strings of her black bonnet and tightened her wool cloak around her shoulders and they went outside into the bitter cold. A block away, they entered a small diner that advertised "*Goot* Food" in blue lettering on the window of the shop.

When they entered, they had both removed their outdoor head coverings and their coats and left them hanging on a pegboard near the door. The restaurant had the look of her mother's kitchen: sparse, but homey with white walls and no adornment save for the wood trim and floors and a pretty sampler between the two windows. Rose couldn't quite read it from where she was standing, but she imagined it was a bible verse. An older Mennonite woman in a white prayer *kapp* and simple green dress stood at the cash register, ringing out a customer.

Rose and Jacob were seated by a young Mennonite girl at a cozy table for two near a fireplace that burned gas instead of wood and were given large paper menus. Rose recognized most of the dishes. They were the home-cooked dishes of her childhood that she had learned to make herself in her mam's kitchen: beef potpies, butter noodles, corn chowder, and fried pork chops. There were also a couple of Englisher dishes Rose didn't know like rigatoni al basilico and pad thai, but there were short descriptions and she was tempted to get something she'd never tried before.

"Order anything you like," Jacob told her from behind his menu. "I'm so hungry, I might order two meals."

A young woman with long blond hair piled haphazardly on top of her head, wearing a blue and white checked apron, brought them each a glass of water. She was definitely not Mennonite. "What can I get you for?" she asked, pulling a little pad of paper and a pencil from the apron pocket.

"Rose?" Jacob asked.

Rose found it interesting how comfortable he seemed with Englishers, which seemed out of character for him; she'd noticed it before back at the market. A pleasant surprise to learn something new about him.

"I . . ." Rose glanced down at the menu, a little overwhelmed by unfamiliar surroundings and choices. "You go, I'm still deciding."

Jacob surprised her by ordering spaghetti and meatballs with garlic toast and a side salad with blue cheese dressing. Definitely not a meal that would be described by any Amish man or woman as "*goot* food," but she admired him for being so adventurous. With her eye on the dessert menu that included shoofly pie with homemade walnut ice cream, Rose ordered ham meatloaf with mashed potatoes and gravy and green beans.

"You want the cornbread or the biscuits?" the girl whose apron matched the tablecloth asked.

"Biscuits, please."

"You know they won't be as good as yours," Jacob said when the waitress had gone.

She smiled but said nothing and Jacob sat back in his chair and looked at her across the small table. "I cannot believe we're here. I can't believe we filled all those fudge orders, Rose. You and me."

She kept smiling. There was a light in Jacob's eyes that she hadn't seen when she first met him. She wondered if she dared consider it might have something to do with her. With them.

"I can't thank you enough," he told her

She took a sip of water. "Well, you *have* thanked me enough. I never had any doubt you wouldn't do it. Couldn't. And what did I do but make boxes and add what you told me at the stove?"

He grinned. He looked younger today than he had in weeks. The worry lines around his mouth had receded and he seemed relaxed. Even happy. He was definitely getting around better, though still using the crutch. After an appointment two days previously, when he found that he was healing faster than expected, his doctor had given him permission to start putting some weight on his knee.

"I don't think you have anything to worry about. It doesn't matter if that big store moves in," she told him. "What you're making, people will pay for, if not in Bluebird, then here in Lancaster. They'll pay the higher prices. I'm sure of that, even more sure now that I've seen the farmer's market. And you said you're selling more in the store than you ever have."

"*Ya,* we have been busy," he admitted. "Maybe when *Mam* comes home next week, I'll keep Lydie on. Give *Mam* more time to visit with friends, go to her quilting circle. Things a woman her age should do. I think Lydie's family could use the extra income, what with them just having their fourteenth little one."

Rose rested her hands on the table in front of her. "You'd best take care, Jacob, or someone will see through that gruff voice of yours and realize how kind-hearted you are."

He scowled, but the scowl turned to a smile and he surprised her by reaching across the small table to take her hand. "I think you've seen through me since the day we met." He looked down, and then back up at her. "Rose, I had no intention of saying this . . . of bringing it up today, but—"

"Here's some bread and butter while you wait," the waitress said, approaching the table.

Rose pulled her hand from Jacob's.

"And some strawberry jam," the waitress continued. "Mrs.

Yoder made it specially for Valentine's Day." She set the basket and little jelly jar down on the table. "Not that you folks celebrate Valentine's Day . . ." She backed away from the table, suddenly seeming to regret the conversation she'd started. Or maybe because she realized she'd interrupted something between them.

When the waitress was gone, Rose met Jacob's gaze. She was unsure what to say now. What to do. She had a feeling Jacob was attempting to discuss their relationship, maybe even wanting to ask if he could court her. Did she encourage him to go on? Or did she let him take the lead. He was just sitting there now. What if he'd thought better of the idea?

"Would you like some bread?" she said after a moment of silence between them.

"Sure." He shifted forward in his chair and accepted the basket she offered. But then he put it down. "No . . . actually, Rose—" He stopped and started again, obviously nervous now. "Rose . . ."

She looked up at him. "*Ya?*"

"Rose . . . I know this is soon, but . . ." He exhaled. "Rose . . . I think we should get married."

She knew her eyes grew round with surprise. She was expecting a discussion of formal courting, which among their people was not entered lightly. An official courting period meant a couple was moving toward possibility of marriage, but for him to suggest marriage outright . . . she was shocked. And a part of her thrilled.

"I didn't say that right." Again, he reached across the table and took her hand. "Rose, will you marry me? Because . . . I care for you deeply. I . . ." He looked into her eyes. "I love you, Rose, and I think . . . I think you could come to love me. I think we're well suited and—"

"*Ya,*" she blurted.

"We both want a family, children if—"

"Didn't you hear me? I'll marry you," she interrupted again, tears springing to her eyes.

He looked startled for a moment and then he squeezed her hand. "You will?"

She pressed her lips together and nodded.

"Not right away of course, but, at our age . . ."

"And me being a widow," she said her voice shaky. "You're right, there's no need for us to wait long. Not if we're both sure." Suddenly she was so happy. She agreed with Jacob that this was all moving very quickly, but in her heart of hearts, she knew Jacob was the husband for her. She had always known that if she had patience, God would bless her with a family again and she knew that blessing was Jacob.

"*Ya,*" he agreed, now seeming pleased with himself. "Exactly."

"Here we go," the young waitress sang, approaching their table again, a serving platter in her hands. "Spaghetti and meatballs and ham meatloaf."

Jacob released Rose's hand and sat back. But as the waitress set the plates before them, filling the table with bowls of pasta and garlic bread and a huge plate of meatloaf and potatoes with gravy and a bowl of green beans, he met Rose's gaze. And Rose felt as if there was no one else in the world but the two of them. No time but this moment.

When the waitress was gone, Jacob smiled. "Just to be sure I heard you correctly. You said yes, you'd marry me. *Ya?*"

Rose laughed, but she wanted to cry, she was so happy. "*Ya,* I said I would marry you. And the sooner the better, I think."

"*Ya?*"

She shrugged. "I imagine a couple of our advanced age," she teased, "your bishop will want to see us married as quickly as possible." She hesitated. "Unless you want to wait. Want to get to know me better?"

He took his gingham napkin off the table and spread it in his lap. "Sooner than later is good to me. I've never been surer of anything in my life." He folded his hands. "Shall we say grace and then eat? And then when we get home, I think I have a phone call to Indiana to make."

They were both smiling.

"Because today," he said, "I think you have made both me and Clara Beechy very, very happy."

Chapter 7

A week later Clara returned from Indiana and Jacob and Rose told her their good news in person.

"I'm so excited for you," Clara exclaimed, grasping first Rose's hand and then Jacob's. Tears filled the older woman's eyes. "I prayed you'd find a good woman, Jacob. Prayed every day for more years now than I can count."

They were all standing in Jacob's kitchen. He had invited Rose for Friday night supper so they could tell his mother the good news of the betrothal together when she arrived home. Jacob had managed to clean the whole house on his own, and had a pot of vegetable beef stew bubbling on the back of the wood stove that he'd started before he left for the candy shop that morning.

"Oh, please don't cry," Rose murmured, reaching into her apron pocket for a white handkerchief embroidered with a tiny yellow rosebud. She pushed it into Clara's hand.

Clara dabbed at her eyes. "I'm just so happy. This might be the happiest day of my life."

Jacob leaned his weight on his crutch. "*Mam* can be dramatic," he explained. "If we're going to all live together once you and I are married, Rose, you're going to have to get used to it."

"Live together!" Clara exclaimed. "Certainly not. Newly-weds need time alone. What makes you think I would want to live with newlyweds?" She marched to the stove and put the pan of buttermilk biscuits Rose had whipped up into the oven.

Rose met Jacob's gaze and lifted her brows.

Jacob took a couple of steps toward his mother while Rose moved to the table to set it with the silverware she'd taken from the drawer.

"Just out of curiosity, *Mam*, where do you intend to live when Rose and I marry?" Jacob turned to Rose. "My aunt Dorcas is a widow as well, and lives not far from here in Bird In Hand." He looked back to his mother at the stove. "You swore you'd never live with your sister, not if you were penniless and without sight or hearing."

Clara chuckled as she removed the quilted hot mitt from her hand. "I did say that, didn't I?" She looked to Rose. "Don't misunderstand. I love my sister, but she's a bit austere for my likes."

"Cheap and cantankerous," Jacob whispered under his breath. Rose hid a smile.

"Colder inside her house than outside on a winter day and she's not much for a smile. Stingy with them," Clara explained.

Again, Jacob met Rose's gaze. Rose pulled out the chair at the end of table for him and he moved toward it, understanding without her having to say so that it was time he got off his knee. They'd been betrothed less than a week, but they were already beginning to communicate the way a couple did. And they were already beginning to enjoy private jokes between them-selves, little things that would help bind them together in mar-riage, Rose knew from experience. They had both worked a full day at the candy shop before the van driver dropped Clara home in time for supper. Jacob's appointment at the doctor's office had confirmed that he was indeed healing, but he was still required to wear the leg brace and use the crutch for at least another two weeks.

"Leave Bluebird? My ladies quilting circle?" Clara continued. "Certainly not. The only way I'm leaving this town is when the good Lord calls me home." She shook her head and dug into a drawer, extracting a big wooden spoon, one Rose recognized as Jacob's handiwork. "I'm going to build myself a *dawdi haus*. Right there in the backyard between the apple and the peach trees." She pointed in the direction with her spoon. "Be in by the Fourth of July, I should think. You don't plan to marry before then, do you? I know November is the month of wedding, but I imagine the bishop would approve an earlier date considering your circumstances of age and Rose being a widow. No need to waste time."

"*Mam,* you don't have to leave your house." Jacob slid down into the chair and Rose took his crutch and leaned it against the wall beside an old pie safe painted green with the customary punched tin panels in the doors.

"Certainly not," Rose agreed. "This is your house, Clara."

"It's Jacob's house," his mother said firmly. She shook her spoon at them. "Meant for him and his wife and his children, God willing."

Rose knew she should have been embarrassed by such a reference, but she was too old and had experienced too much of life to be shy around such talk. She was an adult woman who had given birth and buried a child and husband. She knew where babies came from. And God willing, she did hope to have more children. With Jacob.

"*Mam,* I'm sure you and I and Rose can get along just fine here together. The house is plenty big enough."

"Which is why I want Rose to take over the house when you wed. And take over the housekeeping." She waved the spoon and then commenced to stir the stew. "This house is too big for a woman my age. By the time I've scrubbed every floor on my hands and knees, it's time to start all over again. *Ne.* I want a *dawdi haus* just big enough for a little kitchen and parlor and bedroom and bath."

"We can discuss this later, *Mam.* I've not even yet spoken with the bishop. You're the first we've told except for Rose's cousin Mary and her husband."

"We can certainly talk about it later. Or not at all." Clara took a soup spoon from a drawer and dipped out a sample of the stew and blew on it. "But my mind's made up. It was planned all along. I'd have been in my own little place years ago if you could have convinced someone to marry you sooner." She slurped the stew off the spoon. "Needs more salt." She set down the spoon and walked through the mud room and stepped into the pantry.

"This is silly," Jacob told Rose quietly. "It never occurred to me she wouldn't want to stay here."

She slipped into the chair to his left, where she had set a place setting for herself. Clara's dishes were plain white, but the soup bowls had apple blossoms in the bottom. "You know I'm content to live with Clara, but I understand what she's saying," she said quietly. They could hear Clara rummaging around in the pantry. "She's of an age to do less housecleaning and more visiting. And while she may work fewer hours in the shop, I don't think she has any intention of quitting. She likes the social aspect of it."

"And bossing people around," he pointed out, stretching his hand across the table to cover Rose's.

She smiled up at him. "That, too, probably, but I recall you telling me this morning that I could be bossy."

"It's my lot in life, I suppose, to be bossed around by my women." He brought her hand to his lips and kissed her knuckles. His gesture was unfitting, and Rose didn't care. She hadn't realized how much she'd missed the touch of a man. Of a man who loved her.

"I'll try not to be too bossy," she told him softly, "if you promise to try not to be so grumpy."

"I think both are in our natures," he murmured.

And Rose felt her heart melting. Jacob had told her he loved her the day he proposed, but she'd not said the words yet. She'd still been coming to terms with the idea that she could love Jacob and still love Karl. Because she would always love Karl. But all of a sudden, the words were on the end of her tongue and she wanted to speak them.

"We'll have to put salt on the grocery list, Jacob." Clara came back into the kitchen and Rose released Jacob's hand and stood. If Clara noticed them holding hands and gazing into each other's eyes, she said nothing. "What were you doing with it while I was gone? Making salt dough to play with?"

Rose snickered at the thought. Jacob looked at her, trying to frown and not laugh at the silly thing Clara had said, and that just made it funnier. And it made Rose's heart glad because she knew the home and family she and Jacob would build together would sometimes include frowns, but she knew there would always be laughter, too.

A week later, Jacob sat in his office at the end of the day running numbers from the previous month. Not only had it been a good February, but it had been their best month ever. And their number one seller in the shop, he had learned, was their peanut butter fudge. The new recipe. A part of him wanted to be angry. This was Beechy's Sweets, the old recipe had been *his* recipe. But the truth was that any anger he felt was due to pride, a trait not acceptable in an Amish man. And the other part of him was proud of Rose and the fact that she'd been able to take what was an excellent recipe and improve upon it. What made him even prouder was that she'd been bold enough to change his recipe, to believe in herself enough to do it.

Jacob glanced at the wind-up clock on his desk; it was five fifteen. They had just closed up out front and Rose was ringing out the register. His mother was washing the last of the dishes from a trial run at making chocolate-covered peanut butter eggs for the coming Easter season. While Easter was a time of solemn prayer and even fasting sometimes among the Amish, the Englishers bought a lot of candy for Easter. The idea had been Rose's and together they had come up with some ideas the previous night as to what to make to sell and how to market it to shops in Lancaster. His Rose had a head for business.

His Rose. He couldn't stop smiling. At least not when he was alone. He still couldn't believe it was true, that she was going to marry him. That he would be her husband. As a younger man, Jacob had wanted a wife and children but after Adel's death, he'd lost sight of that dream. He'd become so wrapped up in his grief, and in his fear of loving again, that he'd almost allowed himself to become an old bachelor.

But everything was different now. Now that he had his Rose and she had him. The fact that she had loved another man before him didn't bother him. Because even though he'd only known her a short time, he knew she had enough love in her heart to love him, too. He didn't expect Rose to stop loving her dead husband; he expected her heart to expand to include him, too.

She told him that the previous evening. That she loved him and her words almost brought tears to his eyes. He had no doubt he and Adel had loved each other, but there was something about being older, having experienced more loss, more joy, that made him feel what he felt for Rose went even deeper and wider.

A loud knock on the door startled Jacob and he swung around in the swiveled office chair. His mother stood in the doorway.

"I called your name and you didn't answer. Woolgathering are you?" There was a sly smile on her face. Of course, she'd been smiling since she came home a week ago to learn that he and Rose were betrothed.

He frowned. "Running numbers."

She stepped into the office. She had a dustrag in her hand and she began to run it along a piece of chair rail. "Looked more like you were woolgathering, dreaming of a wedding day, maybe?"

When he didn't respond, she went on. "I'm looking forward to dinner with Mary and Junior and the children tonight with you and Rose. It was kind of you to invite me."

"You're our family." He turned back to the papers on his desk, feeling a little foolish that his mother *had* caught him daydreaming about Rose. "Will be. Rose's," he added gruffly.

"I like being included. I just want you to know that you needn't invite me to every dinner you're invited to. You and Rose need to spend time getting to know each other, making plans. I know I arranged this match, but I needn't be a part of your courting. I only—"

Jacob spun around in the chair. "What did you say?"

She lifted the dustrag, startled by the tone of his voice. "I said I needn't be a part of your courting."

"The bit before." Jacob felt as if he had been slapped. Had his mother just said what he thought she had said? That he had been set up?

She blanched, her rosy, round cheeks growing pale. And then he knew he was right.

"You arranged this how?" he asked, slowly, emphasis on each word.

"Jacob—"

"*Mother,*" he said sharply, coming out of his chair. "Did you bring Rose into my shop with the intention of playing match-maker? Did Rose come here thinking—"

"Jacob, please." She gripped the dustrag. "Lower your voice, Rose will hear you."

Jacob's heart was pounding, his face heated. How could they have done this to him without his knowledge? How could Rose have done this to him? How could she have been so manipulative, so . . . scheming.

"Jacob, come back," Clara called to her son.

He strode out the door, limping, leaving his crutch behind.

Rose was just zipping up the deposit bag and reaching for a pound of fudge she'd boxed to take for dessert when she heard Jacob coming through the doors from the kitchen. "I'm all set here. Door's locked, shades down." She turned to him, holding up the money bag. "We can drop off the deposit as we go by the—" The look on Jacob's face startled her. He looked angry. "What's wrong?"

He was just standing there inside the door, staring at her.

"Where's your crutch?" she asked. "You shouldn't be—"

"You came here for a husband, not a job?" he interrupted.

She stared at him. "What?"

"When you came here to supposedly apply for the job in my shop, you were actually applying to marry me?"

"Jacob, I have no idea what you're talking about."

Clara walked in behind her son. She looked as if she was about to cry.

"Clara, are you all right?" Rose asked, taking a step toward her.

"*Mam,* this is between Rose and me." He didn't look at his mother. "I'll ask you to step out."

"Jacob, what I said was true. I did—"

"*Mam,*" he repeated, his voice practically booming in Rose's ears, "could you please give us a moment."

Clara's teary gaze met Rose's. "I'm so sorry," she said, and then before Rose could answer, she walked back into the kitchen, letting the doors swing shut behind her.

Rose set down the blue vinyl deposit bag. "What's going on? What are you talking about?"

"I'm talking about you and my mother. But mostly about you." He pointed at her. "My mother wasn't interviewing for shopgirls the week she *hired* you. She was interviewing for a wife for me."

Rose's gaze drifted to the door and then back at Jacob again. She'd turned out the overhead lights so just the lights from the candy cases and from the small lamp on the back wall illuminated the shop. It smelled of all the sweets in the cases, but mostly of chocolate. An aroma she'd always loved, one she thought had become a part of her life.

But suddenly she wasn't certain any longer of what was in her future.

"You mother was interviewing to find you a wife?" she asked. As the words came out of her mouth, she realized it was probably true. She remembered, at the time, thinking some of Clara's questions for a shopgirl had been odd, but she'd just come to town and everyone had warned her Clara Beech could be eccentric.

"You manipulated me," Jacob accused.

A lump formed in Rose's throat, but she didn't cry. And she didn't back down.

She picked up the deposit bag again, hugging it to herself.

"What do you have to say?" he asked, tempering his tone a bit this time.

She lifted her gaze until she met the eyes that she thought she would look into until the end of her days, eyes she thought she would see in her children. She took a breath and when she spoke, her voice was soft . . . but strong. Inside she was crumbling, but her words came surprisingly easy.

"What do I have to say?" she asked. "This is what I have to say, Jacob Beechy. If you think I'm the kind of person who would have deceived you in such a way, would have made an agreement with your mother to *manipulate* you, as you worded it, into loving you, then I think you should break our betrothal here and now. If you think I'm the kind of woman who could . . . who would scheme her way into your heart, perhaps even lure you up a ladder and make you fall and break your knee so I could wheedle my way into your life, then I think you should break our engagement." She lifted her chin a notch. Inside she could feel her heart breaking, but if he thought she was that person, did she really want to marry him?

"In fact," she said, pushing the deposit bag into his chest, forcing him to grab it before it fell. "I think you should fire me. I wouldn't want that kind of woman working in *my* shop." And then she made herself walk past him. She would walk out the door, out of the shop, and home to Mary's.

Jacob stood there for a moment, clutching the bag. Rose's response was not at all what he had expected. He had expected excuses, maybe denial, but instead, she had defended her honor . . . and made him feel very small.

"Rose . . . wait," he said, feeling as if the wind had been knocked out of him by a swift kick from a cow.

At that moment, Jacob suddenly came to his senses. He made up his mind that if Rose kept walking, he would go after her. He would follow her home to Delaware if he had to. He would follow her to the ends of the earth because she was the woman for him. Because he loved her. And he was wrong to have jumped to the conclusion that she had been a part of his mother's scheme. Because he knew Rose better than that. And he knew that while his mother might come up with such an outlandish plan because mothers sometime did such things in desperation, he also knew his Rose would never have been a part of it. Had she known what Clara Beechy's intention had been that day she came for the interview, she'd have walked out the door, just as she was now.

"Rose, I'm sorry." He hobbled to her. To her back. She was

just standing there. He tossed the bag on the counter, limped the last couple of steps to her, and he caught her arm and turned her around to face him.

Her eyes were teary, but she wasn't crying.

"I'm sorry," he said again. "I don't know what—when *Mam* accidentally told me that she'd played matchmaker, that she'd arranged all of this, I jumped to the conclusion—" He shook his head. "That you had been a part of it," he whispered. "Will you forgive me?"

When she didn't respond immediately, he went on. "You're right. I do know you better than that. I know you wouldn't have been a part of such an arrangement." He took her hands in his. "I don't know why I thought that for even a moment. I guess I was angry with *Mam,* and . . . Please give me another chance. I know we're just getting to know each other really, but I want you to see that I'm a good man. That I try to be a good man and that I know better than to make such snap judgements. I just—"

"*Ya,*" she whispered. "You are a better man than that."

Jacob wrapped his arms around her and pulled her tight against him. He kissed her neck just below where her prayer *kapp* fell, where there was a curl of hair that was holding him mesmerized.

"You mustn't be too harsh on her," Rose whispered in his ear. "She's your mother. She only wanted what was best for you. She wants you to be happy."

"I know. You're right." He drew back, looking into her eyes again. "Thank you for bringing me to my senses."

She nodded and reached into her pocket, pulling out a hand-kerchief with a rosebud to dab at her eyes. "I was so afraid you were going to let me walk out the door, Jacob. Let me go home. Let me leave Bluebird." She whispered her last words.

"I can be foolish at times, but not stupid. I'm never going to let you go," he said, still gripping her hand.

She gave a little laugh and pulled away. "What would the bishop think of us standing here in near darkness, holding hands? We should go."

She reached for the box of fudge she'd left on the counter.

"What have you got there?"

She lifted the lid to show him.

"Ah, my new peanut butter fudge recipe." He opened the box, picked up a square, took a bite, and then offered it to her.

Rose took a bite. The fudge was creamy and nutty and delicious on her tongue, as sweet as the dreams she had for the future. She knew there would be more disagreements in the coming weeks and months and years of their union, but the fact that Jacob was willing to admit he was wrong made her love him even more.

Jacob reached for another piece and she laughed, pretending to pull the box from his reach. "I'm going to have to get more if you keep eating it."

"I may have to eat the whole box," he said. "How else am I going to figure out what's the secret in my new recipe?"

"It's cheese," she told him softly.

His eyes widened. "*Cheese?* You put *cheese* in my fudge?"

"Just a little soft yellow cheese," she admitted, pinching her thumb and forefinger together.

And then they laughed, and both knew that while their life together wouldn't be without missteps, it would be a sweet one.

The Sweetest Truth

LAURA BRADFORD

For my readers, old and new;
I'm glad you're here.

Dear Reader,

When I sat down to write *The Sweetest Truth*, all I knew is that I wanted it to be a story about the power of love. Because while love, itself, is beautiful, the *true* beauty lies in what love can *do*.

It can lift people up, it can build bridges where none existed, it can right wrongs, it can teach, it can heal, and it can help us to see what's true.

It's that latter part—about love helping us to see what's . true—that led me to Sadie Lapp.

Six years ago, Sadie imagined her life going in much the same way *Mam*'s did. Courtship . . . Marriage . . . Children . . .

But the fire in *Dat*'s barn changed that. Changed *her*.

Or did it?

The answer to that question awaits you in my story, *The Sweetest Truth*. And when you're done, you can see what else I write by visiting my website: www.laurabradford.com.

Happy reading!

Laura Bradford

Monday. 10:45 a.m.

Stepping back, Sadie Fisher drank in the varying shades of yellow that fairly danced across the quilt like rays of sunlight. "Miss Jenny, I think this just might be the prettiest quilt we've ever had in the shop. Ruth Hershberger does fine work. I think this one will sell very fast."

"I certainly hope so." Jenny Duggan pulled her attention from the front window of Bluebird Quilts long enough to beckon Sadie to her side. When Sadie acquiesced, the sixty-five-year-old shop owner pointed out to the street. "I think the buggy-to-car ratio on Main Street today favors the buggy."

Sadie nodded as her own gaze followed three different buggies past the shop, their destination certain. "*Ya.* Ruth's daughter, Miriam, is to be married tomorrow. To Atlee Stutzman. Many people from many communities will be there. I'm going, too—with *Mam* and *Dat*, of course."

"Ooh, a wedding!" Miss Jenny clapped her plump hands beneath her chin. "Is the bride one of your friends?"

"Miriam and I went to school together and she is in our church district."

"Are you close?" Miss Jenny prodded.

"We spoke a little at hymn sings. *Mam* says that is because we were friends as little ones. But I think it is because we were the last of our group to get married. But that will change now as it has with the others." Sadie watched yet another charcoal-colored buggy meander down the road and then hooked her thumb in the direction of the quilts she still needed to price. "I should put the tag on Ruth's quilt before more customers come in."

"What will change, dear?"

"The talking part. We will speak after church, I am sure. But she will be married, like the others, and I will not be. Soon, we will have even less to say to each other than we already did."

Miss Jenny took one last look out the window and then trailed Sadie across the shop to the section earmarked specifically for new additions. "It could happen for you, too, dear."

"What could?" Sadie pulled an empty tag from the drawer beneath the register, noted the price with ink, and then carried it over to Ruth's quilt.

"Getting married."

She felt her throat tighten as it always did when her English boss brought the conversation around to boys. It wasn't that she didn't think of them, because she did. But trying to get Miss Jenny to see things as they were was exhausting. Still, she tried and hoped that maybe, just maybe, the woman would finally come around to the same reality Sadie had been forced to accept six years earlier. "A boy would have to be *interested* for me to marry, Miss Jenny. And there is no one."

Miss Jenny swatted at Sadie's words as if they were a pesky gnat. "I don't believe that, Sadie. I just think you spend too much time here, and in your home when you are not. You should be spending your breaks outside on the front step, or visiting one of the shops where there always seems to be Amish either working or making deliveries of some sort."

"I have gone to hymn sings for many years, Miss Jenny. It is where Miriam and all my other friends met their husbands."

"But the boys I see from the window—like that one who works at the market, and the young man who delivers the milk to the new ice cream shop next door—do not all go to the same hymn sing, do they?" Miss Jenny asked.

Just the mere mention of the handsome, brown-eyed Amos Yoder made it so even the simple act of breathing was difficult. But it did no good to think of him, or to imagine herself living the life of a married woman with children of her own. "No, they do not. But *I* am still the same, Miss Jenny. It does not matter what hymn sing I go to."

"You just need to get out, Sadie. Show them the Sadie I see—a Sadie who is sweet, kind, and has a wonderful little sense of humor."

Sadie fussed with the positioning of the price tag as long as possible and then swept her hands down the sides of her lavender dress. "I do not hide who I am, Miss Jenny. Not here and not at home."

"I know that. I just want you to show it out there"—Miss Jenny motioned toward the front window and its view of Main Street—"to everyone else, too."

Pulling her gaze from the toes of her lace-up boots, Sadie fixed it on the English shopkeeper. "Am I not good with the customers, Miss Jenny?"

"No, you're wonderful with the customers, dear. Everyone who steps foot inside this shop loves you. It's just that *more* people need to see it. People like Amos Yoder and the other boys need to see it."

"I don't even *know* Amos Yoder."

"You see him when he pulls into the alley in his buggy . . . You see him when he hops down off his seat to carry all those milk cans in to his father . . . I know because I've seen you watching him from the side window a time or two."

Oh, how she wanted to dispute her boss's words, to argue that she didn't have any idea about the comings and goings of the ice cream shop owner's son, but she couldn't. To do so would be to lie.

"Perhaps, if you were to actually step outside the shop on a break one of these days, you could say hello and introduce yourself," Miss Jenny said, her blue eyes sparkling at the thought. "He looks like such a nice young man."

She closed her eyes against the oft-imagined moment that had her outside Bluebird Quilts, sweeping, as Amos drove up, the left side of her face positioned outward. As always, she saw him jump down from his buggy seat, reach for a milk can, and then freeze as he spotted her. The smile she'd spied from the window while Miss Jenny was otherwise occupied would spread across his face as he stepped forward, eager to meet her. She would prop the broom against the railing and then turn to greet him and—

Shaking the ridiculous image from her thoughts, she stared, unseeingly, out the window. "I do not need to introduce myself. There is no reason."

"No reason?" Miss Jenny echoed. "But he could be the one, Sadie! The one that will make it so buggy after buggy drives down Main Street for *your* wedding one day."

Breathing in the courage she needed to smile through the pain, Sadie shrugged. "There will be no buggies for me, Miss Jenny. Not until it is God's will for me to pass."

"Sadie! Don't talk like that! You are only twenty-two!"

"But death brings lots of buggies, too." Rising up onto the toes of her boots, Sadie spun back toward the counter and the next quilt she needed to display—this one from Leddy Miller, the girl who'd sat behind her in school when they were young, and now had two little ones of her own. "If it is okay, Miss Jenny, when I am done with this quilt, I think I'll take my lunch outside and read."

"On the front porch?" Miss Jenny asked, her voice hopeful.

"No. Out back. On the stoop."

For a moment, the woman said nothing, her bright blue eyes fixed on Sadie's hazel ones as if she was searching for something. Eventually, though, she stepped forward and gathered Sadie's hands inside her own. "You are *beautiful*, dear. Inside and out. The scars on your face don't change that. Not for people with eyes that truly see, anyway. Remember that. Always."

Swallowing against the lump that was now firmly lodged inside her throat, Sadie tugged her hands free, scooped up the next quilt, and headed back across the shop. When she reached the recently emptied rack, she arranged Leddy's work across the top, careful to showcase the design in such a way that it could be seen by customers the moment they stepped inside. She could feel Miss Jenny watching her as she worked, but that was okay. Watching was better than speaking. At least until she was sure she could engage in the latter without bursting into tears.

The steady *clip-clop* of an approaching buggy wafted through the window overlooking the alleyway between Bluebird Quilts and Yoder's Ice Cream and brought Sadie's focus off Leddy's quilt and onto the gray-topped buggy slowing to a stop. A glance over her shoulder showed that Miss Jenny was otherwise occupied, thus clearing the way for Sadie to take a peek . . .

Sure enough, Amos Yoder had arrived for his afternoon

milk delivery. And, just as he had since his *dat* opened the shop, he jumped down from his seat, said something into the ear of his buggy horse, and then tethered the animal to the hitching post between the two shops. She could never quite make out what he said, even with the window open a little, as it was at that moment, but based on the way the mare turned to look at him, she imagined it was something kind, and reassuring.

Sighing, she leaned against the edge of the window and watched as the man she guessed to be about her age made his way around the back of the buggy. But two steps from his final destination, he turned in her direction, a slow smile and an even slower nod letting her know she'd been seen. Unsure of how to respond or if she should even respond at all, she returned his nod. When he took a step closer as if to engage her, she turned and made her way back to Leddy's quilt.

5:10 p.m.

Sadie lifted her face to the day's waning rays, the momentary encounter with Amos Yoder replaying itself in her mind for the umpteenth time as she made the quiet trek toward *Dat*'s farm on foot. She knew she'd been rude to turn her back the way she had, but somehow, the notion of seeing *that* look on his handsome face was more than she could bear.

It was a look she knew well, a look she'd come to expect since the fire in *Dat*'s barn six years earlier. In the beginning, a glimpse at the right side of her face had sent her running for her bedroom only to be reminded by *Mam* that vanity was wrong. In the mornings, when she'd wake up, she'd touch the left side of her face and actually imagine the time she'd spent in the hospital had been a bad dream. Of course, when she touched her right cheek, reality always won.

Memories of the first hymn sing she'd attended after being released from the hospital still weighed on her heart. Friends she'd known her whole life—friends she'd once laughed and played with so easily—suddenly avoided eye contact. They'd smile as she approached and then drop their eyes to the earth when they saw the damage to her face.

She remembered coming home that night and finding *Mam* waiting at the kitchen table, the quiet hope she held for Sadie as tangible as the suspenders she'd been mending. More than anything, Sadie had wanted to cry on *Mam*'s shoulder—to share the whispered things she'd overheard and the pain she'd felt every time someone looked away. Instead, she'd managed a smile and shared details of the evening that weren't entirely truthful. Still, the taste of the lie on her lips was preferable to seeing *Mam*'s hope fade.

Over time, she'd gotten used to it, or as used to it as one could get when half their face was pretty and half their face looked like some mask the English children wore for their Halloween celebrations. Some friends even stopped casting their eyes away whenever she got near, though in all fairness her effort to stand to everyone's right certainly helped in that regard.

Now, it was just the new people she encountered that served as a reminder of something she tried to forget—customers at the quilt shop, tourists walking by the shop while she was outside sweeping, and Amish who lived in one of Bluebird's surrounding communities. And while she couldn't do anything about the customers, she found that taking lunch in the alleyway and saving certain tasks for less crowded times helped minimize the stares and whispers.

Somedays, if she was careful enough, she could actually make it from morning to night without thinking about the one thing that made her different from everyone else. Then again, most of those instances fell on her day off, when the only eyes looking at her belonged to the chickens and cows on *Dat*'s farm. But leaving her job at Bluebird Quilts wasn't an option. Not a good one anyway. Working alongside Miss Jenny was fun. And if she ever wanted to own a shop of her own one day, she needed to learn everything she could.

At the sound of an approaching car, Sadie stepped onto the graveled shoulder and glanced back, her heart sinking at the familiar flash of red and its equally familiar driver.

"Hey there, Saaa-die . . . What's wrong with your face? Did you get stepped on by a cow?"

Forcing her gaze forward, she kept walking, the teenage boy's cruel comments nothing she hadn't heard a million times before. She tried to tell herself each time that there would come a day when the Englisher would grow tired of planning his evening around her walk home, but she wasn't entirely sure she believed that anymore.

"Hey! I'm talking to you!"

She tightened her hold on her lunch pail and willed herself to stay calm. Some days, her lack of response made him give up and drive away. Other times, six years of looks and whispers and comments boiled up inside her until she couldn't stand it anymore. On those days she either walked the remaining half mile with wet cheeks, which he loved, or spent it biting back the kind of things she knew she should not say.

"Your daddy use some sandpaper on your face or something?"

Do not pay him any mind . . .

Do not pay him any mind . . .

Do not—

The hurried *clip-clop* of a horse broke through her thoughts and sent her eyes back toward the road in time to see the Englisher race off in his car, sneering at her through his open window as he passed. For a moment, she simply watched as he disappeared around an upcoming bend, the answering relief she felt sagging her shoulders.

"Hello there!"

Lifting her hand as a shield against the sun, she was stunned to find Amos Yoder looking back at her. "Um . . . hello."

The same smile that had stolen her breath nearly every day since November overtook his face, taking with it her ability to breathe and think. "You work in the quilt shop next to my family's ice cream shop, don't you?"

"*Ya.*"

"I think I saw you in the side window earlier today. But when I came closer to say hello, you were gone."

"I . . ." She looked down at the gravel and pinched her eyes closed. "I had to take care of a customer."

It was a lie, of course, but at that moment it was preferable to the private truth that was making it so her face felt as hot as fire.

Fire . . .

On instinct, she reached up and felt, first, her good cheek, and then her—

A quiet gasp from the direction of the buggy pulled her attention back to Amos in time to see his warm brown eyes widen with curiosity and . . .

Pity?

Dropping her hand to her side, she shifted her slight frame across her legs. "I was in a fire. Six years ago. My *dat*'s barn burned to the ground."

"You were *inside*?" he asked, his voice little more than a raspy whisper.

"I ran inside to free the horses."

Silence filled the space between them as he looked from his horse, to the countryside in front of them, to the reins in his hand. She knew the reaction well. She'd seen it hundreds, maybe *thousands* of times since the fire . . .

"I should go," she finally said. "*Mam* will be wondering where I am and I do not like to make her worry."

His head snapped upward, his eyes traveling in the direction the Englisher's car had gone. "Could I give you a ride the rest of the way?"

"No. It's okay. I do not have far to go."

"Please. I would feel better knowing you got home safely." Reaching down, he extended his hand to her. "Grab hold, I will pull you up."

She started to protest but stopped as her own gaze fell on the headlights of an approaching car in the distance. The car didn't look shiny and red from where she stood, but . . . "If it's no trouble, a ride would actually be nice," she said, looking up at Amos.

"No, no trouble at all."

Bypassing his outstretched hand, she used the edge of the buggy to lift herself onto the seat. When she was safely in place, he loosened his grip on the reins and urged the horse forward. "I'm Amos, by the way. Amos Yoder."

"I know who you are."

His eyebrow cocked upward. "You do?"

"*Ya*. Miss Jenny told me your name."

"I don't know a Miss Jenny . . ."

"She owns Bluebird Quilts."

"Ahhh, then my *dat* has told her my name."

"*Ya*." She pointed straight ahead. "That is my *dat*'s farm coming up on the right."

"I don't come out this way often, but *Dat* needed me to make a delivery to the Hochstetler farm."

"They live one farm over from ours." She directed his gaze from her own driveway to the land beyond. "Abram Hochstetler is our bishop."

When they reached the mailbox with *Dat*'s name painted on the side, Amos slowed the buggy to peek across Sadie. "Mose Fisher . . . So your name is Fisher?"

"*Ya.*"

"Do you have a first name?" he asked.

She pulled a face. "Of course, I have a first name. It is Sadie. Sadie Fisher."

"Sadie. That is a nice name."

"Thank you."

He slowed the horse even more as the turnoff to her house drew nearer. "I'm sorry if your friend left because I drove up."

"My friend?" she echoed.

"The Englisher. In the shiny red car just now."

She tried to relax the instant set to her jaw, but it was difficult. Still, she was glad Amos was looking ahead rather than at her. "He is not my friend."

A momentary silence, peppered only by the sound of *Dat*'s chickens, fell around them as Amos turned up the driveway. When they reached the barn, he stopped and motioned to it with his chin. "Was anyone else hurt in the barn fire?" he asked.

"No. Just me." She climbed down from the buggy, quickly smoothed away the creases from her dress, and then swept her focus back to the barn. "As you can see, *Dat* and the others worked hard to build the new one. You cannot tell there was ever a fire here, can you?" When he didn't respond, she turned to find him looking at her, his eyes unreadable. "Unless you look at my face, of course."

He opened his mouth as if to reply but closed it as she gestured toward the house. "It is time for me to go inside. Thank you for the ride. It was very kind."

Wednesday. 9:20 a.m.

She waited for the bell to finish signaling her arrival and then lifted up the plate of cookies she'd made especially for her boss. "I made you your favorite oatmeal cookies last night, Miss Jenny."

"Oh, Sadie. You just made my morning. I love your special oatmeal—wait." The quilt shop owner stepped out from behind the counter to give Sadie her usual morning once over. Only this time, instead of following it up with a smile, there was only confusion. "Wasn't your friend's wedding yesterday?"

"*Ya.*" She made her way around the woman and set the plate of cookies on the counter. "I am sorry I was not here a little sooner, but I was just passing the Weaver's Farm when I remembered the cookies."

Miss Jenny returned to her own post behind the counter, eyeing Sadie as she did. "Don't get me wrong, dear, I'm pleased as punch about these cookies, but weren't you supposed to be *at* your friend's wedding?"

"I was."

"But Amish weddings last all day," Miss Jenny protested. "Weren't you visiting with family and friends and . . . *eating*?"

She knew where this was going. In fact, she'd gone down this very road last night. With *Mam.* "I did a little of that. For a while."

Reaching past Miss Jenny, she deposited her lunch pail and her book on the shelf beneath the register and plucked the clipboard with the day's tasks from the wall. "So, what would you like me to do first? Dust the quilt racks or go through the consignment ledger?"

"Neither." Miss Jenny liberated the clipboard from Sadie's hands and held it to her own chest. "I want you to tell me why you were making oatmeal cookies for me instead of enjoying your friend's wedding."

"I enjoyed it, Miss Jenny. I-I just didn't stay until dark like *Mam* and *Dat*."

"Why not?"

For a moment, it was as if Sadie was back in her room the previous night. Only instead of sitting on the edge of her bed, unlacing her boots, and trying not to notice the ever-present worry in *Mam*'s eyes, she was standing in the middle of Blue-bird Quilts, trying to smile away a similar worry in Miss Jenny. "I do not fit with them anymore."

"Fit with whom?"

"Miriam and the others—from my old hymn sings."

"But they're your friends, Sadie!"

"*Ya*. But now they are all married—and some even have children of their own."

"So?"

She stilled her finger along the crack in the counter she'd been tracing and shrugged. "They understand each other in a different way now. A way I am not part of. So, after a while, after we had eaten and I had spoken to many, I walked home and made cookies. For you."

"*I'm* not married, dear. And I talk to all sorts of people."

"You are kind and funny," Sadie pointed out.

"As are you."

She drew back. "I'm not funny. Not anymore, anyway."

Miss Jenny reached beneath the counter's eave and tugged out the stool on which she often sat. When she was settled on the cushion, she dipped her chin to afford a clear view of Sadie across the upper rim of her glasses. "You're funny, dear. You always have me chuckling about some such thing."

"That is because I'm here. In the shop. With you."

"I don't understand. What difference does that make?"

She passed behind Miss Jenny and wandered onto the floor, the colors and patterns of the various quilts displayed around the shop little more than background clutter to the sudden dull noise in her head. "You don't see *this* most days," she explained, pointing at her right cheek. "Which means I can be me in a way I can't be at Miriam's wedding or a hymn sing or even inside my own home some days."

Miss Jenny's gasp had Sadie closing her eyes just as she reached the window to the alleyway. "Surely your parents and siblings don't look at your face the way—" The woman stopped, her subsequent breath accompanying Sadie's attention onto the empty alleyway and the side of Yoder's ice cream shop. "Sadie, I'm sorry. I didn't mean anything by that."

"It's okay, Miss Jenny. I know people look at me funny when they first come in the shop. I know people point at me when they see me walking down the porch steps at the end of my shift here. And no, my mam and dat do not look at me like that. But Mam? She has worry in her eyes when she looks at me now—worry she didn't have before the fire." She heard Miss Jenny's steps approaching but didn't turn. "When I forget and I say something funny or I try a new recipe and set it on the table for Mam, I see that worry. So I try not to do those things around her."

"You mean be yourself?"

"*Ya*. It makes her sad. Because when I am the way I used to be, she sees only the husband and children I might not have now because of . . ." This time, Sadie didn't even bother touching her face. She didn't need to. Miss Jenny knew what she meant. *Everyone* knew what she meant . . .

"Oh, Sadie, it doesn't have to be like that. I see Amish men your age looking up at you when you are out front sweeping. I see it all the time."

She resisted the urge to roll her eyes in favor of asking the obvious. "Who do you see looking at me?" she countered.

"There is that young man who unpacks the trucks that come to the market . . . And that other young man who works part-time at the hardware store . . . And the Yoder boy from next door looks to be about your age, as well."

Amos . . .

Sadie took in the corner of the ice cream shop's sign that she could see from where she stood and then swung her focus back to the empty cobblestoned alley in time to hear Miss Jenny prattling on. "Maybe, if you would just look at them or, better yet, engage them in conversation, something might grow. They'd get to know you in a way they can't when you take all your breaks in the back with your books."

"I've looked up plenty of times, Miss Jenny. You just don't see the way the smiles disappear the moment I do."

Miss Jenny touched Sadie's shoulder. "But that is why they need to get to know you, dear. Why you need to be yourself with everyone. So they can stop seeing the scars the way I have."

It sounded so simple when Miss Jenny said it. It really did. But it wasn't real. One only had to walk beside her on the way home from work most evenings to know that . . .

Shaking the image of the familiar red car and its equally familiar driver from her thoughts, she made herself smile in the hopes the effort would reach into her voice. "I can be me when I'm here, Miss Jenny. I can be me with *Dat* when *Mam* is busy. I can be me with my siblings when *Mam* is busy. And I can be me with the chickens and the barn cats, and all of the animals on *Dat*'s farm. That is good enough for me."

Movement at the mouth of the alley pulled her gaze left and onto the very face that had consumed her thoughts more than normal the past day and a half. *Before* Monday evening, when she'd thought of him, it had been from the angle of this very window—snippets of his strong shoulders beneath his suspenders, the thump of his boots as he jumped down from his buggy seat, and the rich, hearty sound of his hello as he pushed open the ice cream shop door and stepped out of view. *Since* Monday evening, her mind's eye had widened to include his warm brown eyes as he looked down at her from his buggy seat as the Englisher drove off, the way her name sounded when he repeated it, and the hand she wished she'd taken if for no other reason than to know how it felt against her own . . .

"The Yoder boy seems so nice, so respectful, doesn't he?"

She watched the buggy come to a stop. "There are many who are nice and respectful, Miss Jenny. That is not the problem. *I* am."

"Pishposh, Sadie Fisher, don't say such a thing!"

Turning her back to the window, she took Miss Jenny's hands in her own and squeezed. "I'm not saying it to be unkind or to make you feel sorry for me. I say it because it's true and it is important to speak the truth."

"No, Sadie, it's *not* true. What *is* true is that you are beautiful. You are kind, funny, creative, and so very bright. You have a real business mind, you know."

"But that is not what people see *first*, Miss Jenny. They see the outside stuff. They see hair color and eye color and . . . *scars*. It is why, when I look up at those men you spoke of a minute ago, they do not stay to talk."

"Is it that they don't stay because of your scars, or because you have decided what their reaction will be before you ever look up?" Miss Jenny argued.

Sadie released Miss Jenny's hands and motioned toward the quilt racks. "I think I'll start on the dusting now. Perhaps I can get to that and the ledger before you need me to help with customers."

"Sadie, you need to believe you're—"

"Please, Miss Jenny. I'd really like to just do my work right now."

Seconds turned to minutes as Miss Jenny studied her with eyes so full of love Sadie had to look away. But as she did, she caught sight of Amos standing near the back of his buggy, his brown eyes moving between the milk cans she knew he was gathering and—

The corner of the window where she normally stood?

No.

It couldn't be . . .

Unsure of whether to step into his sight line or to step away completely, she took a moment to steady her breath. A second peek yielded his free hand held high in a wave and his gaze fixed on a pair of English children skipping by her window with ice-cream cones from his *dat*'s shop.

"Sadie? Are you—"

Shaking off her silent pity party, Sadie met Miss Jenny's curious eye with a smile. "I'll start on the racks closest to the window."

Hour by hour she made her way through the morning, dusting quilt racks, refolding quilts, double-checking the consignment ledger so it was ready for Miss Jenny, answering customers' questions, and ringing up two quilt purchases. The customers who came in to look but not buy didn't pay Sadie much mind. They simply came in, shook their heads when she asked if she could help them with anything, and then wandered back outside to their respective tour groups. The customers who were serious about making a purchase either already knew the quilt they wanted, or spent considerable time looking at the shop's inventory before making their selection. Questions invariably followed regarding the craftsmanship or the person who made it and it was then that they'd notice Sadie.

Or, rather, her face.

It was hard not to think of her life in two distinct parts—the first sixteen years as Sadie, and the last six as the girl with something terribly wrong. In the immediate aftermath of the fire, it had all been so overwhelming. The pain, the time alone in the hospital, the scars . . . She'd put so much on the day she'd be released that the ensuing reality had taken her by surprise. Suddenly, the people and faces she'd been so anxious to see again, could hardly look at her. They'd pull back, they'd gasp, they'd wince, and sometimes, they'd even turn away.

Today's quilt-buying customers were no different. Quilt buyer number one pulled back. Quilt buyer number two had gasped and covered her mouth. And while Sadie knew it shouldn't bother her, somehow talking about Miriam's wedding and the reason behind her decision to leave the celebration early had left her feeling unsettled.

Or maybe it was the sadness she'd seen in Miss Jenny's eyes—a sadness not unlike the kind *Mam* wore whenever she saw Sadie. On *Mam*, though, the sadness had become normal, like the scars on Sadie's face. But on Miss Jenny? It was out of place, if not downright disquieting.

Looking up from the ledger she wasn't really paying attention to, Sadie surveyed the wall clock and set down her pencil. "Miss Jenny? If it's okay, maybe I could take my lunch outside now? That way, if it gets busy in the afternoon, I'll be here to help."

Miss Jenny turned from her temporary post beside the alleyway window and nodded. "Of course, dear. I've got things covered for now. Why don't you take forty-five minutes instead of your usual thirty? You've been working hard all morning."

"I-I don't need that long," she protested.

"I know you don't. But I'm giving it to you. No arguments."

Sadie shrugged, swapped the ledger for her lunch pail and book, and made her way down the rear hallway and out into the surprisingly mild February day. For a moment, she simply stood there, in the back door, breathing in the smells and sounds of her surroundings. Miss Jenny's mums . . . The smell of chocolate wafting across the street from Beechy's Sweets . . . The sound of car doors closing in the distance . . . The gentle *clip-clop* of a buggy horse making its way down Main Street . . .

Slowly but surely, the peace that was Bluebird and its effect on her mood began to work its magic in much the same way time with the barn cats or going for a walk by the pond always did. Here, as in those places, there was no need to worry about how to angle her face as she greeted someone or whether the redheaded Englisher was going to come up behind her with his hurtful words. Here, she could just be herself.

Giving in to the smile she could feel just as surely as the fresh air on her skin, Sadie let the screen door close and slowly lowered herself to the second step. The noon hour, especially at this time of year, meant her favorite lunch spot was inundated with sun and for that, she was glad. There was something about the warmth of the sun's winter rays that always gave her hope.

She allowed herself a single sigh as she settled back against the edge of the top step and then reached inside her lunch pail, her hand closing over the chicken leg *Mam* had insisted she take.

"And here I was thinking I'd be eating lunch all by myself out here today."

Startled, she snapped up her head to find Amos Yoder standing atop the ice cream shop's back stoop. "I'm sorry," she said, dropping her food back into her pail and rising to her feet. "I-I didn't see you when I came out and I—"

He drew back, his own lunch pail brushing against the brick exterior of his father's shop. "I did not say that to make you go."

"It's okay. I know that it is nice to sit outside here alone with the birds and the sun."

"I have time alone with the birds and the sun on my way to *Dat*'s shop every day. But as nice as that is, talking to a real person is even nicer." He stepped down off the stoop and crossed the alleyway, his gaze moving between Sadie and her book. "Do you like to read?"

She followed his eyes to her hand and tried to slow her breath. "*Ya.*"

"What's it about?"

"A sick girl. She is working very hard to climb a mountain."

"Why does she want to climb a mountain if she is sick?" he asked as he stopped at the bottom of Miss Jenny's steps.

"Because she does not have much time. She wants to know what she will see from the mountaintop. Soon, she will see."

"Are there pictures?"

"No, but her words make it so I can see what she sees in my head." With a quick shrug, she tucked the book under her arm and gestured from it to her lunch pail. "It is something to do when I eat."

"You could sit on the front porch and watch the people walk by. Sometimes they say hello."

"To you, perhaps." The second she spoke, she wished she could grab her words from the air and stuff them back inside her heart. But it was too late. Instead, she motioned to the step she abandoned and hoped her voice revealed a steadiness she didn't feel. "Besides, I like to sit back here. It is quiet. And . . . safe."

His left eyebrow cocked upward. "It is not *safe* on the front porch?"

"No, it's safe. It's just . . ." She let the rest of her words trail off in favor of a shrug. "Anyway, I'll leave you to your lunch and—"

"Sit with me? Please?"

Unsure of what to say or do, she peeked inside the screen door of the quilt shop and listened for anything resembling an excuse to go inside. When she heard nothing, she cast a side-long glance at Amos. "I guess I could sit. For a few minutes."

Small divots appeared in his cheeks as he pointed at the spot she'd vacated upon his arrival. "Shall we?"

"I suppose." Tightening her hold on the handle of her lunch pail, Sadie lowered herself back to the second step.

When she was situated with her pail beside her, he claimed a spot on one of the lower steps. "So how long have you been working here at the quilt shop?"

"A few years. Almost four, I think."

"Do you like it?" he asked, pulling a thick sandwich from his pail. "Do you make some of the quilts?"

"I've only ever made one quilt and it wasn't very good." She reached inside her own pail and plucked out a grape instead of the chicken. "I was always better at being outside. In the garden. Or helping *Dat* in the barn."

"Why a quilt shop, then?"

Rolling the grape between her thumb and index finger, she considered the question. "Because Miss Jenny was the only one hiring at the time."

"Perhaps there are others now?"

"Oh no. I wouldn't want to work anywhere else unless I had my own shop. Miss Jenny is my friend now."

"Your own shop?"

She shrugged. "*Ya*. Maybe. One day."

"I think about that sometimes, too. But I'd have to get a whole lot faster with my tools to have enough things to sell in a shop." He took a bite of his sandwich and leaned back, his upper arm brushing against her boot so briefly she suspected he didn't even notice. After a few more bites, he moved his pail onto the step beside him and looked up at her. "That car the other day? The red one? Why was he driving so slow next to you?"

She stared at the grape between her now still fingers. "I don't know."

"His window was open and he seemed to be talking to you. But you did not talk back."

Feeling her heart begin to thud inside her chest, she tossed the grape back into her pail and stood, her destination any-where in the vicinity that would buy her time to breathe. "*Ya.*"

"Why did you not speak to him?"

"I-I just didn't." She wandered over to his tethered horse and ran her hand down the side of the mare's head. When the mare didn't pull back, she spoke softly to it in Pennsylvania Dutch before looking back at Amos. "What is her name?"

"Her name was Bell, but *Dat* has taken to calling her Grumpy."

As if on command, the horse let out a snort of disgust, fol-lowed by a clap of its hoof on the cobblestoned alley.

"*Grumpy?*" she echoed. "Do you call her that, too?"

"Sometimes. When it fits."

The mare let loose a tired exhale before bringing her head down to Sadie's. Sadie, in turn, rested her scarred cheek against the mare and inhaled the scent of earth and soap that clung to the animal's skin. "I don't think Grumpy fits her at all."

"Sitting here, watching her with you, I'd have to say I agree."

Sadie parted company with the horse in favor of an uninhibited view of the steps and the hatted man watching her intently. "Is she not like this with you?"

"You remember the snort and the smack of her hoof just now?"

"*Ya . . .*"

"That is what *Dat* and I get when we are near."

"Perhaps if you went back to calling her Bell, she would not be so grumpy."

His eyes sparkled in the sun. "Perhaps you are right."

"I am."

Again, she spoke to the horse in quiet, hushed tones before turning back toward the quilt shop steps and the man now heading in her direction with both of his dimples on full display. "So in addition to being able to quiet grumpy horses, what else should I know about you?"

She stepped away from the mare, careful to keep her good cheek angled toward Amos. "There is nothing else. I work at the quilt shop, I think Grumpy is not a nice name for your horse, and my name is Sadie. There is nothing else to know."

"Somehow I do not think that is true."

Placing her hands on her hips she widened her gaze on Amos. "I do not tell lies."

"I didn't mean you were telling a lie, I just . . ." He splayed his hands at his sides. "I'm just sure there is more to you than those three things."

When she maneuvered past him to retrieve her abandoned lunch pail and book, he followed. "Wait! I know! You love horses . . . See? That's four!"

"Wanting a horse to have a proper name doesn't mean I love horses," she protested.

"Maybe. But running into a burning barn"—he motioned toward her face and winced—"to save them *does.*"

Feeling the answering prick of tears she refused to shed in front of anyone, Sadie turned toward the door. "I should head inside now. Miss Jenny will wonder where I've gone."

4:30 p.m.

She was gathering her things to go home when Miss Jenny stepped through the front door, setting off the overhead bell. "Sadie, dear! You got a note!"

"A note?"

"Yes!" The jingle faded into silence as the woman propped the shop's broom against the wall, crossed the room to where Sadie was standing, and held out a plain white folded piece of paper with Sadie's name written across the outside. "I found it outside . . . On the steps where you eat your lunch . . . I think it's from an admirer."

She took the folded note and looked back up at her boss. "Did you read it?"

"No, of course not. But I saw that young man—the one who works at the market in the mornings—near the porch earlier, and I think he probably left it for you."

"You mean Samuel Zook?"

"Yes! Samuel! That's the one!"

Working against the sudden tremble in her fingers, Sadie unfolded the page and stared down at the familiar handwriting.

> Dear Sadie,
>
> I have seen you outside, sweeping,
> many times and wish that you would
> speak to me. You are quite beautiful,
> and kind. Your smile is like Lap's
> Pond when it shimmers in the sun.
>
> Yours truly,
> Your Secret Admirer

Slowly, deliberately, she returned the note to its previously folded state and handed it back to her boss. "There are *two p*'s in Lapp, Miss Jenny."

"So he can't spell! That doesn't mean he wouldn't make a fine mate for the right gal!"

"I am sure Esther Troyer agrees . . ."

"Esther Troyer?" Miss Jenny echoed, her brows furrowed. "Isn't that the Amish gal who helps out at the Bed and Breakfast?"

"*Ya.*"

"Okay. But what does she have to do with Samuel being able to spell?"

"They're getting married next month."

Miss Jenny's cheeks turned crimson. "I didn't know . . ."

"I see that." Drawing in a breath she tried to match with patience, Sadie closed her hand around Miss Jenny's and waited until eye contact was made. "Miss Jenny, I know you are trying to help, but it only makes things harder for me. I don't want to believe something that is not real. I know you care for me and I am glad. But *you* did not need to be married to be happy, so *I* do not need to be married to be happy."

"But that's what the Amish do. They don't stay single—they marry!"

She squeezed her friend's hand. "I'll be okay, Miss Jenny. I *am* okay."

"But you're so good and so special. I don't want you to be alone!"

"I'm *not* alone. I have *Mam* and *Dat* and my brothers and sisters. And I have you. That is enough."

Miss Jenny's throat moved with her swallow.

"I can't change this," Sadie continued, touching her cheek. "*No one* can, Miss Jenny. Please. I need my time here to be a-a . . ." She cast about for the right word only to have Miss Jenny deliver it along with a gentle kiss on Sadie's forehead.

"You need this shop to be your refuge, dear."

Sadie nodded.

"Okay. I hear you. And I want this place—and me—to be that for you, too." Miss Jenny withdrew her hand and gently brought it to Sadie's scarred cheek. "But know in your heart, dear, that the young men in this town who don't take the time to see your beauty are the ones missing out."

5:20 p.m.

She was just passing the turnoff to Lapp's Pond when she heard him coming. The slow crunch of the gravel . . . The momentary thump of music through the now opened window . . . The knowing thud in her chest . . .

For a few glorious minutes, she'd almost thought he'd given up when she made it past the Grabers' farm without seeing his car. And when she approached and then passed the Beilers', she'd actually smiled.

Now that he was here, though, she knew why she'd made it so much farther than normal. Miss Jenny had let her go early. And even with the whole pretend-note thing having eaten up some of that time, she'd still gotten out ten minutes earlier than normal—ten minutes that had allowed her to pass those two farms without incident.

"Hey there, Saaa-die! Scare anybody off with that face of yours yet today?"

She continued walking, her thoughts moving to the book in her left hand and the lunch pail in her right. Soon, she'd be home . . . Soon, she'd be carrying the milk bottle out to the orphan calf . . . Soon, she'd—

"It's probably good your kind isn't big into using mirrors. Keeps you from having to see what the rest of us see! Then again, maybe if you did, you'd stay home and make it a prettier world for the rest of us."

Turning her chin toward the stretch of woods just north of the Beiler property, she willed herself to imagine running through the trees, chasing her brother as her sisters stood by, giggling. It wasn't something they'd done in that exact spot, but that didn't matter. She knew the sound of her sisters' laughter. She knew the way her brother loved to tease. Surely, if given the time and the chance, they would—

"I know your kind probably doesn't celebrate Valentine's Day, but if they did, you wouldn't get anything. You've got to be *pretty* to get a card and chocolates!"

She tried to blink away the mist making it so the woods suddenly looked foggy, but try as she did, the fog turned into something resembling rain.

"Hey!"

Swiping the back of her hand across her eyes, Sadie turned toward the road and the fast-moving buggy she had failed to hear over the thumping in her chest and ears. Before she could fully process the scene, Amos pulled Bell alongside the red car, his focus trained on the driver. "If you do not want trouble, I think it is best that you keep driving."

"Trouble?" the Englisher echoed. "Oh please . . . You're *Amish*."

Amos tucked the reins onto his seat and jumped down onto the road. "*Ya*. I am Amish. And you need to keep driving."

She tightened her hold on her lunch pail and prepared to run for help, but stopped as the Englisher sped off, his tires raining dust over Amos in the process. Amos, in turn, let loose a cough, and then waved away the rest of the cloud until his brown eyes were locked on hers. "Are you okay?"

"*Ya*. I am . . ." She took a moment to breathe away the tremble in her voice. "I am fine."

"That was the same car as yesterday, wasn't it?" he asked.

"It is the same car every day."

"I thought you said you do not know him."

"I don't. I know only his car, his hair, and his voice."

"His hair?"

"It is what I see before I walk faster."

Amos hurried over to where she stood. "And his voice?"

She felt the tears returning and squeezed her eyes closed against them.

"Sadie?"

"It is the part I know best," she whispered.

"He says things to you?"

When she was pretty sure the tears would hold, she opened her eyes. "*Ya.*"

"What kind of things?"

She looked from Amos, to the sky, and back again, the reality that was her life finally bringing her heartbeat back to normal. "It does not matter. He is gone now."

"But you said he does this every day."

"He is gone now," she repeated.

Amos's brown eyes left their hold on hers and traveled down to her right cheek. "He says unkind things, doesn't he?"

"Some say them, others just . . ." She waited until his gaze returned to hers before looking away. "I should be going. It's getting late."

Her skin tingled at his touch as he reached out and stopped her. "Please. Finish what you were saying. Some say unkind things and others . . . *what*?"

"Look away, whisper, clear their throats,"—she returned her gaze to his—"*wince*. But it's all the same thing."

"But—"

"I thank you for coming when you did. It has made it so the rest of my walk will be better."

Amos cupped a hand to his mouth only to let it fall back to his side. "Can I at least bring you the rest of the way home? In case he comes back again?"

"You say that as if he won't be back tomorrow and every day after."

"Maybe he won't. Maybe he'll—"

She laughed away the rest of his delusion. "It is as if you and Miss Jenny are the same."

"Your boss? Why?"

"It is like our old barn cat, Willow, who went blind. He would take off running the way he once did when he could see. But he couldn't, so he would bump into things."

He folded his arms across his chest, studying her closely. "I don't understand."

"*Miss Jenny* thinks someone would leave a secret note for me on the front porch as if I am the way I once was. But I am not."

"A secret note?"

"*Ya.* She wanted me to believe an Amish man would find me pretty and . . ." She waved off the rest of her answer and, instead, wandered her focus off Amos and down the very road the Englisher had traveled. "And *you* speak as if the boy in the red car might not come back. But he will."

"How can you be so sure?"

"Because, come tomorrow and every day after, I'll still look like"—she turned so as to afford him a bird's-eye view of the scars she couldn't hide any better than Willow could pretend he had sight—"*this.* It's who I am, who I'll always be."

Thursday. 11:30 a.m.

Breathing in the laughter that was Miss Jenny's weekly quilting group, Sadie made her way back into the shop's main room. Often times, when Miss Jenny's friends gathered with their coffee cups and quilting tools, Sadie imagined what it would be like to have such a group—to sit alongside people she'd known for decades and know they saw her in a way no one else did.

Sure, the weekly hymn sings before the fire had been fun. There'd even been some girls—like Miriam and Esther—whom she'd laughed and chatted with in much the same way Miss Jenny and her friends were at that moment. But the fire had changed that just as it had changed her. Suddenly, the easy conversations about boys and siblings had become . . . *awkward.* At first, she'd thought it was because she'd missed so much during her recovery that she just needed to get caught up on everything. But as time went on, and she began to see beyond herself, she knew it was about so much more.

Because of her scars, she looked different. Because she looked different, the likelihood she would marry was slim. And when she was not courting as the others were, they no longer had things they could talk about together.

It was as if the fire had somehow made it so she couldn't possibly understand about crushes and courting and hand holding any longer. And maybe that was true, on some level. Because pre-fire, she could imagine riding in a buggy with Jakob or Atlee or Eli or any of the boys she'd caught looking at her during a volleyball game or while laughing with her friends under a shady tree. Post fire, all those same boys who her friends had teased her about were either married or courting someone. Now it wasn't a matter of who liked whom, but rather who was getting married next, who was moving where, and, in some cases, who was expecting their first or second child.

The life she'd known had stopped the moment she ran into *Dat*'s barn to free the horses. What was left looked very different than she ever could have imagined during those early days in the hospital.

A quick glance outside the quilt shop's front window yielded a handful of tourists who'd already been in the shop that morning. Most had simply come in and browsed as so many did, but one woman, from somewhere in Connecticut, had purchased one of Sadie's favorite quilts. It had been a good sale and one she knew Miss Jenny would be pleased to hear about when her quilting hour was done, but for now, Sadie was on her own.

Grabbing the broom from its hook behind the counter, Sadie stepped onto the front porch and began to sweep, the rhythmic motion of her arms helping to put a little distance between herself and the things she couldn't change. Life was good. *Dat*'s last crops had been good, *Mam*'s jams and jellies were selling well in the market, her brother had gotten a few pieces in the furniture store on the other end of Main Street, her youngest sister was becoming quite the quilter, and Sadie, well, she . . . what?

"I have read six books in the past two weeks," she murmured in tandem with the sound of the broom moving back and forth against the wooden slats of the porch. "I have sold three—no, *four* quilts in the past week. And I tried a new recipe on *Mam* and *Dat* that everyone seemed to like."

"Do you always talk to yourself?"

Stopping, mid-sweep, she looked up, her gaze traveling the width of the porch to the sidewalk beyond. "Amos! I did not hear your buggy!"

"That is because it is down by the market."

"Oh." She loosened her grip on the broom handle in time with a slow inhale. "Mmmm . . . Do you smell that?" she asked.

He, too, sniffed in, his eyes widening as he did. "What *is* that?"

"That is Beechy's Sweets."

"The sweet shop?"

"*Ya*. They make the most wonderful smells, don't they?" She rested the broom against the shop wall and ventured closer to the steps. "One day, I peeked inside the window, and they had a whole glass case filled with chocolate—flat pieces, big pieces, small pieces, squares . . . It was hard to keep walking when all I really wanted to do was go inside and try some."

She savored the memory responsible for the smile she didn't need to verify in Miss Jenny's front window and let loose a quiet laugh. "A few weeks ago, when I was eating my lunch in the alley, I saw Samuel Zook coming out of Beechy's Sweets with a small bag in his hand. Later on that same day, when I was sweeping right here"—she splayed her hands wide—"I saw him tuck the bag into his buggy. I know he was bringing it to Esther, I'm sure of it."

"Esther?"

"Troyer. She and Samuel are to be married next month." Dropping her hands to her sides, she shook her head. "I wanted to tell him she doesn't like chocolate, but I didn't. If he is to be her husband next month, he should know she doesn't like sweets."

He grinned. "Maybe if you told him, he'd have given it to you, instead."

Like a goat's horn to the stomach, his words pulled her from her woolgathering and set her on a fast path back to the broom. She'd already completed everything on the day's to-do list, but surely she could find something to—

"Sadie? Are you okay?"

She turned to find him looking at her scars with an expression she knew all too well. Only this time, the pity that normally made her rush to console, had her clenching the broom handle so hard she actually heard a faint snapping sound. "I am fine! This"—she touched her cheek—"doesn't hurt any longer. It hasn't for a long time. What *does* hurt is all these things that you and Miss Jenny want to be true for me but aren't."

He drew back as if he'd been slapped. "Things? What things?"

"Thinking someone would like me enough to leave a note . . . Or that the boy in the red car will grow tired of saying such hateful things when I am walking home . . . Or that Samuel Zook or *any* man would ever think I am special enough for chocolate . . . Or-or that I am not ugly!"

"U-Ugly?" he stammered. "You're not—"

"Stop it! The Bible says, 'Wherefore putting away lying, speak every man truth with his neighbor!' I am *your neighbor*, Amos. You must speak the truth, not lies!" Now that the words were tumbling from her mouth it was as if she had no ability to make them stop. "The fire did not take my eyesight, Amos! I can see these"—she fingered the rough, taunt skin—"just as well as you and everyone else can. But I can live this life if everyone would just *let me*."

She swung her focus back to the road and the small grouping of people—both Amish and English who'd gathered on the sidewalk to listen and point. At her.

Squeezing her eyes closed, she counted to ten in her thoughts only to open them at the sound of Amos cresting the top steps "No. Please." She crossed to the door, turned the knob, and, as the door swung inward, cleared her throat of the sadness she didn't want him to hear. "It is time for me to go inside and do my job. Miss Jenny's group should be finishing up soon and I really should be at the counter when they do."

Friday. 12:45 p.m.

"Good book?"

Clapping her hand to her chest, Sadie looked up to find Amos standing not more than a few feet away, a cup of ice cream in each of his hands. "I-I didn't hear you come outside."

"Or drive up."

"Drive up?" she echoed, glancing around his legs toward the road. Sure enough, Bell, his chestnut-colored mare, was tethered to a post near the mouth of the alley. "I must have been inside with a customer when you arrived."

"No. You were sitting right where you are now, your nose buried in that same book." He took a step closer and held out the ice cream cup in his right hand. "I scooped up a bit of ice cream for us both. It's vanilla."

She looked from the cup, to her uneaten lunch, and back again before sliding her full attention back onto the *Plain* yet handsome man smiling back at her. "I guess I got so busy with my book, I forgot to eat my lunch."

"That's okay. Sometimes, when I was young, I would sneak a cookie before dinner. Now that we are old enough, we don't have to sneak." Stepping still closer, he lowered the ice cream cup to her seated eye level and, when she finally took it, made a spot for himself on the step just below hers. "So, your book . . . You're enjoying it, then?"

"*Ya*. It is wonderful." Slipping the first spoonful of ice cream past her lips, she moaned. "Mmmm, Amos, this is so good! It is no wonder your *dat* has so many customers even when it is cold outside."

"I'm glad you like it." After another taste or two for himself, he again returned her attention to the still-open book in her lap. "Tell me about the book. Has she gotten to the top of the mountain yet?"

She savored another bite of the unexpected treat and then set the cup next to her on the step. "This is a different book. It is filled with poetry and proverbs and sayings."

"Are you enjoying it?" he asked.

"*Ya*. Some of the sayings make me laugh, like this one . . ."

Flipping back a few pages, she skimmed both sides until she found the right one. "In a closed mouth, flies do not enter."

He halted his spoon just shy of his mouth. "In a closed mouth, flies do not enter," he repeated, laughing. "*Ya*, that is funny."

"It took me a few minutes to know what it meant, but I think I know now. It means sometimes it is best not to say anything at all." She looked up from the page, only to cast her eyes down at her boots. "Like yesterday, on the front porch. I did not mean to snap at you like that. I should have just gone inside."

"But if you had, I wouldn't know I'd upset you," he protested before finishing his next bite of ice cream and pointing her attention back to the book. "Are they all silly like that?"

"No. Some make you think, some make you think *and* smile."

"Ahhh, so that is why you were smiling when I first stepped outside just now. I wanted to think it was seeing me with two ice creams, but since you did not look up, I knew it was because of something in your book."

At a loss for how best to respond, she simply dropped her attention back to the page and the quote she'd been reading and rereading when he appeared in the alley. Tapping the applicable quote, she read aloud: " 'Faith is the bird that feels the light and sings when the dawn is still dark.' Isn't that lovely? It's how . . ."

She shook off the rest of her sentence and, instead, reached for her treat, smiling at him as she did. "This is very good. Thank you for sharing it with me."

"Thank *you* for sharing it with *me*. But please, finish what you were going to say. About what you just read."

"It was nothing."

"I heard the way your voice changed when you read it just now, Sadie. It would not do that if it was nothing. So please"—

he motioned her attention back to the book—"read it again. Slower this time."

She looked at him over her latest scoop of ice cream and then lowered it back to the step in favor of the book. " 'Faith is the bird that feels the light and sings when the dawn is still dark.' That is how I *want* to feel—how I *do* feel when I am with the barn cats or taking a walk in the woods."

"How you *feel*?"

"I am like that bird when I am by myself or with animals who do not see what everyone else sees. I can sing in those places because I know I am still me—the same me I always was. But everywhere else—here, at home, at hymn sings, on my walk home after the shop is closed—I am not just Sadie. I am Sadie, the girl who was burned."

Slowly, he lowered his near empty cup to the step and turned to face her. "Why can't you be the way you once were?"

"Because in all those places I just spoke of, I am reminded of what I am able to forget when I am alone. I am reminded by a mirror, by a mean Englisher in a red car, by *Mam*'s sad eyes, by Miss Jenny's"—she lifted the book off her lap and gave it a little shake—"silly games."

"Silly games?"

"*Ya*. After Miss Jenny's quilting hour yesterday, I came outside here to have my lunch. And just as she left that silly note on the porch for me the other day and pretended it was from a secret admirer, she left this book with my name written inside. See?" She flipped back through the book, stopping as she reached the inside cover. "It says, 'For Sadie.' Only this time, she was clever enough to change her handwriting or to have someone else write it for her."

"Did you ask her if she did it?"

"*Ya*. She said no. But . . ." Sadie waved away the mental replay of the previous day's conversation and looked up, his gaze meeting and holding hers as she continued. "Miss Jenny is the only one who would do such a thing."

"The only one? Are you sure?"

"*Ya.*"

"But why would she do that? Especially when she knew you'd caught her the first time."

"Miss Jenny believes there is someone out there who will see past my scars to *me.*"

"And you don't agree?"

"No."

"But why? Why is that so hard to believe? Miss Jenny sees past them, right? And surely your family sees past them at this point?"

"No, they don't. If Miss Jenny *did*, she'd stop pushing so hard. She wouldn't look at me and think, *if only someone could see past those scars* . . . And if *Mam* saw past them, she wouldn't look as if she's going to cry whenever we learn of another friend who is getting married."

"But—"

"No buts, *please.*" She closed the book, returned her un-eaten lunch to her pail, and reclaimed what was left of her ice cream for the trek back inside the shop. "I have enjoyed talking to you just now. Let's just leave it at that, okay?"

5:06 p.m.

She heard him the second her feet hit the graveled country road, the flood of noise scattering squirrels and birds just as convincingly as any hawk ever could. So much of this moment had become routine she found herself running through the order of things in her head . . .

The loud engine . . .

The ping of the gravel against the tires as he slowed . . .

The initial blast of music as the window lowered . . .

The rapid beat of her heart in her ears as the music bowed to his voice . . .

And the way her hand invariably tightened on her lunch pail in tandem with her quickened pace . . .

"Hey there, Saaa-die. Scare anybody with that face of yours today?" His laughter rang through the air as he inched the car forward in time with her steps. "So . . . Yesterday . . . I take it that doofus who showed up in the buggy was your brother or something?"

She veered as far to her right as she could go without hitting the Grabers' fence and kept walking, the growing clamminess in her hands necessitating a wipe down on the sides of her lavender dress.

"Because, well, you've got the kind of face only a mother can love, so maybe that holds for a brother, too. *Maybe.*"

Feeling the tears that were no more than a few blinks away from announcing their presence on her cheeks, she lifted her eyes to the sky and willed herself to focus on the clouds. Ever since she was a little girl, she'd always made a game of trying to find the shape of a horse or a chicken or a goat in the clouds. Sometimes, the search could take seconds—with a particular stretch of clouds yielding a veritable white, puffy barnyard. And other times, her eyes would grow so tired from looking, she'd doze off in the warmth of the sun only to be awoken in short order by a barn cat or one of her siblings in need of something. Today, though, it would be okay if her search took her all the way to the safety of her farm.

"Stumble across that mirror yet? Bet you scared yourself if you did."

She scanned the clouds above her head and when she found

little more than a goat's tail without an accompanying goat, she looked toward the horizon and—

The quick snap of a twig up ahead near the stretch of woods between the Grabers' and the Beilers' farms halted her search and sent her thoughts racing in time with her heartbeat. A glance toward the road and the Englisher, however, yielded nothing to indicate he'd heard it, too.

"Don't worry, Saaa-die. I'm still here . . ."

A second, louder snap ricocheted her focus back to the tree line in time to see Amos step out from behind a large maple tree and sprint onto the road. For several beats of her heart, Sadie remained in place, her feet seemingly rooted to the ground even as her thoughts sped away with the Englisher.

"You okay?"

She shook herself back to the moment and the young Amish man now heading in her direction. Sagging against the fence post, she took a moment to inhale the peace and safety that was hers once again. "*Ya*. I am okay."

"I don't like that he bothers you," Amos said, glancing, again, in the direction the Englisher had gone. "It is not right."

"It's okay. I've gotten used to it in some ways."

He turned back to her, his brown eyes void of their usual warmth and crackle. "You should not have to get used to such a thing, Sadie. It is not right. *He* is not right."

"He is gone." She scanned the road for some much-needed verification and then turned back to Amos. "Where is Bell and your buggy?"

"In town."

She looked a question at him and, when he didn't respond, added words. "But you were in the woods just now."

"You said he'd be back," he said by way of explanation. "So I came back, too."

"But you can't do that every day! You don't live out this way!"

"You are right. I don't. But *you* do."

She felt a tightening in her throat and swallowed it away long enough to set him straight. "Amos, I thank you for-for chasing the Englisher off just now. But I cannot ask you to do so every day."

"You're not."

"But you live in the other direction!"

"It does not take long to drive out this way."

"Today you did not drive your buggy. You walked."

"You're right, I did."

"But why?" she asked.

Amos hooked his thumb beneath his suspender and shrugged. "I wanted to hear the things that he says to you."

Her cheeks flamed hot as her thoughts rewound to the moment the music stopped and the Englisher's voice began to fill the quiet countryside air . . .

"Scare anybody with that face of yours today?"

"I take it that doofus who showed up in the buggy was your brother or something?"

She blinked hard against the parade of insults, each fresh new memory, now imagined through Amos's ears, making it harder and harder to breathe . . .

"Because, well, you've got the kind of face only a mother can love."

"Stumble across that mirror yet? Bet you scared yourself if you did."

Aware of the tears that were no more than two, maybe three blinks away, Sadie cocked her head in the direction of home. "Did you hear that?"

Amos paused and listened. "No. What was it?"

"It was . . . *Dat.* I-I should go."

Again, Amos paused and listened. "Are you sure? Because I didn't hear—"

"*Ya*. It was *Dat*." She hated the way the lie tasted on her tongue, but she hated the truth of her impending tears even more. "Goodbye, Amos."

Monday. 3:20 p.m.

She saw it the second she stepped outside with the day's trash a few days later, the attention to detail and vivid colors so startling she actually thought it real for a moment. But when it didn't take flight as she inched closer, she knew the bird on the quilt shop's back step had actually been whittled out of wood.

Setting the garbage bag at her feet, Sadie squatted down for a closer look, her mind's eye soaking up every last detail.

The round orange belly . . .

The dark gray–feathered back that seemed to gather together to create a tail . . .

The perfect yellow beak . . .

And the dark, almost brooding eyes . . .

Every minute detail was so spot-on, so authentic, she half expected it to burst into song the way its living breathing counterparts did outside her bedroom window during the spring and summer months. Instead, she lifted it up off the concrete, and held it at eye level to afford a second and even closer inspection.

Slowly, carefully, Sadie turned the bird over only to suck in a breath as her gaze came to rest on two words written in pencil across the underside. "For *Sadie*?" she whispered. "But who would—"

She let the rest of the question go as an image of the person responsible for the whittled surprise stepped into the forefront of her thoughts. She wanted to be angry, to be strong enough to stand up, throw the garbage bag into the dumpster, and then march herself back inside the shop for a long overdue talk with

Miss Jenny. Yet every time she really looked at the bird in her hands, she knew she couldn't be angry. Not really, anyway.

Did she wish Miss Jenny would stop this whole secret admirer thing once and for all? Of course. But she'd tried to make the woman understand her displeasure after the letter and it had gotten Sadie nowhere. Instead, after a day or so with no mention of men in relation to Sadie, the book of quotes and poetry had shown up on the back step with her name written neatly on the inside cover. Same writing, same pencil.

Miss Jenny, of course, had denied leaving the book for Sadie. And Sadie, in turn, had let it go in favor of keeping the reins on her own growing frustration. It wasn't the ideal way to handle it, but Miss Jenny was stubborn, plain and simple. Besides, it was because of that book that Sadie had taken the full forty-five-minute lunch break suggested by Miss Jenny—a lunch break that had culminated in ice cream and some real conversation with the handsome Amos Yoder.

She knew, too, that she should probably say something about the bird—and maybe she would—but for now, its detailed beauty was actually starting to part the very clouds that had hovered over her mood since Amos stepped out of the woods. In the grand scheme of things, it shouldn't matter whether or not Amos had overheard the awful things the Englisher had said about Sadie. Because even if he hadn't, Sadie's scars were still there for Amos and everyone else to see. The Englisher simply gave voice to the kinds of things others thought but were too polite to say.

The telltale sound of a door opening on the opposite side of the alley lifted her gaze just long enough to see that Amos was stepping out of the ice cream shop and heading in her direction. "Good afternoon, Sadie. I haven't seen you the past few days."

"I never work on Sunday, as I'm sure you don't. And Miss Jenny gave me Saturday off this week."

He stepped down off his father's back stoop and headed in her direction. "Ahhhh, okay, now it makes sense why I did not see you walking home after work on Saturday."

"See me walking home?" she echoed.

"*Ya*. I did not see the red car, either."

Pulling the bird to her chest, she forced herself to respond despite the memory of their last meeting now filtering though her head. "He has figured out when I work, I guess."

Amos stopped, mid-stride, and drew back. "*He?*"

"The Englisher."

"If that is true, it is not good."

"*Ya*, but it can't be helped." Then, anxious to change the subject, she held the bird out where he could see. "Isn't this lovely? It looks just like the robins that wake me with their beautiful songs."

He closed the remaining gap with several easy steps and then leaned forward for a closer look. She, in turn, tried to hold the bird steady so he could see it, but the feel of his breath against her skin made it difficult to think, let alone stand still. "Is it yours?" he asked.

"*Ya*. Look." She flipped the bird over to reveal her name. "See? Miss Jenny is at it again."

"At what again?"

"Leaving surprises for me outside—surprises I am to think are from a secret admirer. Like the note, and the book of quotes and poetry."

"But you said you spoke to her after the note."

"I did, but she did not listen. That is why there was a book, and now, a bird."

"Perhaps it is not Miss Jenny," he said, his voice husky.

She grabbed the trash bag with her free hand but stayed put. "Of course, it is Miss Jenny. Only now I am to believe it is not from Samuel as the letter was supposed to be."

"Samuel? Do you mean Samuel Zook?"

"*Ya.*"

"But he is to marry the one who works at the English inn."

"Miss Jenny didn't know that when she wrote the letter." She made a beeline for the dumpster only to have Amos take the bag from her hand before she'd taken more than five or six steps. "I can throw that away!"

Amos shook his head. "I am here, I will do it."

She stepped aside to give him access to the large black trash bin and then brought the conversation back to the bird now safely encased in her hand once again. "The book and this bird just have my name. That way I cannot catch her with another mistake."

"I don't know why you think your boss would give you such things."

"Because she knows no one else will." She gazed down at the bird and immediately felt her smile return. "But it's okay. This bird . . . it's—"

"A reminder to sing even in the darkness?"

Startled, she looked up to find him studying her with so much intensity she could barely remember how to breathe. "You-you remember that?"

"I do." He stepped away from the bin and nudged his chin in the direction of the road. "I should be heading back to the farm. But if it is okay, I would like to give you a ride home when you are done."

There was no denying the excitement that pinged through her body at the notion of spending more time with Amos. But there was also no denying the reason behind his offer and it had to stop. She didn't want to get used to something that would surely stop when Amos began courting. As it was, she'd been working on ways to tune out the nasty comments when Amos came along that first time, anyway.

"Sadie?"

She shook off the introspection and looked up to find his eyes hadn't budged from her face. "It is very kind of you to offer, Amos. But today, Miss Jenny will drive me home."

It wasn't necessarily true, but it could happen. Miss Jenny did, in fact, offer to do so on many occasions. The fact that Sadie turned the woman down more times than not was unimportant. She simply didn't need or want offers born on pity from Amos or anyone else.

"Oh. Okay. Good." He recovered an odd yet quick slump to his shoulders and, slowly, backed his way toward the road. "It was nice to see you again, Sadie. I am glad Miss Jenny's bird has made you smile."

Miss Jenny . . .

With a quick flick of her hand she returned his wave and, when he disappeared around the corner of his *dat*'s shop, she climbed the trio of steps to the quilt shop's back door and stepped inside. "Miss Jenny? I'm back. I'm sorry that took so long but—"

The answering flurry of footsteps Sadie barely had time to process were followed just as quickly by Miss Jenny's hands clamping down on her shoulders. "Is he as nice as he looks?" the woman fairly squealed.

"*He?* Who is *he* . . ." And then she knew. Miss Jenny must have looked out into the alley and seen Sadie talking to Amos. "*Ya.* He is nice. But we have talked many times this past week. It is nothing."

Miss Jenny's cheeks rose with her smile. "Is he courting anyone?"

"*Ya.*" The second she uttered the guess aloud, she wished she could take it back for the lie it might be. But she couldn't. Not yet, anyway. Instead, she took advantage of Miss Jenny's disappointment to wiggle free and lead the way back into the shop's main room.

"That is too bad," Miss Jenny said, following behind.

When she reached the counter and its vantage point for confirming the absence of customers, Sadie inhaled the courage she needed and turned back to her boss. "Miss Jenny, we must talk."

"About what, dear?"

Thrusting her hand out, Sadie folded back her fingers to reveal the hand-carved bird she held inside. "About *this*."

"What is—" Miss Jenny leaned forward, readjusted her glasses atop the bridge of her nose, and sighed. "Oh, Sadie, where did you get this? It's beautiful."

The answering tap of her boot against the carpeted floor seemed to echo off the walls. "Miss Jenny, please. I know it was you."

"*Me*?" Miss Jenny echoed, drawing back. "What was me?"

She elevated her bird-holding hand to eye level while keeping her own sight firmly on the woman. "I found it on the steps outside just now."

"Perhaps someone dropped it?"

"It has my name on it." Reaching over with her free hand, she turned the bird over so Miss Jenny could see its underside.

Miss Jenny squealed. "Oh, Sadie! It must be from the same person who left that book the other day."

"And the note a few days before that," she reminded.

"Note? I didn't know there was a note!" Miss Jenny clapped once, twice. "What did it say?"

She made a face. "You know what it said, Miss Jenny, because *you* wrote it."

Again, Miss Jenny drew back, but this time it was in conjunction with a quiet gasp. "I didn't write you a note!"

"Yes, you did." She marched around the counter, yanked open the drawer housed beneath her lunch pail, and plucked out the note she was now glad she hadn't thrown away. After a quick cough solely for the purpose of making sure every word was heard, she began to read. "Dear Sadie. I have seen you outside, sweeping, many times and wish that you would speak to me."

Stopping, she looked up. "Should I keep reading?"

Miss Jenny's eyebrows dipped with obvious confusion. "That is the note from the other day. The one that—"

"*You* wrote," Sadie finished. "I know."

"But you just said you got a note along with the book and that bird."

"*Ya.*"

"So what does *that* note say?"

She lifted Miss Jenny's note just enough to give it a little shake. "It says what I just read."

Several beats of silence filled the room as Miss Jenny looked from the note to Sadie and back again. "I don't understand."

"*You* wrote the note! *You* left the book! And *you* put that bird on the back step for me just now!" She heard her voice beginning to rise and rushed to bring it in check. "I-I'm sorry, Miss Jenny, I do not mean to yell at you. It is just that *these* things"—she shook the note again and then traded it for the bird—"do not change what is true no matter how much you want to think they will."

"I've never seen that bird before, dear."

"Miss Jenny, please . . ."

"Dear, it's true. I wrote that note, yes. And you were right, I shouldn't have. But I only did it because I truly believe there is someone out there for you—someone who will see you as I see you if you would just *look up* sometimes."

"But—"

Miss Jenny halted the rest of Sadie's words with a splayed palm. "Stop, please. Let me finish. Is your cheek scarred? Of course. But it is one cheek—*one!* The fire did not get the rest of you and it did not get what is"—the woman touched Sadie's chest—"right here. And that, more than anything else in the world, is what truly makes a person."

"I don't have *to marry* to be happy, Miss Jenny. You didn't marry and you're happy!"

Dropping her hand to Sadie's, Miss Jenny held on tight. "But you're not me, Sadie. You're different. You're fun, you're creative, and you have a way about you that just makes it so I know you'd be a wonderful wife . . . And the way you are with the little ones who come in here with their parents and grandparents? Why, I just know you'd make a great little mother one day, too."

"I can be wonderful as an aunt to my siblings' children when that day comes!"

"Oh, Sadie . . ."

"Don't you see that pretending to be someone who can see past my scars doesn't make it so?"

Miss Jenny's gasp echoed around them. "I'm not pretending to see past them, Sadie!"

"I don't mean *you*. I mean the way you're pretending others do with that note and"—again she reached for the bird—"this bird."

"But I didn't leave that bird, dear. Or the book."

She searched for anything to indicate Miss Jenny was being less than honest, but unlike the flushed face and downward glances that had accompanied the letter, there were none. "But I don't understand," she whispered. "Both the book and this bird had my name on them. And they were left on the back step *here*. At the shop."

"The answer seems pretty clear to me. Especially with Valentine's Day coming up so soon." Miss Jenny rocked back on her heels as a smile spread across her plump face. "You, my dear sweet Sadie, really *do* have a secret admirer."

5:10 p.m.

Somehow, she'd made it through the rest of the afternoon. She'd refolded and stacked the quilts on the shelves, she'd answered questions about specific quilts, and she'd covered the shop while Miss Jenny stepped out for a late afternoon coffee with one of the other English shop owners. For most of that time, she'd even managed to put aside Miss Jenny's ridiculous belief that Sadie had a secret admirer. But on occasion, when there was a lull in tasks or customers, she'd found herself looking at the wall calendar and wondering if maybe, just maybe, her boss was right.

After all, Valentine's Day was little more than a week away . . .

"It is possible?" she mumbled as she rounded the bend near the Grabers' farm. "Really truly—"

"Hey there, Saaa-die!"

Stunned into the moment, she looked over her shoulder and felt her heart sink. She'd been so wrapped up in the notion someone may have actually noticed her, she'd missed the usual tells that the Englisher was near. Yet there he was in his shiny red car, peering at her through the open passenger side window with the same mocking smile he always wore.

"What? You're surprised to see *me*? Your biggest admirer?"

She froze in place and turned toward the car. "My *what*?"

"Wait. You're right. *Biggest* implies there are others. And"— he stopped to chew something and then spit it across the seat and onto the road not more than a foot or two away from where she stood. "And *admirer* doesn't fit, either, on account of your face and all. So let's just start this over, shall we?"

Fisting her hands at her sides, she continued on her path toward home, the urge to run tempered only by her need to show she was stronger and more resilient than his cruel words.

"Sooo . . . Where's your brother?"

"He's not my brother," she hissed.

The car stopped. "Uncle?"

"No."

"Cousin?"

"No."

He rolled forward until he was in line with her once again.
"Preacher?"

"No."

"The only thing left is boyfriend and that can't be it . . . Not
with *that* face, anyway." He rolled forward again. "So who is
he? And why is he making it so I have to come up with different ways to mess with you?"

"Please leave."

"Why would I do that? I plan my whole day around this."

"You must have a boring life if this is fun for you," she re-
torted.

The car lurched forward only to stop hard beside her. "*What
was that*, Amish girl?"

"I said—"

The plunk of rock against metal stole the rest of her sentence. Amos's voice stole her breath.

"This is the last time I will tell you to leave," Amos thun-
dered.

The Englisher turned his undivided attention on Amos.
"Get lost, Hat Boy. Your services would be better spent growing me some corn or some tobacco."

"But then I would miss the moment the English police come
around that bend." Amos pointed over his shoulder toward
town. "Which should be happening in the next minute or so . . ."

She followed the Englisher's eyes to the mirror on his windshield and then hurried away from the spray of pebbles kicked
up by his rapid exit.

When he was out of sight, Amos stepped into the spot previously taken up by the red car and studied her from head to toe. "I thought Miss Jenny was driving you home."

"Then why are you here?" she countered.

"I don't know. I guess I needed to be sure."

"Sure of what?"

"That you're okay."

"Why?"

"I just did." He pointed to her lunch pail and the top of the bird peeking out from the cloth cover. "So was it Miss Jenny?"

She, too, looked down at the bird and grinned. "No."

"Then who?"

"I don't know. Miss Jenny thinks it has to do with Valentine's Day coming up. But I don't know. It doesn't make any sense considering . . ." Her words trailed off as the Englisher's voice loomed loud in her ears.

"*Why is he making it so I have to come up with different ways to mess with you?*"

"No," she whispered. "Please no . . ."

"Sadie? What's wrong?"

Was it possible? Was the book and the bird just another way to hurt her?

"Sadie?"

She knew she owed Amos an answer, or, at the very least, a thank you for coming to her rescue yet again, but at that moment, the urge to run the rest of the way home could no longer be denied.

Tuesday. 4:50 p.m.

She wiped her face with her dress sleeve and did her best to steady her breathing before he made it across the alley. If she'd had her druthers, it would be fifteen minutes later and the ice cream shop would already be closed and locked for the evening. But it wasn't fifteen minutes later, it was now. And she didn't need to look up to know Amos was fast approaching.

"Good evening, Sadie. I'm glad to see that you have not set out for home yet."

She wasn't. In fact, had she not taken it upon herself to take out the end-of-the-day trash and sweep the back step, she'd be halfway to home by now instead of sitting there, crying. She tried to stop, several times, but every time she did, the sight of her latest surprise set her off all over again.

"I wish you hadn't run off the way you did yesterday. If I upset you somehow, I'd like to know."

"No, it wasn't you. It's just that . . . I was right." She heard the hitch to her voice and followed it up with yet another swipe of her eyes. "It was all a joke."

"What was a . . . Wait. Are you crying?" he asked, dropping down onto the step beside her.

She didn't answer. She couldn't. Instead, she lifted her forehead away from her palms and stared down at her latest gift, sniffling as she did. "Miss Jenny was telling the truth—about the bird and the book."

"I—"

Pinching her eyes closed, she pressed her fingers against her trembling lips. "It is why I ran yesterday, because I . . ." She tried to strangle back her sob, but it was no use.

"Hey . . . hey . . ." Amos reached across the gap between them and, with the help of his finger, guided her sights off her lap and onto him. "Why are you so upset?"

Part of her wanted nothing more than to disappear from that very spot—from anywhere that wasn't her bedroom or her favorite rock by Lapp's Pond. When she was alone, she could think. When she was alone, she could cry. And when she was alone, she could forget about the one thing no one else around her could. Yet, for whatever reason, the urge to get up, to walk to the road, and set off in the direction of home, seemed bigger than her at that moment.

"Sadie . . ."

"For a little while, after I spoke to Miss Jenny yesterday, I thought maybe it was true. That maybe—"She waved off the rest of her words, dropping her gaze to her lap as she did. "Anyway, it is as he said yesterday. He has found new ways to mess with me."

"*He?*" Amos repeated.

"Even when he would say the things he said as I walked, I could look up at the clouds and find shapes until I reached our farm. I could think of funny things from my day to keep from hearing his words. But this"—she thrust the gray handled mirror forward on her lap—"makes it so he doesn't have to speak at all."

He followed her gaze to her latest gift and, when she looked up after noting her scars, his Adam's apple was moving with a swallow. "You think the *Englisher* left this mirror?" he rasped.

"*Ya.* Amish would not leave a mirror as a gift. But he would." She drew her legs up and under her chin, cringing as the gift she wished she'd never found clattered off her lap and onto the concrete step between them. "He wants me to see what I want to pretend is not there—what I want to believe someone else can pretend is not there, too.

"And he is right," she half hissed, half sobbed. "If it is hard for me to look at myself, how can I really think someone will one day *choose* to look at me?"

Wrapping her arms around her legs, she gave into the fresh round of tears she could no longer hold back. It wasn't that she relished the idea of crying in front of Amos, it's just that she couldn't help it. Still, when she finally got herself under control, she lifted her head off her knees and apologized.

Amos, in turn, shrugged, picked up the mirror, and stared down at his own reflection. "You don't see it, do you?" he asked, his voice strained.

"See what?"

"Your face . . ."

She swiped her eyes with her dampened sleeve. "Did you not hear what I just said? Of course, I see my face."

"You see it as a half, not a whole."

"That is because half is me, and half is something different—something *awful*."

"Do you remember the first time you saw the Englisher in his red car?"

Thrown off by the sudden shift in direction, she shrugged.

"Try," he prompted.

Sighing, she dropped her thighs flat against the concrete. "I thought he was lost or maybe looking for *Mam*'s jam stand."

"Okay. So when you thought that, what did you do?"

"I walked over to the car to help."

"And what did you think of him when you saw him?"

She turned to face him. "I just told you. I thought he was lost or—"

"Looking for your *Mam*'s jam stand. I know. That is not what I am asking." He too, turned, brushing his knees against hers as he did. "What did you think of *him* when you walked over to the car?"

"I thought he looked to be about my age, maybe a few years younger."

"And?" Amos prodded.

"He looked . . . kind." She shook her head at the memory of her naïveté and sighed again. "It is why I told him my name. But now, when I see him, I do not know how I could think such a thing."

"Why? Has something happened to his face?"

"No."

"But you said he looks different now."

"It is as if the mean in his words has made his face mean."

Silence filled the space between them as Amos, once again, studied the mirror. But just as she was trying to gather her own thoughts, he spoke, his voice quiet yet sure. "I think it works the other way, too."

"What does?" she asked, studying him.

"I think kindness can change the way someone looks, too."

She considered his words as her mind's eye filled in images of Miss Jenny and *Mam*. "Miss Jenny's eyes always remind me of the sun shimmering on top of Lapp's Pond. And *Mam*? *Dat* says *Mam*'s smile makes rainy days seem less gray."

For a moment, he said nothing, and then, just as she wondered whether he'd heard her answer, he positioned the mirror so the reflection it held was hers. "What do you see when you look in this?"

The emotion she'd managed to stuff down in favor of the odd conversation, resurfaced, rendering her momentarily speechless.

"Look toward *Dat*'s shop." When she obliged, he continued. "Now, with just your eyes, tell me what you see in the mirror."

Slowly, deliberately, she did as he said, the image reflecting back at her more than a little startling. For there, in the mirror was her old self—the smooth skin so like *Mam*'s, the curve of the nose she shared with two of her five younger siblings, the faint dimple she could see as her lip curved upward . . .

"What do you see, Sadie?"

"I see me, the way I was." She tilted her cheek up, down, and up again. "*Before* the fire."

She could feel him watching every tilt of her head, but at that moment, all she could do was stare at herself.

"Who is *that* girl?" he asked.

"That is a silly question," she said, glancing back at him.

"I don't think so." He pointed her head back to the ice cream shop and then reminded her to look in the mirror with just her eyes. "The girl you see right now—tell me about her."

"I don't understand—"

"What makes her happy? What makes her sad? What scares her? That sort of thing . . ."

Lowering the mirror down to her lap, she mulled the question. "So I'm answering about the Sadie I used to be? Before the fire?"

"I'm asking about the Sadie you saw in the mirror just now."

Again, she lifted the mirror, and again she looked into it so only her left cheek was reflected. "The happy stuff was always easy—playing with my siblings, helping *Mam* in the garden, sitting under a tree with one of the barn cats, helping *Dat* with the horses, and seeing my friends at the weekly hymn sing."

"And now? Those things don't make you happy anymore?"

Her gaze ricocheted to Amos's. "Of course, they do!"

"So that is the same?"

"*Ya.*"

He redirected her back to the mirror. "And the things that made you sad back then?"

"I didn't like seeing one of my siblings sick, or *Dat* worrying about a crop. Those things made me sad. But mostly I was happy."

"Any fears?"

She scanned the alley and then lowered her voice. "I didn't like spiders."

"And now?" he asked as his laugh returned.

"I still don't like spiders."

"Good to know." He looked up at the sky and then back at her, the sparkle in his brown eyes suddenly subdued. "Now it is time to look at me and then turn just your eyes to the mirror."

"Why? I know what I will see."

"Tell me."

Grabbing the mirror, she turned her burned cheek to the reflection, her breaths becoming shallower, more labored. "I see a monster."

He drew back so hard he almost toppled off the step. "A monster?"

"*Ya*. My cheek"—she fingered the outer edges of her scars—"is not a cheek anymore. It is not smooth like *Mam*'s. And when I smile, everything gets all funny and . . ."

This time, when she lowered the mirror, she flipped it over so there would be no reflection. "*That* is what everyone sees when they see me now. *Mam* . . . *Dat* . . . my siblings . . . Miss Jenny . . . the Englisher . . . you."

Before he could respond with anything resembling the pity she saw hovering in his every feature, she shot up her hand and stood. "I have worried *Mam* enough these past six years without coming home late. I do not need to add that, too."

"But—"

"Please, Amos. I-I want to leave."

Scrubbing a quick hand over his clean-shaven face, he gave a half nod. "If we take Bell, you will get home quicker."

5:40 p.m.

She gripped the edge of the seat as the chestnut-colored mare heeded Amos's command and stepped off the graveled road. "I didn't mean for you to see Lapp's Pond *now*," she protested.

"I know. But the way you just described it, I want to see it for myself."

She wanted to argue, to remind him she needed to get home, but, truth be told, telling Amos about the pond in lieu of more mirror talk had whet her appetite for a visit, as well. "When I was little, Mam would bring me here on the way home from town sometimes. She would sit under that tree"—Sadie pointed at a large, towering oak tree—"and watch me explore. I would chase butterflies, climb stumps, pick flowers for Mam, and make quiet wishes on the sparkles."

He guided the horse through the grove of trees separating the pond from the road, his attention as much on her as the setting around them. "Wishes on sparkles?"

"Sometimes, if the sun hits the pond just right, it looks like hundreds of little sparkles are dancing on the water. It was always my favorite part of coming here." She leaned forward in anticipation of the view she knew was just beyond the next tree and felt the day's tension slowly ebb from her body. "I would pick a sparkle near the edge closest to where I sat and make a wish."

"What kind of things would you wish for?" he asked.

"Mam's special apple and cinnamon pie was one I made a lot."

His laugh started deep inside his chest and filled the air around them with such lightness, she couldn't help but join in. "Apple and cinnamon pie, eh?"

"If you had some, you'd understand."

"Any other go-to wishes back then?"

For a moment, she let her thoughts travel back to those childhood moments—moments in time when looking ahead meant pie, new boots, a nice boy to marry one day . . . "No, not really."

"Did you ever throw rocks into the water?" he asked.

"No."

"My older brother saw me doing that into a small pond on the edge of Dat's farm one day and he taught me how to skip them across the top. It took much practice, and I was not good at it at first, but soon, I could skip them many times."

She couldn't help but smile at the image of a young Amos skipping rocks across a pond. "I have never tried," she admitted.

He halted Belle within view of the pond and lowered the

reins to the spot in front of his feet. "You have *never* skipped a rock?"

"No." Buoyed by the utter shock on his face, she climbed down to the ground and nudged her chin in the direction of the water. "Have you ever wished on a sparkle?"

His laugh was back as he, too, jumped down from the buggy. "I can't say that I have, but I'm willing to try if you are."

"Try? Try what?"

"You try skipping a rock, and I'll try one of your wishes."

She knew she should remind him of her need to get home, but for some reason, that need wasn't as strong as it had been back in the alley. Soon, she was scouring the shoreline for the flat pebbles Amos said worked best. When they had a pile of about fifteen, he beckoned her to the water's edge and showed her how to hold her hand, pull back her wrist, and release the rock. Her first, second, and third attempts sunk to the bottom with a thump. Her fourth managed a half skip and a laugh from Amos as she squealed in celebration.

"You are getting closer."

"*Ya.*"

"Perhaps, if you just hold your wrist a little more like this"— he wrapped his fingers around the base of her hand—"it will work better."

She tried to listen, to feel the motion being directed by his hand, but at that moment the only thing she was truly aware of was the feel of his skin against hers and the way her heart felt as if it was beating funny. With a side-eye, she took in his narrow jaw, his friendly smile, and the way his eyes lit from within as he talked her through the process.

Amos Yoder was a good man.

A kind man.

The kind of man she'd have wished for on one of those sunny sparkles so many years earlier. The kind of man that could never be hers no matter how many wishes she made now . . .

She jumped as her hand flapped to her side in conjunction with his rising into the air in celebration. "You did it, Sadie! Two skips!"

Startled, she looked toward the water and what was left of the ripples still billowing out toward the shoreline. "I-I did?"

He clapped his hands once and then motioned toward the pond once again. "So I guess it is my turn now."

"Your turn?" she echoed as she tried to bring her thoughts around to the present. "To skip rocks?"

"No. To make a wish."

"Oh. Right." She made herself look back at the water and the sun beginning its descent between the trees. "In a few minutes, when the sun is just a little lower, it should make sparkles in that area"—she pointed to the middle of the pond—"right there. So you should have your wish ready."

"It is ready." Reaching up, he readjusted his hat atop his head and then rocked back on his heels, his voice growing hushed. "Were you scared?"

She shifted her thoughts from the soon-to-be sparkles to Amos. "When?"

"When you ran into that barn?"

"You mean the night of the fire?"

"*Ya.*"

"No one has ever asked me that before," she whispered.

"If it's too painful, I—"

Waving his concern aside, she wandered over to a nearby stump and sat down. "I didn't really think about what the fire could do to me. I-I just knew *Dat*'s team was behind those doors and that he needed them to harvest the crops. I didn't want things to be hard for *Dat*."

"And once you were inside?" he prodded.

"I ran to each stall and tried to guide them out. Some ran. Others needed to be pushed. But one—Gus—was too frightened. He rose up on his back legs and knocked me over." She closed her eyes as the horrifying sounds and acrid smells from that long-ago night flocked to the surface. "He-he didn't mean to. Gus was a good horse. He was just so scared. The flames were licking up the wall of his stall and jumping across the hay and he didn't know where to go.

"When I fell, I landed on a patch of burning hay. I rolled over and got up. I knew I'd been burned, but I had to get Gus out. So I ran to the tack room and grabbed some rope. But by the time I got back, it was too late. There were too many flames between me and Gus . . ." She tried to choke back the sobs born on a memory she'd worked so hard to forget, but there, at that moment, in that place, she no longer had any power to keep them away.

But when she looked up to apologize for her breakdown, Amos was there, pulling her to her feet and holding her close. Seconds turned to minutes as she cried into his shoulder, her tears dampening his shirt and his suspenders. She knew she needed to stop, to get her emotions under control, but something about his warmth and his nearness made her feel safe in her grief.

When her cries finally subsided, he stepped back, his brown eyes intent on her face. "You tried, Sadie. You could not have done more."

"But I wish I could have. I wish I had not gone for that rope. I wish I could have gotten myself between Gus and the wall and pushed."

"And if you had, you might not be here now."

They were the same words *Mam* and *Dat* had said in the days immediately following the fire. They were the same words the nurse at the hospital had said when she'd found Sadie crying in her room at night. Yet even now, so many years later, they still felt hollow in her ears.

Wiping her eyes with her sleeve, she wandered over to the water's edge and inhaled the cold, winter air into her lungs.

"How long were you in the hospital?" he asked as he stepped in beside her.

"Many months."

"I bet you were glad when you were finally able to go home."

"I was. At first." He turned, the surprise in his eyes making her stumble out the rest of her words. "It was good to be home with *Mam* and *Dat* and the children. But I was not easy to look at. I'm still not. But back then, when it was still new, it was hard to see *Mam's* sadness, *Dat's* discomfort, and the children trying not to stare.

"When I was well enough to go back to the hymn sings, I would see my friends look away when I would come near. I tried to be the way I always was, to make everyone smile the way they once did when I was near, but soon, when that did not matter, I got quiet. That has made it easier for everyone."

"How so?"

"Now a quick wave or an even quicker smile is enough when they see me. They don't have to come close and look at—" She pointed at her cheek only to drop her hand at the sudden flash of light off to her right. "Look! The sun is just right! It is time to make your wish!"

"You first," he said, his voice husky. "So I know what to do."

Shrugging, she stepped closer, scanned the mass of shimmering sparkles, and, when she found her favorite, pointed. "That is the one I would wish on if I were going to make a wish."

He pulled a face. "You are not going to make a wish?"

"No. It is silly to make the same wish again and again. Especially when it will not come true."

"Then make a new one."

"A new one?"

"*Ya.*"

"Okay. I-I guess I can think of something new." She closed

her eyes, discarded the wish that stood ready to go, and, instead, reverted to one from her childhood days.

"What did you wish for?" he asked as she opened her eyes.

"I cannot tell you that, silly! It won't come true if I tell you!"

"Ahhh, I see. That is a rule I did not know."

"Now it is your—"

"And the other wish?" He leaned forward. "The one you used to make? Can you tell me *that* one since it hasn't come true anyway?"

She looked from the sparkling pond to Amos and back again, her answer barely more than a whisper. "If I tell you, you will think it is silly."

"Did you wish for more of your *mam*'s apple pie?"

Her gasp morphed into a giggle as she stilled her head, mid-nod. "That was not my *old* wish."

He, too, laughed. "Uh-oh."

"*Ya*. Uh-oh." She returned her attention to the waning rays dancing across the pond's surface, wishing for the days when all she truly wanted was *Mam*'s apple pie. It was easier back then because most of the time, it came true. At least by week's end, anyway. "Now, it is time for *you* to pick a sparkle and make a wish."

"I will. But first, I want to know what your other wish was . . . The one you do not make anymore."

She knew he was waiting, she could feel the warmth and intensity of his gaze just as surely as she could the certainty that her wishing days were over. "I wished to be special to someone in the way *Mam* is special to *Dat*."

8:35 p.m.

Pulling her coat closer to her body, Sadie leaned against the stall's half wall and watched as the colt wandered around its mother, exploring the hay, the walls, and the feed bucket. It was getting colder by the minute, but for some reason she couldn't quite bring herself to go inside yet.

"Sadie?"

She turned toward the barn door, her surprise over seeing *Mam* standing there quickly offset by a familiar guilt. All throughout Sadie's childhood, *Mam* had had the biggest smile. It, like the sun, had greeted Sadie's days—always happy, always encouraging, always understanding. Yet because of Sadie's choices six years earlier, it no longer shone as bright as it once did.

At least not in Sadie's presence, anyway . . .

"*Mam*, I-I didn't hear you coming." Sadie stepped away from the wall only to retrace the same step just as quickly. Pointing to the foal, she tried to keep her voice light. "He is very curious about everything. He seems to like the hay in the back corner best."

She felt her shoulders sag with quiet relief as *Mam* came to join her at the wall. "You were like that when you were little, too, Sadie. You would wander around the garden, asking about every plant and flower, and then run into the barn to do the same of *Dat* about . . ." *Mam* turned, a hesitant, yet no less surprising smile playing at the corners of her mouth. "*Dat* said he brought you home again."

"*Dat* didn't bring me . . ." The rest of her words fell away as reality won over her confusion. "You mean, Amos—Amos Yoder. His *dat* owns the ice cream shop next to Miss Jenny's. He drove me so I wouldn't be late to help with dinner."

"But you were still late," *Mam* reminded, not unkindly.

"And I'm sorry for that. He wanted to see Lapp's Pond and, well, we got to talking and"—shame cast her eyes to the floor—"then it was late."

"Perhaps he will want to court you?" *Mam* asked.

"It was just one drive, *Mam*. That is all."

"That is *three* drives, *Dat* said."

"I told him he did not need to those other two times, but he wanted to make sure the Englisher did not come back."

Mam's eyebrows dipped. "Englisher?"

"It does not matter. I am used to it."

"Sadie, please. I must know."

"But—"

"Tell me, Sadie."

And so she did. She spoke of the first time the red car appeared, how she thought the Englisher inside was just lost, and the mean things he said about her face. She heard *Mam*'s gasp, saw the sadness muting the pale blue eyes she'd known since birth, but still Sadie didn't stop. Instead, she talked about his return the next day, and the next day, and every day since. She talked about how it scared her at first but that eventually, when it became routine, she challenged herself to find ways to ignore him by picking out shapes in the clouds, thinking up silly names for the cows she passed, and even the ideas she toyed with for a shop of her own one day.

"You cannot own a shop, Sadie! You must care for your husband and your children."

The colt startled at Sadie's humorless laugh. "There will be no husband and children, *Mam*. Not for me."

"Sadie!"

Oh, how she hated being the cause of *Mam*'s sadness, but maybe, if she could make her see what was real, they could get back to the old smiles again one day. "*Mam*, no one will marry me. Not looking as I do."

"*Plain* people do not concern themselves with such things," *Mam* whispered, fiercely.

"They try not to, but this"—she pointed to her cheek—"is hard not to see."

Mam pressed her knuckles to her face and closed her eyes as if in pain. "Oh, Sadie . . . It is not as bad as you think."

"It is not as good as you want to believe."

"But this boy—this Amos Yoder. Perhaps he—"

She shook away the rest of *Mam*'s hope. "Amos is just kind. I am sure he is courting someone in his own district."

"Maybe there is someone else. Someone other than this Amos."

"I thought there was. For a few days . . ."

Mam's eyes lit with such hope, Sadie felt physically ill. "Oh?"

"It was not real, *Mam*."

"I don't understand."

"The Englisher left things that made Miss Jenny think I had a secret admirer. At first, I did not think I could have such a thing, but then I began to think she was right." She heard the tremor in her voice and did her best to disguise it by making faces at the colt. When she felt as if she could speak again, she did. "The first gift was a book with beautiful words that made me smile and think in a way my other books do not.

"The second gift was a whittled bird—like the birds that sing from the trees in the spring and summer. It looked so real sitting on Miss Jenny's back step that I was certain it was. But it was the third gift—the one he left today—that let me know it was not real."

She looked up at the feel of *Mam*'s hand on her own. "What was the gift?"

"A mirror."

"A mirror?" *Mam* echoed. "But why?"

"To *hurt* me. He knows what I look like, he knows that I am ugly, that—"

"Sadie Fisher you are God's child!"

"God did not make me this way, *Mam*. I did. *My choices* did. I don't blame *God*. I blame myself for tripping . . . for taking so long to get up . . . for not getting Gus out of the barn."

Opening her arms wide, *Mam* beckoned Sadie in for a hug. Soon, a growing dampness on the top of Sadie's prayer *kapp* let her know she wasn't the only one crying. Before she could gather the courage she needed to step away, though, *Mam*'s warm breath filled her ear. "Do you really think someone who could give such a book and a treasure could also talk the way the Englisher does?"

She wiped the last of her tears from her cheek and stepped back, her gaze meeting *Mam*'s. "No, not really. But he is the only one who would leave a mirror."

"*If* it was truly left to be mean . . ."

"Why else would someone leave a mirror for"—she tilted her scarred cheek forward—"*me*? It is not as if I *want* to look!"

"Sadie, please!"

"*Mam*, I know what I look like. *Everyone* does."

"Maybe the person who left the mirror sees you as I do."

"You mean with pity and sadness?"

Mam drew back, her eyes wide. "I do not look at you with *pity* and *sadness!*"

She grabbed hold of *Mam*'s hands and held them tight. "I don't say that to be mean, *Mam*. I say it because it is what I see when you look at me. But I don't want you to worry about me the way you do. A different life does not mean a bad life. Miss Jenny never married and she is okay. And maybe, if I can make a shop of my own, I can be happy, too!"

"Maybe the person who left the mirror is not the same as the one who left the book and the bird," *Mam* protested.

"*Mam*, that doesn't make sense."

"Then maybe it's someone other than the Englisher."

She considered the possibility for less time than it took the colt to return to his favorite corner of the stall after wandering off for a moment. "There is no one else, *Mam*. Not for someone like me."

Wednesday. 11:30 a.m.

She was reattaching a new price tag to one of the quilt displays when Miss Jenny breezed in through the back door, the woman's very pace pulling Sadie to her feet. "Miss Jenny? Is everything o—"

"You got another gift, dear! It was on the back step just now. See?" Miss Jenny thrust the familiar navy-and-white-colored gift sack into Sadie's hand and beamed. "It's from Beechy's Sweets across the street!"

Peeking between the simple white handles, she stumbled back a half step. "Are you sure it's mine? Maybe someone dropped it or set it down and then forgot it was there . . ."

"It was on the back step, Sadie. With your name on it." Miss Jenny reached forward, positioned the attached name tag in Sadie's view, and then did a little dance. "See? It's for you."

She stared at her name. "It looks the same as it did in the book and on the tag that was attached to the—"

"That's because it's from the same person, dear! Your secret admirer!"

"There is no secret admirer." Sadie closed the handles and held out the bag to her boss. "Please. Take this."

Miss Jenny's eyes widened in shock only to narrow to near slits as she refused to take the bag. "Do you still believe I'm behind all these gifts you've been getting? Because I'm not."

"I know." She tried, again, to hand the bag back, but when Miss Jenny's hands remained folded, Sadie bypassed her boss and headed straight to the counter and the newly emptied trash can it shielded from customers' view. "I know it is wrong to waste food, but I cannot keep this."

Reaching inside the bag, she pulled out the single heart-shaped chocolate with its clear plastic covering and big red bow. So many times, she'd imagined this moment, yet never in

all those instances had it ended with her throwing the treat
away . . . until now—

"Sadie Fisher, freeze!"

She lingered the treat over the trash can and looked back at
Miss Jenny. "I-I can't keep this."

"Why on earth not?"

"Because it is not from a true admirer. It is from someone
who is not nice."

"Not nice?" Miss Jenny crossed to the counter, her eyes
locked on Sadie's. "How could someone who leaves you a
book, a hand-carved bird, and a heart-shaped piece of chocolate not be nice?"

She looked between the chocolate and Miss Jenny as the
timing behind yesterday's gift clicked in her thoughts. "You
don't know about the other gift . . . The one I found while I
was closing up yesterday . . ."

Miss Jenny leaned forward with a smile. "Another gift?"

"*Ya.*"

"What was it?"

"It was something mean." Aware of yesterday's sadness returning, she swapped the chocolate heart for a dustcloth and
ran it across the top of the already-clean counter. "He wanted
to hurt me, and he did. For a while. But thanks to Amos and
Mam, I did not go to bed sad."

"What was the gift?" Miss Jenny repeated.

"A mirror."

It was fast and it was fleeting, but there was also no denying
the shock and subsequent sadness that dulled the woman's normal sparkle. "But—"

She waved the dustcloth until Miss Jenny grew silent. "It is
okay. It was because of that gift that I knew who was pretending to like me."

"*Pretending?* Oh, Sadie you can't know that."

So she told Miss Jenny about her walks home and the cruel things the Englisher in the red car said to her each and every afternoon. As she spoke, she watched Miss Jenny's reaction move from curiosity, to surprise, and, finally, to anger. And when she was done, she tossed the dustcloth back on the counter and grabbed hold of the heart-shaped chocolate once again. "So that is why I will not keep this. Because it is given in meanness."

"But what if it's not?" Miss Jenny said, resting her hand atop Sadie's. "What if these gifts have nothing to do with that awful person?"

"A *kind* person would not give someone who looks like me a mirror!"

"Would a *mean* person give you a book of quotes? Would a *mean* person give you a hand-carved bird? Would a *mean* person give you"—Miss Jenny released Sadie's hand just long enough to extract the chocolate and hold it up—"a heart-shaped piece of chocolate?"

"He gave me *a mirror*, Miss Jenny!" she protested.

"I don't think that means anything, dear. Except that whoever your admirer is knows you're beautiful even if you don't."

She didn't mean to laugh, she really didn't. But considering the pain her tears would likely cause Miss Jenny, it was preferable.

"You can laugh if you want, dear, but there is a very simple way you can find out once and for all."

"Find out?" she echoed. "Find out what?"

"The identity of your secret admirer."

Sadie drew back. "How?"

"Go across the street to Beechy's Sweets and ask Clara who bought that chocolate."

12:15 p.m.

In some quiet corner of her brain, she heard the welcoming jingle that greeted her first step into the sweet shop. She was even vaguely aware of the few sets of eyes that looked up from the various treat stations around the room. But the only thing she knew for certain was her stomach's response to the mouth-watering smell of Jacob Beechy's famous fudge. She'd sampled a piece on occasion thanks to Miss Jenny's insatiable sweet tooth, but getting a quick sniff from a carefully packaged box was nothing compared to breathing it in, firsthand.

"Welcome to Beechy's Sweets, how can we—oh, Sadie! Isn't this a nice surprise..." With a quick word to her new employee, Rose Bontrager, Clara Beechy came out from behind the counter, wiping her plump hands on a simple white cloth. "How is your *mam*? Your *dat*?"

"They are well, thank you."

"Come closer, child. Let me have a look at you."

With quick steps, Sadie met the fifty-something halfway across the century-old hardwood floor and lowered her chin for the inevitable inspection. Clara, in turn, lifted her free hand to Sadie's cheek and smiled. "It's healing nicely."

She knew it wasn't true. Her scars were no different than they were a month ago, six months ago, even six *years* ago. But still, the fact that Clara could look at Sadie without wincing as so many others did, was refreshing.

"So what brings you by the sweet shop today?" Clara dropped her hand to her side and motioned toward the counter with her cloth. "Did you know Rose is working here now?"

"I did. Miss Jenny told me."

"She's working out very well." Clara smiled at Rose and then turned back to Sadie. "Did Jenny send you over for some fudge? Because Jacob is making a fresh batch right now."

Leaning to the left, Sadie followed Clara's finger toward the swinging wooden door and the narrow view it afforded of the kitchen and the shop's owner, Jacob Beechy. She couldn't see much, but it was enough to know he was spreading chocolate across a wide slab.

"I'm surprised Jenny sent you. She usually likes to come herself."

She turned back to Clara. "I'm actually here because I'd like to ask you a question. About a piece of heart-shaped chocolate you may have sold earlier today. I-I was hoping you could tell me who bought it?"

Clara's laugh filled the room, earning them more than a few curious glances from the pair of customers happily indulging in some fudge samples at a nearby table. "You *do* realize Valentine's Day is right around the corner, don't you, Sadie?"

"I do."

"Then you have to know that I've probably sold close to two dozen of those heart-shaped chocolates over the last day or so. And I expect we'll sell ten times that amount"—Clara directed Sadie's attention to the display case behind which Rose was standing—"between now and the big day."

"But this one was in a clear bag and tied closed with a red ribbon."

"They *all* leave the shop like that, Sadie."

She tried to hide her disappointment by pretending to look at the case, but Clara was as observant as she was kind. "Sadie? Is everything okay?"

"No, it's fine. It's just . . ." The rest of her words faded off as the jingled arrival of a new customer pulled the Amish woman's attention off Sadie and fixed it, instead, on the door.

While Clara greeted the couple and offered them samples of Jacob's fudge, Sadie stepped over to the window and its view of the quilt shop on the other side of Main Street. On any other day, the sight of the wide front porch and colorful quilts displayed in the large picture window made her happy. Today, though, it was as if everything were muted by the sound of Miss Jenny casting doubt on her theory—a theory that, while sad, was far more realistic than the one her boss wanted to believe.

A familiar buggy pulled through her view, directing it off Bluebird Quilts and leading it to a stop just beyond the mouth of the alley. Seconds later, her handsome friend dropped down from his seat, whispered something in Bell's ear, and then, glancing toward Miss Jenny's shop, pulled a basket from behind his seat and carried it up the alley.

Curious, Sadie stepped to the left, her gaze riveted on Amos as he headed toward his *dat*'s shop while looking back at Miss Jenny's window every few steps. When she lost sight of him, she took another step to the left only to stop as Clara finished up with the customers and returned to Sadie's side.

"I'm sorry I couldn't help you with your question, Sadie, but perhaps there is something else I can do for you?" Clara asked. "Maybe a sample of Jacob's fudge for yourself? Or some candy to take home to the little ones?"

"No thank you, Clara." She met the woman's worried eyes with what she hoped was a reassuring smile. "I really should be heading back to work. Miss Jenny will be wondering where I am if I don't get back."

"Don't be such a stranger, Sadie. It's lovely seeing you here."

"Thank you, Clara." With a quick squeeze of the woman's hand, Sadie turned, yanked open the door, and made haste across the street to Miss Jenny's shop.

As she approached the front porch, she could see Miss Jenny standing just inside the door with a pair of customers. Not wanting to interrupt, Sadie cut through the alley toward the back door, stopping mid-step as her gaze fell on the same basket she'd seen in Amos's hands not more than five minutes earlier.

Confused, she stepped closer, her steps and her eyes guided forward by a familiar sight hanging from the basket's handle.

4:25 p.m.

She moved through the rest of the afternoon in a daze, her thoughts and her feet returning again and again to the basket she'd placed on the shelf behind the counter. Even before she'd pulled back the cloth cover she'd known what was inside. The medley of apple and cinnamon aromas had been evident even before she'd gotten close enough to read the tag.

Stilling her hand atop the quilt she'd just finished folding, Sadie traveled her thoughts back to the moment she'd first turned over the tag and saw her name written exactly as it had been on all the other gifts.

Including the mirror.

Only now, instead of wondering whether Miss Jenny was trying to be kind or the Englisher in the red car was intentionally being cruel, she knew who was behind it all.

Amos had left the book of quotes.

Amos had left the whittled and hand-painted songbird.

Amos had left the heart-shaped chocolate from Beechy's.

Amos had left the apple cinnamon pie solely responsible for her stomach's persistent growling.

And *Amos* had left the mirror.

Amos. As in Amos Yoder . . . The handsome Amish man with the dark hair, warm brown eyes, kind voice, and dimple-accompanied smile that had made her heart flutter more than a few times the past week or so.

"I'm sorry Clara didn't have any information for you, dear . . ."

Shrugging away Miss Jenny's disappointment, Sadie deposited the newly folded quilt on its proper shelf and reached for another. "It's okay. It's not really anything I should be worrying about."

"That's quite a switch."

She stopped folding. "What do you mean, Miss Jenny?"

"Is this still about you thinking that awful young man in the red car is behind all of these gifts? Because it still doesn't make sense to me. Not with all the other gifts beyond the—"

"It wasn't him." Propelled forward by Miss Jenny's answering gasp, Sadie set the quilt on a different shelf and wandered over to the window overlooking the alley. A quick visual sweep of the area netted no sighting of Amos or his buggy.

Miss Jenny's footsteps grew louder as she, too, made her way to the window and Sadie. "I thought you said Clara couldn't help you. That she's sold too many heart-shaped chocolates the past few days to know who all bought them . . . Though, I still think if you'd described the Englisher to her the way you did to me, she might have been able to at least say if he'd been into her shop or not."

"There is no need." She turned her attention to the part of Main Street she could see from her vantage point and wondered when Amos would return. If he followed the same pattern she'd begun to piece together for him over the past few days, his buggy would reappear about the same time she was starting the various closing tasks around the shop. And then, sometime after she set out for home, he'd show up to chase off the Englisher. Or, in the case of the day the mirror came, he'd step outside the ice cream shop's door and find her crying on the back step.

But not today. Today, *she* would be waiting for *him*.

"Of course, there was a need, dear. If you know the chocolate came from him, I could make sure that all subsequent gifts go straight into the trash without you even having to see them. And if it *wasn't* from him, then—"

"It wasn't from him," she whispered.

This time, when Miss Jenny gasped, the sound was immediately followed by the feel of the woman's hands on Sadie's shoulders, turning her. "I thought you said Clara was unable to help."

"Because she wasn't."

"Then how do you know who it wasn't?"

She took one last look over her shoulder at the empty alleyway and then beckoned for Miss Jenny to follow. When she reached the counter, she made her way around it to the basket she'd yet to share. "Because I know who it was now," she said, setting the basket on the countertop between them. "He left this for me while I was at Beechy's."

"What . . ." Miss Jenny's words trailed away in favor of a hearty laugh as she peeled back the cloth cover and looked into the basket. "So *this* is why I've been smelling apple and cinnamon since you got back! I thought I was imagining it. Although, I'm not sure if you noticed or not, but just after you got back, a customer in a blue sweater came in. I noticed the smell about that time and thought maybe it was a new kind of perfume. I even commented on her necklace just so I could get close enough for a whiff. But it wasn't her *or* my always hungry imagination, was it?"

"I'm sorry, Miss Jenny. I should have mentioned it, but I was having trouble thinking and I just wanted to stick it under the counter so I could get back to work and think later. Only"—she stopped, her focus dropping to the tag bearing her name in bold, penciled lettering—"I haven't been able to think about much of anything besides this pie . . . and the book . . . and the bird . . . and the chocolate . . . and . . . the mirror."

"So, who is it?" Miss Jenny asked, mid-squeal. "Who is your secret admirer?"

"He's not a secret admirer. Not a real one, anyway." Sadie

stepped back against the wall and cocked her head up toward the ceiling. "He was simply doing what you did, Miss Jenny."

"What *I* did?" Miss Jenny echoed.

"*Ya*. He was pretending. To be nice."

"He was *pretending* to be nice? You mean like the Englisher?"

She considered Miss Jenny's words against everything he'd shown her that week and, finally, shook her head. "No. He wasn't pretending to be nice. He was pretending to be my secret admirer *because* he's nice."

"How do you know this?" Miss Jenny asked.

"Because he is handsome and smart. He could court any girl in any district if he wanted."

Miss Jenny joined her behind the counter and waited until Sadie relinquished her visual hold on the tiled ceiling above her head. "Perhaps he wants to court *you*, Sadie."

"No, Miss Jenny. He doesn't." She inhaled the courage she needed to give Miss Jenny a proper, carefree smile but it froze midway across her mouth at the sound of a buggy in the alley.

Stepping around Miss Jenny, Sadie grabbed hold of the basket and headed toward the back door. "There is something I need to take care of, but I shouldn't be long."

Before Miss Jenny could say or ask anything, she stepped outside, the sudden sadness she felt as she looked at the back door of Yoder's Ice Cream rendering her momentarily immobile. Yes, she knew she needed to speak to Amos . . . And yes, she knew she needed to ask him to stop . . . But when he did, so, too, would the brief moments she'd had of feeling special.

It wasn't the gifts, per se, that had done that. In fact, just the lingering question mark over the various treats had made that difficult. It was the *time* she'd spent with Amos that had done that.

Sharing her favorite quote from the book . . .

Having him chase off the Englisher . . .

Confiding in him about the fire . . .

Letting him wipe her tears . . .

Making wishes together on sparkles . . .

"Got something special in that basket?"

Startled from her thoughts, she shifted her focus to the opposite side of the alley and the living embodiment of her oft-made wish. Because, right or wrong, Amos Yoder had made her feel special. And even if it had been for all the wrong reasons, it had still felt nice for the brief moment it lasted.

"Sadie?"

"The new wish you told me to make came true," she said, stepping down off the step and brandishing the basket in the air.

"Oh?"

"*Ya.* I was given an apple pie today. It is not *Mam's*, but it smells delicious."

"Smells delicious? Does that mean you haven't tried it yet?"

She forced herself to meet his eye and hold it while simultaneously praying for the courage she needed to say what needed to be said. When she was sure she was ready, she returned his smile. "I will. Tonight. Along with the chocolate you left me."

Shifting his weight, he palmed his mouth only to let his hand fall back to his side. "I almost told you yesterday, when you were so upset about the mirror, but I wanted to give you the chocolate as my last surprise. But then, after your wish, I knew I had to add one more thing. Especially since I'd guessed it out loud."

"But that's just it, Amos. You didn't have to do any of it. Not the book, not the bird, not the . . ." She heard the tears hovering around her words and made herself stop.

Amos jumped down off the stoop and slowly crossed the alley, his every step seemingly labored. "You have to know I didn't mean for that mirror to bring you pain, Sadie. I mean,

I-I knew it was wrong, that it is not a proper Amish gift, but I was hoping—"

She had to stop him, had to let him off the hook. But to do so meant the end of her real wish . . .

"I was hoping that maybe you'd look at it and see what I—"

Squaring her shoulders, she stopped him with her hand. "Please, Amos. I know why you did what you did and it was very sweet. But I *need* you to stop."

Her words seemed to push him backward. "Stop? Stop what?"

"Giving me things." She lifted the basket into the air again, then swept it toward Miss Jenny's stoop. "Trying to be nice. It's sweet, it really is, but I don't want you feeling sorry for me anymore than I want Miss Jenny feeling sorry for me."

"Feeling sorry for you?"

"For *this*." She gestured her free hand toward her cheek and then returned it to the basket handle in the hopes its incessant trembling would stop. "Miss Jenny only sees it when I am here in the shop, working. And you . . . you only see it if you happen to come out to the alley when I am having lunch or taking out the trash. But I see my reflection in my bedroom window every morning. I see it in the mirror in the kitchen before I leave to come here. I see it in *Mam*'s eyes when she hears of yet another friend who is to be married. I am used to it, Amos. It is normal for me now. I don't need pity."

He stared back at her, his mouth gaping and closing and gaping again.

"But I *would* like a friend," she added. "A friend who will laugh with me like you do, Amos."

"A friend? I don't want to be your *friend*."

It was as if his words were a hand, smacking her across the face. "But—"

He closed the gap between them with three determined

strides. When he was not more than a foot away, he reached out, took the basket from her hands, and set it at her feet. Then, gathering her hands in his, he held them tight. "I didn't give you that book because I felt sorry for you, Sadie. I gave it to you because I know you like to read and I thought you would like it. And I gave you that bird because that quote you read from your book—the reason you liked it—made me want to make you a reminder of those words. The chocolate was because I remember the way your eyes got all shiny when you spoke of the treat your friend Esther would not eat. And the pie? That was because I didn't want your wish to be ruined because I guessed what it was out loud."

Too stunned to speak, she remained quiet, her head trying hard to keep up with her ears.

"And the mirror? I gave that to you because I wanted to help you see what *I* see every time I look at you."

"What you see?" she rasped.

"*Ya.*"

"There is nothing to see but ugly scars . . ."

"That's where you're wrong, Sadie. There is *everything* to see." His voice deepened as he stepped still closer. "You are hardworking . . . You are kind . . . You are funny . . . You are brave . . . And you are—"

"Amos, please stop."

Releasing her from his grasp, he cradled her cheeks inside his strong, calloused hands. "I can't stop. Maybe I should have just said this last night, at the pond, instead of wanting to get in two more surprises. But I'm saying it now . . . You, Sadie Fisher, are the most beautiful woman I have ever seen—inside *and* out."

"But my face. It's—"

"Your face—your *whole* face—is what I see in my thoughts when I'm driving to *Dat*'s shop each day. And when I finally get here, it is what I hope to see when I look at Miss Jenny's steps or into Miss Jenny's . . ."

She followed his eyes as they left hers and traveled toward the very same window where she'd so often stood, never quite daring to imagine a moment like this. A moment so perfect she might actually think she was dreaming if it weren't for the happy squeal and the not so hushed *"I knew it"* coming from the other side of the screen.

"Uh-oh," she murmured, looking back at Amos.

"What's wrong?"

"I think Miss Jenny just heard everything you said."

His brown eyes flashed with joy. "I think my *dat* did, too."

"Your dat?" Sadie peeked around Amos to the ice cream shop's back door—and the outer edge of a black brimmed hat she hadn't noticed until just that moment.

"Ya. He has heard me speak of little else since I met you."

She stumbled back a step. "You have spoken about *me?"*

"Every day. *All* day."

Amos's laugh filled the air around them as he gathered her hands inside his own once more, his eyes so full of love she could hardly breathe. *"Dat's* right, Sadie. You're *all* I think about. All I *want* to think about. So please . . . If it's alright with your *dat*, may I court you, Sadie Fisher?"

"Yes! Yes!"

She waited until Amos's eyes returned to hers and added the smile she couldn't hold back even if she tried. "What Miss Jenny said."

Nothing Tastes So Sweet

MARY ELLIS

*This book is dedicated
to Joycelyn Sullivan.
I will always be grateful
for your proofreading
of my novels.*

Acknowledgments

It was an honor to be able to work with Emma Miller and Laura Bradford.

Special thanks to my editor, Alicia Condon, and my production editor, Paula Reedy, at Kensington Publishing. I also wish to thank my fabulous agent, Nicole Resciniti; my former proofreader, Joycelyn; and my darling husband, Ken, who has always been supportive of me.

Chapter 1

"Daniel," Hannah called from the stove. "Your breakfast is ready."

"What are we having—Eggs Benedict?" he teased. "Corned beef hash?"

She laughed. Daniel always requested the same menu each Monday morning and today was no different. "Two eggs, over hard, four strips of bacon, and three pieces of buttered toast. Better hurry before everything gets cold." She filled his mug with coffee.

"Ahh, my favorite. How did you know?" He winked while adding jam to a slice of toast.

Hannah took her coffee over to the window seat. Normally she ate with her husband, but today her stomach didn't feel right. In fact the thought of bacon grease and butter made her downright queasy.

"Any plans this week, other than work?" he asked between bites of egg.

"If Wednesday's weather is nice, I may call for a ride to

Mam's. She's hosting a quilting at her house. Then *Dat* can bring me home."

"What does weather have to do with quilting?"

"I don't want him out late if it's snowing. That makes it too hard to see buggy reflectors."

Daniel nodded and refilled his mug.

Hannah peered down on the street below. "Oh my, your ride is here already."

"Tell Mr. McCourt I'll be down right now." Daniel built a sandwich with his remaining eggs and toast and then headed to their bedroom to finish packing.

Hannah wiped the glass and squinted, but couldn't distinguish whether it was Mr. McCourt—her husband's regular driver—or not. "I hate screaming out the window while everyone in town is sleeping," she called on her way to the stove. "After I fill your thermos, I'll carry down a cup of hot coffee. Mr. McCourt might have asked someone to fill in today."

Without warning, her husband of eight years crept up behind her, enfolded her in his massive arms, and lifted her off her feet.

"Goodness," Hannah squawked in surprise. "Put me down. You're lucky I wasn't still holding the pot of coffee."

Daniel lowered her to the floor but didn't release his embrace. "I sure hate leaving you for five days at a time."

Hannah squirmed away. It was Daniel's standard Monday complaint, but she needed to pack yesterday's blueberry muffins in with his lunches and load his cooler with bottles of water. "Good paying jobs like yours are hard to find. In another year or two we should have enough to buy our own farm."

"That day can't come soon enough." Shrugging into his work coat, Daniel tightened the lid on his thermos. "Is there any of Jacob's fudge left?"

"No. After supper you ate the last piece of maple and I finished the vanilla." Hannah pressed the extra travel mug into his hand just as they heard a car horn.

"For certain it's not Mr. McCourt. He knows better than to blast his horn. Maybe he arranged a replacement through Uber." Daniel buzzed a kiss across her forehead. "Stay well, dear *fraa*. I'll see you Friday night."

As he hurried down the steps of their second-floor apartment, Hannah swallowed a lump of emotion in her throat. It was the same routine week after week, yet it never seemed to get any easier. Only during the month of August when Daniel took his three-week vacation were they together during the week. But considering the cabinet factory was forty miles away in Reading, there wasn't time for him to come home each night.

Hannah waved from the window as Daniel jostled his over-stuffed duffle and cooler into the back seat and climbed in the passenger side. Then she watched the deserted street long after the hired car disappeared around the corner. So much had changed in Bluebird since they'd moved from her parents' attic to the apartment above the hardware store. It had been an easy adjustment for her. Mr. and Mrs. Howard kept the rent cheap since they loved having people living upstairs, sort of like resident night watchmen. And with her odd hours at the store, going home after work was a simple matter of climbing the stairs.

Although they both had been born and raised on farms, living in town gave Hannah a chance to talk to people other than her family. With more Amish moving to the area, Bluebird businesses catered to both Amish and English needs, as well as a steady influx of tourists. It was odd for a *Plain* woman to admit, but Hannah had felt lonely and isolated surrounded by corn and hay fields—a sentiment not shared by her sisters or her mother.

For Daniel, the transition from the country to town had

been more difficult. The small four rooms—kitchen, dining room, living room, and bath—felt claustrophobic to someone who'd grown up in a rambling, six-bedroom farmhouse. The Klines' living room was so spacious they could easily accommodate the entire district when it was their turn to host the preaching service. Plus, Daniel loved the smell of newly mown hay and the crow of the rooster each morning. He couldn't wait for Saturdays when he harnessed his *dat's* Percherons for spring plowing or the corn harvest in the fall when the whole district pitched in. Despite the fact he made oak and walnut cabinets all day, sold at prices nobody Amish would ever pay, Daniel was a farmer from the soles of his boots to the top of his black felt hat.

Thanks to his job and hers, someday they would save enough money to buy a farm or at least some acreage, which wasn't easy this close to Lancaster, a popular spot with English tourists. Then they would quit their jobs and fulfill his lifelong dream. Hannah would take her rightful place at his side as his wife and hopefully by then, a mother. Until that day, she enjoyed seeing a steady stream of new faces and having neighbors close by. And who wouldn't love having a candy shop across the street where every type of sweet was only a few steps away?

Hannah washed the breakfast dishes, made the bed, and wrapped her long hair in a bun. After a quick trip down the back stairs, she turned her key in the front door and punched in an hour early at Howard's Hardware. Since idling in four empty rooms upstairs would be wasteful, she switched on the lights and got started with the weekly inventory, another of her standard Monday routines.

Within the hour, the diner would open for breakfast, the bakery would have fresh donuts and pastries, and Jacob Beechy would be in his kitchen making the world's best fudge. The rest of Bluebird—the quilt shop, the ice cream store, and the grocery store—opened a bit later in the day. But the one bed and breakfast kept some lights on both night and day, hoping to attract the attention of those passing through.

Ready for her second cup of coffee, Hannah entered the back room just as the door to the parking lot opened. "Good morning, Mrs. Howard," she greeted.

"Good morning, dear child. And I've told you a thousand times to call me Martha." The fiftyish woman set down two take-out bags and a tray holding three Styrofoam cups. "I bought us breakfast tacos, hash brown potatoes, and yogurt parfaits." Her employer smiled and ran a hand through her salt-and-pepper hair.

Tacos and greasy potatoes didn't sound any more appealing than what she'd cooked for Daniel that morning. "Thanks for the coffee, but I'm not very hungry." Hannah took off the lid to let the liquid cool.

When Hannah shook her head, Martha's big smile faded. "Not even for strawberry and blueberry yogurt? You usually love that."

"I'll stick it in the fridge and eat it for lunch. Where is Mr. Howard? Didn't he ride in with you?" Hannah would never be able to call her elderly employer by his given name, Lawrence, no matter how much he scolded.

Martha pulled a chair to the table that served as their work surface, lunch counter, and conference room for infrequent employee meetings. "Lawrence's breathing treatment took longer than usual. He told me to go ahead and he'd see us later." She added three packets of hot sauce to her burrito, something few Amish people would do at nine in the morning.

"Oh dear. Is Mr. Howard's COPD getting worse?"

"I don't think so, but we won't know for sure until his doctor's appointment next week." Martha nibbled the burrito and took a sip of coffee. Despite her assurance, deep worry lines creased her forehead.

"I'll remember him in my prayers tonight."

"Thank you, but that's enough about us old folks. What's new with you and Daniel?" She broke off a piece of hash brown to eat.

Hannah was grateful for the change in subject. "We visited his family on Saturday, stayed overnight, and came home yesterday after church. Daniel has so many nieces and nephews these days I can't keep their names straight. Every one of his six brothers and sisters is married with several children."

Martha's expression turned downright bewildered. "How does his mother serve dinner to so many people?"

"Dinner is never served sit-down in Daniel's household. All the women cook on Saturday, either at home or they come early to help *Mam* Kline that day. Then the food is kept cold overnight and set out on several tables after church. People fix a plate and find a spot to sit in the dining room, kitchen, or on one of the three porches. If there's one thing the Klines have, it's plenty of room. We don't cook on the Sabbath."

The older woman clucked her tongue. "Each Thanksgiving and Christmas I kick myself for not buying a house with a bigger dining room. Now all Lawrence and I talk about is moving to Florida to be closer to our son. He wants me to put my feet up while someone else does the holiday cooking."

Hannah was momentarily speechless. This was the first time she'd heard anything about the Howards relocating. "I'm sure your daughter or daughter-in-law would welcome the opportunity," she murmured.

"We'll see how true that is when the time comes. Hopefully, you'll soon have your own babies to chase after at family get-togethers. Then you won't worry about your nieces' and nephews' names." Martha laughed so hard her belly shook.

"I hope so," she agreed. "But it hasn't happened yet and we've been wed eight years."

"And for most of those years Daniel's been gone four nights

a week. On Friday, I'll bet he comes home so tired he can't do more than lift his fork for supper."

Hannah felt her cheeks redden with shame. "The Amish don't discuss such things. We patiently wait on the will of God."

"I know, but sometimes even the Lord needs a little help from us."

She felt another uncomfortable rumble in her gut, while her queasiness escalated threefold. "Excuse me a moment, Mrs. Howard." Hannah jumped up and fled to the bathroom, where she lost the little bit she'd eaten, along with two cups of coffee.

When she returned to the table, Martha had put away the food and thrown out both coffee cups. "I'm sorry I embarrassed you. It's not my place to stick my nose in your business." She wrung her hands.

Hannah reached for a bottle of water from the shelf. "You were trying to help. No apology is necessary. Besides, I've been feeling sick all morning. Maybe I'm coming down with a bug."

"Is this the first time you've felt this way?" Martha asked.

Hannah pondered the question. "No, last Tuesday the crunchy peanut butter on my toast didn't agree with me."

"It could be the flu . . . or maybe a little Kline is on the way."

She shook her head. "You just have babies on the mind this morning, that's all."

"Maybe, maybe not. But the pharmacy sells little kits that could solve the mystery right quick." Martha pushed to her feet and slipped a long apron over her clothes.

"I wouldn't spend my money on such foolishness." Hannah regretted her words the moment they left her tongue. She had no business talking that way to her employer. "Shouldn't we get the store ready to open?" she asked sweetly.

The comment had rolled off Martha's back. "Absolutely right, dear girl. Don't tell Mr. Howard about my dawdling, or he might fire me on the spot." Martha issued another belly laugh and marched through the swinging doors to turn on the overhead lights, dust, and straighten the displays.

Hannah breathed a sigh of relief and slipped on her long white apron. She would rather update the accounting and inventory software than contemplate looking for a new job . . . or the possibility of being pregnant. Since the bishop had given her permission to use the store's computer during business hours, she'd grown invaluable to her employers and was well compensated for the new responsibilities. But her job security would last only as long as the Howards owned the hardware store and she remained childless. Married Amish women didn't work outside the home after they had babies.

She knew there would be plenty to do once they owned a farm. The henhouse was usually the wife's domain, along with a large vegetable garden. Canning, drying herbs, and quilting augmented the everyday tasks of cooking, cleaning, and laundry. Unlike English households, children made life *easier*, not harder for farm wives because once they were old enough, they would help with chores. But until she and Daniel saved enough money, Hannah wanted to keep working.

As soon as she finished the updates, Hannah printed spreadsheets for Mr. Howard's inspection. However, when the owner finally walked through the front door, he didn't seem up to assessing anything. His complexion looked sallow, almost pasty, and his usually spry step was now a slow, unsteady shuffle.

"Mr. Howard, are you all right? Let me get your wife. She's in the stockroom."

"No, no, Hannah. I'm fine. Let Martha keep working. She takes enough breaks as it is." His dark eyes twinkled with mischief. "I just need to sit for a spell." Mr. Howard slumped onto a stool at the counter, looking much older than he had yesterday.

"Can I bring you some water?" she asked. Just then the bell

over the door chimed and a young couple with two children walked in.

"No, no. Go take care of the customers. That's what you enjoy most. I'll just sit here and watch." When he smiled, the expression erased a decade from his face. As long as his blood stayed oxygenated, Mr. Howard functioned well for a seventy-year-old man. But a bad night's sleep robbed him of vitality, despite sleeping in an oxygen tent.

Buoyed by the compliment, Hannah approached the wife, trying to gauge what she might be interested in. She did have a knack for turning a one-item shopping trip for a toilet plunger or roll of duct tape into a bag of time-saving gadgets for Amish customers or energy-saving gizmos for Englishers. Who didn't need birdseed after buying a feeder, or drop cloths and extra brushes if buying paint? Most people thanked her for sparing them another trip back to town.

Once the young couple left with a full bag of household cleaning products, Hannah checked on Mr. Howard. He had moved to the tall chair behind the cash register, his usual perch, with far more color in his cheeks.

"How are you feeling?" she asked.

"Good. You fuss over me as much as my wife. That walk from the parking lot gets longer every day, but I'm fine now."

So began their regular, daily routine: Hannah waiting on customers and answering questions on the floor, Mr. Howard ringing sales and fielding questions on plumbing and electrical, and Mrs. Howard refilling shelves as needed. Since replacing inventory didn't take all day, Martha usually went down the street to chat and gossip at other businesses.

Hannah loved the established routine. She loved her job and forced any thoughts of the Howards selling the store from her mind. After all, didn't most people dream for *years* before actually doing something about it?

The idea she couldn't force from her mind was Martha's suggestion she might be with child. It wasn't the second time she'd had morning sickness, it was the fourth. Although most *Plain* women would wait until they were fairly far along before seeing a doctor for confirmation, patience had never been one of her virtues. As soon as she finished her shift, Hannah hurried to the drug store, purchased one of those overpriced kits, and ran all the way home. Once she read through the directions twice and followed them to the letter, she couldn't bear to look at the results. After all, her husband was forty miles away. Her mother and sister were at least ten. Even Mr. and Mrs. Howard had locked up the store and gone home.

She felt so alone.

But sitting there like a ninny wouldn't do any good.

So Hannah bowed her head and whispered a short prayer. "Thy will be done, Lord." Then she picked up the stick, looked at the indicator, and realized she wasn't alone at all.

Chapter 2

On Tuesday, Hannah bathed, dressed, ate two pieces of dry toast, and reported to work as usual, even though nothing felt the same. Hidden deep inside her grew the miracle she and Daniel had been waiting for. Yet Hannah didn't say a word when Mrs. Howard arrived and started cleaning light fixtures with a long-handled duster and wiping down the counters with Windex. Hannah knew Martha would be overjoyed for her. She had mentioned more than once that Hannah could set a cradle behind the counter and spare the cost of daycare.

Daycare. As though an Amish mother would ever consider such a thing.

As fond as Hannah was of her employers, she didn't want to tell them the news until after she told Daniel on Friday. Her husband should be the first to know. Hadn't he yearned for a son to take fishing and teach the proper way to milk a cow? Secretly, Hannah hoped their first child would be a girl since she longed to sew tiny *kapps* and dresses. Either way, as long as the child was healthy, they both would be grateful.

When Wednesday arrived markedly colder and with snow beginning to fall, Hannah felt no disappointment. As much as she enjoyed quilting bees, she didn't want her father out with the buggy in the snow. Plus, she wasn't good at keeping secrets. No way could she sit next to *Mam* and her sister, Lydia, without spilling the beans. Maybe she and Daniel would spend this weekend with her family, giving her the perfect opportunity to tell them.

Despite the nasty weather, the store enjoyed a flurry of customers all day. Staying busy made the hours fly by. And since her stomach had settled down, she accepted Martha Howard's invitation for supper at the diner. Mr. Howard hadn't come to the store today, preferring to stay home with a Crock-Pot of hot soup and a thermos of lemon tea.

Over a delicious meal of meatloaf, mashed potatoes, and fresh green beans, Martha kept up a steady stream of conversation. Besides the ladies at the quilt shop and the couple who ran the bulk food store, Hannah didn't know any of the Englishers Martha talked about. So she merely nodded and murmured, "Goodness, me" or "Is that right?" every now and then.

That evening Hannah went to bed early, exhausted. But at least her sleep was free from troubling dreams and she awoke refreshed. To repay Martha for her generosity, Hannah packed two extra turkey and Swiss cheese sandwiches in her lunch, along with several apples for both the Howards. With the sun rising in a cloudless sky, nice weather should bring in plenty of customers, all but guaranteeing a good day. But in the end, there was nothing good about Thursday.

At eleven fifteen, Mrs. Howard's cell phone rang. When she noticed the caller ID, she stepped into the back room to talk. Hannah continued to watch for customers who might need help. A few minutes later, Martha walked back into the store looking pale. "Hannah, may I speak with you a moment?" she asked.

"Of course." Hannah left the spinner rack of kitchen tools

and hurried to the counter. "What is it? Isn't Mr. Howard feeling well? Do you need to leave?"

"Yes, we both need to leave."

"We can't both leave. Someone needs to tend the store."

"No, I'm closing the store for the day. We must get to the hospital in Reading."

Fear turned her blood cold, but when Hannah opened her mouth to speak, not a word came out. Instead she stood motionless while Mrs. Howard whispered to each customer milling through the aisles and flipped the sign from *Open* to *Closed*. As though Hannah were helpless, Martha wrapped her in a heavy shawl, guided her out to the car and buckled the seat belt across her midsection.

Then she spoke in a soft, controlled fashion. "The call was from your husband's boss. There was an industrial accident at the cabinet factory. I am to bring you to the hospital where they took Daniel."

An industrial accident? The term made no sense to Hannah. "What kind of accident?" she asked.

"I don't know. His boss didn't elaborate." Heading north, Martha drove through Bluebird well above the speed limit. "We'll find out soon enough."

"I'm glad we gave your number as an emergency contact," whispered Hannah, desperate for something to say.

"Me, too. Try not to worry." Martha took one hand off the wheel long enough to squeeze Hannah's fingers.

She stared out the windshield at the road, trying to imagine what had happened. Surely they wouldn't call if Daniel had bashed his thumb with a hammer again. *Did he lose a finger? Did he drop a heavy cabinet on his foot? Maybe he slipped in a puddle of varnish and hurt his spine.* One by one, a variety of mishaps ran through her mind, along with the subsequent consequences for a farmer.

Martha said little for the rest of the drive. Once they reached the parking lot of the Reading Hospital, she pulled up to the emergency entrance and braked hard. Hannah jumped out the moment the car stopped and ran to the revolving doors, banging her head on the glass. Once inside, she scanned a sea of faces until she found a familiar one—Daniel's boss. Though she'd met the man only once, she recognized him instantly, even before he started toward her. His damp cheeks and red-rimmed eyes indicated that no matter what type of accident Daniel had had, the consequences were both dire and permanent.

In many respects, making arrangements after the death of a loved one was easier for the *Plain* than for Englishers. Hannah only felt confused for a few brief minutes after hearing the dreadful news. Then she remembered the name of the English mortician familiar with Amish traditions and set the wheels into motion.

"Mrs. Howard, would you please call Mr. Ross on Walnut Street in Lancaster?" she asked in a calm voice. "Ask him to come to this hospital for Daniel."

"Of course." Martha wrapped her arm around Hannah's waist. "Will you have visitation at his facility?"

"No, that's not how we do things," Hannah answered after a short hesitation. "Since our apartment above the store is too small, Mr. Ross will probably take Daniel to his parents' home in Paradise. They will want the wake there. Now until Mr. Ross arrives, I would like to sit with my husband."

That was the last decision Hannah had to make.

Martha took her home to pack a suitcase, then to her parents' home to tell them what had happened, and finally to the Kline farm. She would stay with Daniel's parents until after Monday's funeral. Thanks to her family and his, news would spread throughout the Amish community by word of mouth. People would spring into action, notifying out-of-town relatives. Some folks would arrive to clean the Klines' home and cook a vast quantity of food for the mourners. More food would be prepared for the meal following Monday's funeral. Hannah's and Daniel's families would be free to focus on the friends, relatives, and coworkers who came to pay their respects.

The next three days passed in a blur, but finally Hannah found herself alone in the Klines' living room after the funeral.

"Well, that's the last of the dishes," announced her mother, Sarah Troyer. "And all the leftover food has been packed up." When Hannah didn't reply, Sarah continued, "We'll take you back to our house tonight, daughter."

Hannah roused herself from her stupor. "There's no need, *Mam*. I'll call a driver to take me back to Bluebird."

"Why are you going back there?" Sarah's brows knitted together over the bridge of her nose.

"Because Bluebird is where I live."

"Well, at least come home with us tonight. You haven't eaten a bite all day. I'll heat up a bowl of chicken soup for you." Sarah patted Hannah's hand.

Chicken soup—a mother's cure for every ill, whether she was Amish or English. Hannah was too tired to argue, so she acquiesced. Tomorrow would be soon enough to return to the apartment she'd shared with Daniel.

During the ninety-minute ride home, she sat in the back of the buggy with her sister. Lydia talked the entire time, filling the family in on district news and the gossip gleaned from out-of-town relatives. *Mam* kept her eyes on the road to help *Dat*, with her ears open to Lydia. Hannah stared out the window, not paying attention to either the scenery or her sister.

Once they pulled up the Troyers' tree-lined driveway, Hannah climbed out and picked up several large roasting pans of leftovers. Her parents would eat for a week on the food *Mam* Kline had sent home with them. Since Lydia volunteered to help their father with livestock, Hannah headed to the house.

"Don't you dare go upstairs, daughter," Sarah warned, apparently able to read minds. "Not until you eat some soup."

Hannah placed the roaster in the fridge and slumped into a kitchen chair, overwhelmingly exhausted. Dropping her head in her hands, she let the tears run down her face unchecked.

After her mother put away the rest of the food and placed the soup on the stove, she wrapped her arms around Hannah's neck. "Go ahead and cry. Tomorrow you'll feel better. This is God's will. We must not question his plan for our lives."

Hannah nodded, knowing it was pointless to argue. This was how she'd been raised. This was their faith. Those were the same words she'd said to others in similar situations. For several moments she sat mutely, allowing herself to be comforted.

When her mother placed a warm bowl of soup in front of her, Hannah picked up a spoon and began to eat. The sooner she finished, the sooner she would be able to sleep. And escape the five most horrible days of her life.

"These truly are dark days now, but someday you'll remarry. Life will go on, until the Lord calls you home as well."

Hannah's head snapped up. "*Remarry?* How can you even speak of such a thing?"

"Perhaps I shouldn't, but what other path is open to you?"

"There are other paths. I could keep doing what I am doing. Besides, what man would want a woman my age with . . . with . . . with a baby to raise?" She'd sputtered the words in haste. This wasn't how she'd planned to tell her family the good news. Yet the deed was done and there was no turning back.

"*A baby?*" asked Sarah, as though she hadn't heard correctly.

"A baby!" Lydia exclaimed as she entered the kitchen from the porch. "I'm overjoyed for you." She hugged Hannah tightly. "Just when you and Daniel had all but given up hope."

"Thank you, sister." Hannah squirmed out of the embrace and carried her bowl to the sink. "Truly, it is a blessing."

"Now the blessing comes along?" asked her mother.

"Yes, *now*," Hannah stated with as much dignity as she could muster. "As you pointed out, we must not question God's plan for our lives."

"Of course not. Forgive me, daughter, but certainly you must stay on the farm with a baby on the way. Your place is with your family."

"I have a job, a responsibility to Mr. and Mrs. Howard. We'll see what the future holds, but tomorrow I return to Bluebird."

Before her mother could say another word, Hannah climbed the steps to the bedroom she'd shared with Lydia for eighteen years. Her sister stayed downstairs to wash dishes . . . and calm their mother's anxieties. By the time Lydia came to bed, Hannah had fallen blissfully asleep.

In the morning while Lydia still slept and her parents tended livestock, Hannah wrote a brief note and slipped out the front door. She walked to the closest English neighbor and called for a ride back to Bluebird. She didn't like being evasive but couldn't deal with any more arguments. She was a grown woman. If she chose to spend her life selling hardware, it was her choice to make.

After the driver dropped her off, Hannah carried her suitcase upstairs and entered the shop through the back door. Donning her long white apron, she marched into the store as if today were any other Tuesday.

"What are you doing here?" said Mrs. Howard. Luckily, no customers milled around the displays.

"Why, have I been fired?" she asked.

"Of course not, but no one expected you in this week. You should take time off."

"To do what? Sit upstairs and sew? I do that every evening."

"To be with your family." The older woman rubbed her knuckles, a sure sign her arthritis was flaring up.

"I've been with my family for days. If it's okay with you, I would like to work." To prove her sincerity, Hannah started sorting misplaced bolts and latches into their rightful bins.

"You go ahead, then," Martha said with a smile. "I'm glad to have you back, since Lawrence isn't coming until later. I'll check in the back order that arrived. If you need help, just holler."

Hannah watched her employer walk away, glad she would have a couple hours to herself. As fond as she was of the Howards, she needed time to think.

For the next few hours she waited on customers, answered the phone, and assembled several bird feeders. They always sold faster if already put together. At noon, Martha brought her a ham sandwich from the diner and an iced tea. Then just about quitting time—six o'clock on Tuesdays—Mr. Howard entered the store with someone Hannah didn't recognize. Judging by the man's briefcase and business suit, he wasn't a supplier of farm implements or handheld appliances.

Hannah rose from her crouched position where she'd been retagging a display. "Hi, Mr. Howard. You're looking well today."

"Thank you, Hannah." To the gentleman, he said, "Mr. Salvatore, this is Mrs. Kline, our right-hand woman in the store. Martha and I don't know what we would've done without her all these years."

"How do you do, Mrs. Kline. Richard Salvatore, from Kings Hardware, Corporate Headquarters, but please call me Rich." He extended his hand.

Hannah shook it, while her mind raced a mile a minute. "The national hardware chain, Kings?" she asked.

"Yes, ma'am. And with any luck, the new owner of Howard's." Salvatore's smile stretched from ear to ear. "Bluebird has been growing by leaps and bounds. Kings can help it grow."

This man wants to change Howard's into a carbon copy of all those suburban stores. Hannah slipped her fingers from his hand.

"But an excellent worker like yourself has nothing to worry about," he added.

"That's good to hear, Mr. Salvatore."

Nothing indeed. The bad feeling she had lived with for days returned with a vengeance.

Chapter 3

Hannah was never so glad to see a workday end. But instead of heading up the steps to her apartment, she bundled up and walked down Main Street at a brisk pace. She considered stopping at the diner for a cup of coffee or something to eat, but caffeine would only keep her awake and she wasn't the least bit hungry. She waved at the quilt shop ladies, but didn't dare venture inside. They might not have heard about her husband and Hannah didn't want to recite the details yet again: *There was a freak accident at the factory. A load of stacked pallets slipped off a tow-motor and struck Daniel, killing him instantly.* Since the owner was an Englisher, she would ask about her plans to sue the company, something she had no intention of doing. No one Amish would ask such a question since lawsuits weren't their way.

Next, she passed Beechy's Sweets, where the delicious smell of fudge wafted on the breeze every time a customer opened the door. One of her cousins from Delaware had recently started working there. She had met Rose Bontrager at the funeral, but hadn't had much time to get acquainted. Yet her heart wasn't in making polite conversation at the moment.

So Hannah wandered up and down the street, peering into the window of the ice cream shop and the B & B, wondering what the residents' lives were like. Had any of them suffered a recent loss like her? Did any of their hopes and dreams vanish like smoke up the chimney? Hannah walked until her feet ached and her stomach growled with hunger. Then she felt a stirring deep in her gut, reminding her that not all of her hopes were gone. She had a very real baby inside her, a baby that needed nourishment to grow.

Hurrying home, Hannah climbed the steps to her apartment. At least being alone felt normal, since Daniel had been gone more than he'd been home. She fried up some ham and eggs for supper and read in the recliner until her eyelids refused to stay open. Then she pulled on her long nightgown, said her prayers, and slept for eight dreamless hours.

In the morning, Hannah reported for duty as usual, where she found the inventory and sales spreadsheets surprisingly up to date. Mr. Howard must have felt strong enough to update the books in her absence. So she swept the oak plank floor and dusted the displays until time to open.

Promptly at nine o'clock, Mr. and Mrs. Howard arrived, dressed to work, and looking surprised to see her. "Hannah, you poor dear," said Martha. "We don't deserve someone as loyal as you."

"Why don't you?" she asked, bewildered.

"Sit here, Hannah." Mr. Howard patted the tall stool on the customer side of the counter while he walked to the other side.

"Have I done something wrong?"

"Not in the least, but it's time Martha and I explained what's going on."

"I wish somebody would." Hannah spoke solely out of nervousness.

He smiled patiently. "This was a hard decision to make, but it's time for us to retire. Martha has wanted to move closer to our grandchildren for a long time. I'm the one who's been stubbornly holding on to my independence. Can you see me sitting in a lawn chair, sipping lemonade?"

Hannah wasn't sure if he wished an answer or not. "I know you enjoy keeping busy."

"I do, but everything in life comes to an end. You need not worry. I'm sure whoever buys the store will keep you on the payroll. In fact, I plan to insist on it, along with keeping the upstairs apartment rent controlled for the next two years."

Martha bobbed her head enthusiastically. "You'll still have a job, if you wish to stay in Bluebird. Of course, we'll also understand if you choose to move home with your family."

"I'm not worried about me or where I'll live. God will provide. But what will happen to Howard's Hardware? We have a fine assortment of nonelectric tools and appliances for *Plain* folk and for those Englishers who wish to be less dependent on the power grid." She heard that explanation from customers so often she knew it by heart. "The Amish moving into the area rely on us, along with those who don't like feeling helpless when the electricity goes out."

Both of her employers stared, slack-jawed.

"My, you have been listening to the customers," said Mr. Howard.

"I have, because I love my job here. What will happen to our customers, those who travel a long distance to shop here, should Kings buy your store?" Hannah imbued the chain's name with a tone of contempt.

The couple exchanged a glance. "We'd definitely prefer to sell to a local, someone who will serve both Amish and English customers. We put an ad in newspapers as far away as Harrisburg that the store is for sale. We'll make no rash decisions and promise to keep you informed every step of the way."

Martha wrapped her arms around her. "I think of you as my second daughter."

Hannah felt hot tears flood her eyes. For a moment her head pounded, her vision clouded, and she thought she might faint. Was this emotional overflow due to Daniel's passing, Martha's declaration, or her body's hormonal changes?

She gripped the edge of the counter. "Thank you, ma'am. I feel the same."

Mr. Howard patted her arm with his leathery hand. "I'm calling Uber to take you to your parents' house. Daniel's death was traumatic enough, now this. Spend a few days in the sunshine with your family. They will help you decide whether you wish to remain on the farm or continue living in Bluebird and working at the store. Come back when you're ready. We only want what's best for you."

Hannah knew it was pointless to argue. After all, Mr. Howard was her boss. Plus, he was right. She'd have no time to think inside the store. Perhaps she'd find solace walking between the rows of corn or along the path by the river. Impulsively, she threw her arms around Mr. Howard's neck and squeezed. Then she duplicated the gesture with Martha. "Thank you. Maybe it's me who doesn't deserve the two of you. I'll go up and repack my bag, then wait for Uber in front of the store." She fled out the door before she burst into tears. She couldn't let herself start crying. She was afraid if she started, she wouldn't be able to stop.

When Hannah walked up the driveway and into their house, her parents and sister were sitting at the kitchen table. "I'm sorry we argued, *Mam*," Hannah said, breaking the silence.

"Don't give it another thought." Her mother scrambled to her feet. "I keep forgetting you're a grown woman now."

"Welcome home, sister. I'll make your bed and do your share of the dishes. But just for a day or two." Lydia punctuated her offer with a wink.

"And I'll prepare your favorite dish for tonight—chicken

and dumplings." Sarah took her Dutch oven down from the cupboard.

"I'm just happy to see you, daughter." *Dat* placed a clumsy kiss atop her *kapp* on his way to the stove. "How 'bout some coffee?"

"No, but I'd love some tea." Hannah reached for her favorite mug.

"There's a stack of cards and letters for you on the mantel. They arrived after you left." Her mother carried the kettle to the stove. "Why don't you sit by the fire and read? I'll bring you a hot cup of tea. A day to yourself will do you good, Hannah."

Truer words were never spoken. Hannah did exactly as she was told. For several hours she sipped tea and read messages of sympathy—everything from a few lines scribbled in a card to four pages of youthful memories. She helped her mother and sister make dinner just like in the old days. Then she slept soundly in her twin bed, despite Lydia's snoring. But the next day was a very different story.

Hannah had always been an early riser, but when she came downstairs in the morning, everyone else was already up and dressed.

"Good morning, daughter. The coffee is hot and we have leftover carrot cake or banana bread for breakfast."

"Both sound good." Hannah poured a cup of coffee and took her usual place at the table. But before she could cut a slice of either, her mother demanded that she make a decision.

"Which would you prefer—helping me in the henhouse or helping your sister can the last apples from cold storage?"

Could I opt for choice number three?

Hannah waited until she'd swallowed the first delicious bite of banana bread to reply. "I'll help you today, *Mam*. Do we just have to feed and water the chickens?"

"Unfortunately, no. It's time for a thorough cleaning from

floor to ceiling. Your sister holds her nose whenever she gathers eggs for me."

Almost choking on her second bite of breakfast, Hannah washed the piece down with coffee and pushed away the plate.

"Don't you like it?" Sarah asked. "Try some carrot cake. It might be more to your liking. Maybe you got spoiled with all that fancy English cooking."

"I rarely eat English cooking. My stomach just feels a bit off. I'll eat more after we finish with the chickens. I'd better go change my clothes." Hannah ran upstairs to put on her oldest dress and then slipped on a pair of muck boots from the back porch. When she reached the henhouse, her mother had already shooed the hens into the fenced yard and closed the entrances to their nesting boxes.

"Here," said Sarah. "Put this clothespin on your nose. You're not used to the smell anymore."

Hannah didn't like clamping her nose shut with green plastic, but she liked breathing in the fumes even less. The clothespin at least made the chore tolerable. Breathing through her mouth, Hannah carefully gathered brown eggs from each box, while Sarah followed behind, scooping out the soiled bedding. After Hannah had collected four dozen eggs, she carried the basket to the stationary tub in the barn, where they would be washed and sorted. By the time she returned, her mother had hauled away the soiled straw and filled two buckets with soapy water.

"Time to scrub." Sarah handed Hannah a bucket and brush with a gleam in her eye.

For several hours mother and daughter washed every inch of the henhouse, including the nesting boxes, ramps, and interior walls. When finally done, Hannah had a crick in her neck and a sour taste in her mouth, but the palace of the county's best-laying hens was clean. Then Hannah filled the grain and water dispensers, while Sarah opened the doors so that the feathered ladies could roost. In they marched, clucking and cooing and talking amongst themselves like school children after recess.

Hannah pulled off her rubber gloves. "I'm going to the barn to clean up, *Mam*."

"Oh no, dearie. We still must wash the eggs, crate them, and store them in the refrigerator." Sarah headed toward the barn, but Hannah stopped her.

"I'll do that. Why don't you start lunch? *Dat* will be in soon from the barn and hungry as a bear."

Her mother grinned. "Good idea. My, it sure is nice having you home again." Sarah started toward the house with a definite spring in her step.

As much as Hannah loved seeing her mother happy, she didn't share her outlook. Although most Amish women liked farm work, or at least performed their chores stoically, Hannah found the work tedious and boring. But time alone in the barn would give her a chance to think about her future . . . or lack thereof.

For so many years, her goal had been to buy a farm. But with Daniel gone, buying a farm was out of the question. She would always have a roof over her head and plenty of work to do here. But it was difficult to move back to your parents' home once you'd lived on your own. She loved working at the hardware store, but with Mr. and Mrs. Howard retiring, those days were numbered. But instead of pondering possible solutions, her thoughts of Daniel triggered a wave of grief that left her weak-kneed and breathless. When Hannah finished with the eggs an hour later, she was no closer to a solution than when she'd started. With a heavy heart, she climbed the rickety porch steps and entered a kitchen that needed a coat of paint. One thing was for certain about farms . . . there was always something to do.

The next morning after breakfast Hannah chose Lydia to work with. Her sister had washed, peeled, cored, and blanched two bushels of apples yesterday but still had more to do. After filling a thermos with coffee, Hannah joined her sister on the porch, where a stack of empty bushel baskets waited.

"Here, let's put this on you." Lydia pulled an apron with a giant front pocket over Hannah's head. "I use these aprons when picking apples, but today they'll keep our dresses tidier. Let's take the empty baskets back to the barn and get more apples from cold storage."

Hannah chuckled as she hefted several empty baskets to her hip. "I have harvested apples before. I've been living in Bluebird, not on Mars."

"Yes, but *Dat* just bought these aprons last year." Lydia picked up the other stack of baskets.

"We sell these aprons in my store."

"Oh yeah, I forgot." Lydia impulsively kissed Hannah's cheek. "I'm so glad to have my sister back, even if it's just for a few days."

With her emotions barely beneath the surface, all Hannah could do was nod in agreement. "Tell me *your* news, Lydia. Sounds like you've met someone special."

With a cold wind fluttering their *kapp* strings, twenty-two-year-old Lydia launched into a tale of summer picnics, hayrides, bonfires, and rides in his courting buggy. Seeing her sister so happy filled Hannah with joy during their multiple trips to the barn's basement for apples.

"I think Nathan will propose soon. I hope to get married this December. It's about time, no?"

"Any time is perfect as long as this Nathan is the right one."

"Oh he is. I met him when he came to live with an aunt after his uncle broke his leg. Nathan's from Ohio, but he said last week he wants to make Lancaster County his home."

"I'm very happy for you," she said with fond memories of her own courting days.

For hours while they washed, peeled, and cored, they chatted and enjoyed each other's company, as they had years ago. But with so many apples, their workday was nowhere near over. Most Englishers buying a jar of pie filling or applesauce at the store have no idea how much preparation takes place before canning jars can be filled.

By the time they'd finished processing today's load of apples, it was well past dinner and they had turned *Mam*'s tidy kitchen into a disaster zone. Their parents had already eaten cold leftovers and gone upstairs. Hannah was starving. Her hands were red and chapped. She'd cut herself twice and felt like she'd fallen into the steam bath along with the apples.

"A job well done," said Lydia. "Thanks for your help."

"I would like a few jars to take home." Hannah dropped her voice to a whisper, knowing her mother might be somewhere close by.

"We'll consider it your day's pay." Lydia placed six jars on the windowsill. "Let's eat supper by the fire and clean up later. Why don't you carry in two glasses of tea while I fix our plates?"

Hannah poured the drinks, then rocked in *Mam*'s rocker while the fire on the hearth crackled and popped. After a long day, the heat warmed and soothed her sore muscles, but it also nearly put her to sleep. Through the window, a million stars and a full moon illuminated the cornfields and rolling hills in the distance.

It was beautiful on a farm . . . but a person was usually too busy to notice.

Lydia carefully carried in two plates of food. "Glad you didn't fall asleep. We've got fried chicken, buttered lima beans, and pickled beets, courtesy of some unknown kinfolk." She handed Hannah a plate.

Hannah bit into a crispy drumstick. "Daniel's aunt Sophie made the chicken and beans. Not sure who pickled the beets. Every one of his *mam*'s sisters is a wonderful cook. If we had bought a place near his parents' farm, those women would have fattened us both up in no time flat." Without warning, Hannah burst into tears. She set her plate on a table and covered her face with her apron.

Lydia put her dinner aside too, pulled over her chair, and wrapped an arm around Hannah's shoulders. For several minutes the two sisters remained linked while one wept and the other consoled.

Then Hannah dried her eyes, wiped her mouth, and swiveled around to face Lydia. "At least I won't gain too much weight while working in a hardware store."

"Sounds like you're going back to Bluebird."

"I am. I love my job at Howard's.

"I don't know how you keep those facts and figures straight, but since you can, that's where you need to be." Lydia's smile couldn't have been more genuine.

"You have no idea how much your approval means to me," said Hannah. Then she drew in a deep breath and updated her sister on the latest developments, including the national corporation's interest in buying the store.

"Howard's will become like every other chain hardware store. Won't be much there for Amish folk," Lydia commented.

Hannah sighed wearily. "I agree, but at least the new owner will most likely keep me on. After all, I've almost run the store singlehandedly for the last six months. And I can keep my apartment at the same rent."

Lydia nodded. "Even if they don't hire you, maybe you

could work at Beechy's Sweets. Cousin Rose seems very nice and she seems to enjoy it there."

"Yes, she does." But wheels were already turning in Hannah's head as she jumped up to pace the porch.

"If that doesn't work out, *Mam* and *Dat* would love to have you back. Or I would love it if you and your little one lived with Nathan and me. That is, if we get our own place, and if Nathan asks me to marry him," she added. "And if I happen to say *yes*."

Hannah stopped pacing and met Lydia's gaze. Then they broke into peals of laughter. "I have missed you so much," she said, rejoining her sister on the swing. "I appreciate the offer, but I've come to a decision just now."

The corners of Lydia's mouth curved up. "What are you up to?"

"I'm going to buy Howard's Hardware. I'll go write them a letter right now. Mr. Howard should get it by the weekend."

"Have you lost your mind? What will you use to buy it with?"

"The money Daniel and I saved for a farm."

"Do you think he would have approved of such an idea?"

"Well, he sure wouldn't want me buying a farm alone." Hannah fought back another round of tears.

"Will it be enough?" Lydia asked after a moment's pause.

The question quelled some of Hannah's emotion. "I have no idea, but I must try."

"I have two hundred dollars from selling eggs. You can have it."

"Absolutely not. You'll need that when you marry Nathan. That is, if he asks and if you say yes."

"I will pray for your success each night."

"And I will pray for yours." Hannah hugged Lydia with a strength that belied their long workday. "In the meantime, don't say anything to *Mam* and *Dat*. I'll tell them when the time is right." She picked up her plate to finish her dinner.

Lydia nodded and reached for her plate, too. "Feels like the old days when we were young, no?"

"You, dear sister, are still young." But Hannah knew exactly what Lydia meant. When they were both young, everything felt possible.

Chapter 4

Seth Miller sat in his pickup, waiting for his brother to emerge from the house where they both were born. One Saturday each month, Seth drove Adam around to do his errands. More than likely, they would end the outing with a burger and fries. Not a single car passed by on the road, only Amish buggies. Would any of his former district members still recognize him? Did any of them wonder where he lived or if he still lived?

Seth forced random thoughts of the past from his mind, concentrating instead on the Holsteins around the feed stanchion in a barren pasture. For many generations Miller land had been handed down from father to oldest son. If the situation had been different, the house, barn, and profitable milking operation would one day be his. But since he'd never joined the Amish church, Adam and his wife would take over when his parents were ready for the *dawdi haus* and Adam would eventually inherit the farm.

Seth felt no jealousy and no animosity toward his younger brother. He didn't miss the sixteen-hour days necessary to run a dairy operation. But he did miss his mother and two sisters.

Both sisters had homes somewhere on the Millers' three-hundred acres. With Mary and her family living on the back acres, and Rachel's brood in a house around the corner, seeing either sister was a rare occurrence. At least whenever Adam mentioned that Seth would pick him up, *Mam* chose that time to hang out the wash. Today was no exception. Just as Adam emerged from the house carrying a plastic crate, *Mam* followed on his heels with her clothes basket. Once a month, the routine remained the same. She would carry her basket to the highest sunny spot, and wave at him like a tourist from a bus window. Seth always returned the gesture with equal enthusiasm.

His brother climbed into the truck with his usual greeting. "I have no idea why you can't walk to the porch in a civilized fashion."

Seth responded with his usual retort: "Good morning, brother. And you know why. *Dat* said never to darken his doorstep again."

"A doorstep doesn't include the porch. There's no reason to park on the street and make me walk so far."

"A little exercise is good for you." Seth clapped a hand on Adam's shoulder before shifting the truck into gear. "Where to today?"

"I want to check on grain prices at the elevator, pick up boots I had re-heeled, and stop at the hardware store in Bluebird."

"Why go all the way to Bluebird? There are closer hardware stores." Seth cast him a sidelong glance.

"Because Howard's expanded its selection of hand tools. And because Amanda begged me to bring her vanilla bean fudge from Beechy's. That skinny gal craves sweets, but then she only eats one piece. Guess who finishes the rest?" Grinning, Adam patted his belly.

"A few pounds will do you good. In fact, I think marriage has done wonders for you in general." Seth pointed at the crate covered with a checkered cloth. "What did you bring me?"

"*Mam* baked you pies, one apple, and one peach. And she added two loaves of whole grain bread. That sliced, store-bought stuff isn't healthy."

"Tell her I said thank-you." Seth ignored the nutrition comment.

"Plus, Mary knitted you a hat and pair of gloves. And not to be outdone, Rachel knitted you three pairs of socks."

Seth felt a familiar pang of guilt and longing. "They shouldn't fuss over me. Both have husbands and children to take care of."

"You try telling them that. Rachel said she won't rest until you're back where you belong."

"Maybe I already am. I have a nice apartment, a decent vehicle, and a good job." Seth turned on the radio.

"You forget who you're talking to." Adam switched the radio off. "The way I see it, you're no longer Amish but you're not English, either."

"I think you've been out in the sun too long."

"Sure, you wear Levi's but your shirts are still plain."

"Maybe I haven't had a chance to go shopping."

"In five years? Plus, you still hold up your pants with suspenders, not a belt."

"That doesn't mean anything!" Seth struggled not to lose his temper. "I assure you, this particular carpenter uses a nail gun and a power drill. Please, let's not go down this road again."

"Whatever you say, but I'm starting to agree with Rachel. You're just stubborn. You ain't been shunned, yet you've cut ties with the whole family."

Anger spiked up Seth's spine. "It's still *Dat*'s house and that man called me a thief and a liar."

Adam sighed wearily. "But I know if you came around, hat in hand, you two could put this behind you. He's getting old. Why can't you forgive him?"

Same old argument, the same old outcome. Just once, couldn't someone see their father as the stubborn one? Braking hard, Seth pulled to the side of the road. "Look, let's drop it. I don't want to argue on a Saturday."

Adam nodded, but his jaw remained tight and he said nothing the rest of the way. Seth knew that Adam was trying to find a logical solution to the conundrum, but their sister Rachel was right: He was stubborn—a regular chip off the old block.

Once they reached the grain elevator, a beehive of activity on Saturdays, Adam found too many friends to talk with to continue an argument. Seth kept to himself on the sidelines until Adam was ready to leave. After a quick stop at the harness maker, who also repaired boots on the side, the brothers headed to Bluebird in better moods. Seth liked the charming little town, frequented these days by as many Amish as Englishers. Bluebird's Main Street had thrived while other downtowns had fallen victim to big-box discounters by the interstates.

After parallel parking in front of Howard's Hardware, Seth climbed from the truck slowly, stretching his back one vertebra at a time. Adam hopped out and bounded inside like a much younger man. Although Seth had no use for nonelectric implements and already owned all the power tools he needed, he wandered inside to pass the time. He found his brother at a spinner rack, where all sizes of batteries were buy one, get one free.

"Can you believe this price? All the popular sizes, too." Adam placed several packs of C's, D's, and nine-volts into his basket.

"Good deal, as long as you need them," said Seth. "Not sure why you want nine-volts. Did the bishop change his mind about allowing smoke detectors in district homes?"

Adam shrugged. "No, but I have an alarm clock that uses them."

While his brother pawed through the bins of fasteners, Seth waited close to the door, admiring the way the store combined old-fashioned ambience with new-fangled practicality. Overhead, brass fixtures resembled converted gaslights, yet contained energy efficient electric bulbs. Underfoot were the original oak floorboards, but they had been sanded smooth and varnished for easy maintenance. Walnut cabinets had been refitted with metal shelves for displaying merchandise. And Adam was right about Howard's having a great selection for such a small store. When his brother still didn't appear after ten minutes, Seth went looking and found him at a display of flower and vegetable seeds, along with small pots of violets.

"I didn't know you were into gardening," Seth teased.

"I'm not, but my wife thinks something should be blooming all year round. Here are some spring wildflower seeds she can sprinkle on the slopes as soon as the snow is gone." He put several packets in his basket. "And I think I'll surprise her with potted violets for her windowsill. Then she can plant them outside after the last frost."

"You're a hopeless romantic and I'm . . . a little jealous." Seth punched his shoulder lightly.

Before Adam could comment, an elderly man stepped through the swinging doors. "Yep, I've got one of those rain barrels with a spigot left. I put it on the loading dock for you. You can drive around back to pick it up."

"What do you need one of those for?" asked Seth. "You've got running water."

"Amanda can fill her watering can for the flowers by the house. Say, Mr. Howard, where is Hannah today? I can't remember a Saturday when she wasn't working."

The man's pleasant expression disappeared. "She's staying with her family for a few days. Her husband was killed last week at work. The funeral was on Monday."

Adam swept off his hat. "Somehow the news never reached us. Please give Hannah my sincere sympathy."

"Will do, son. Now who is this quiet young man?" Mr. Howard gazed curiously at Seth.

"Sorry. This is my brother, Seth. He lives near Harrisburg and works as a commercial carpenter."

Seth touched the brim of his black hat. "How do you do, sir?"

"I'm fine. Say, are you Amish, young man, or not?" Mr. Howard didn't beat around the bush.

"No, not anymore." Seth bristled at the question. But considering his clothing, he couldn't blame the man

Mr. Howard waited for someone to elaborate, but no one did. "Is that all you need, Adam?" he finally asked. "Should I ring you up?"

"Yep, it's time for us to hit the candy shop. My bride has quite a sweet tooth."

The elderly man grinned, deepening the wrinkles around his eyes. "I had forgotten—you and Amanda are still newlyweds." Reaching into the bin of flower seeds, Mr. Howard added several more packets to the pile.

"My brother doesn't need charity, sir." Seth spoke without thinking.

"Of course, he doesn't. But can't I give a belated wedding gift to a long-time customer?" He gazed from one brother to the other.

"Yes, you can and thanks." Adam crossed his arms and glared at Seth.

"I beg your pardon, sir." Seth felt much smaller than his six-foot-two inches. "That was uncalled for."

"No harm done, young man." Howard rang up the sale while Adam inspected the new variety of seeds.

"When those come up in the spring, I'll tell Amanda they're from you."

"I'll be living in Florida by the spring. We both need to make our *brides* happy."

"But what about your store?" asked Seth. "What will happen to this place?"

"Hopefully nothing. I've got it up for sale."

"It won't be the same without you." Adam put the purchases into a brown bag as they were rung up.

"That's nice of you to say. Maybe you two can do something to help."

Adam was quick to respond. "Just name it."

"This store has been my pride and joy for years, so I'll sell it to who I want. I prefer to sell to someone Amish, if any happen to be interested in buying. With more Amish moving into the area, I've expanded my inventory to meet their needs. So an Amish buyer makes the most sense." Again, Mr. Howard looked from one brother to the other.

"I left the district, sir, a long time ago," Seth said softly.

"Maybe, but you can help spread the word."

"That I will do, everywhere I can."

Adam puffed out his chest. "And I'll tell our bishop, who will tell every other bishop in the three-county area. If there's someone *Plain* with money to invest in a store, my bishop will find him." Enthusiasm almost poured from his ears.

"Good, that's what I want to hear." Mr. Howard handed him the bill.

After Adam counted out the correct amount, they both told the man goodbye. "Ready for lunch at the diner or the candy store first?"

"I'm good with either. You pick." Seth was too busy thinking to worry about inconsequential choices.

Adam led the way into Beechy's Sweets, where he bought candy for Amanda and Seth paid for their sisters' favorites. "Now I'm ready for Coke, fries, and a cheeseburger loaded with grilled mushrooms. Smelling that fudge always makes me hungry."

Seth ordered the same, but the waitress had to ask twice whether he wanted lettuce and tomato and how he wanted the burger cooked.

When the poor woman finally had the order correct and walked away, Adam grabbed Seth's arm and shook. "What's the matter with you? Are you coming down with something? I've never seen you this distracted."

Seth took a gulp of water. "Sorry, I was thinking about Mr. Howard's store."

"Will you help him find an Amish buyer?"

"I don't think so."

"Why not? I've never known you to act this rude." Adam dropped his voice to a growl.

Seth sucked in a deep breath and looked his brother in the eye. "Because I'm thinking about buying the place."

There was complete and total silence. Then Adam blinked like an owl. "But you're not Amish anymore."

"True, but I still know exactly what they want. Plus, I've lived with Englishers long enough to know what they like, too."

"I thought you enjoyed building houses in developments."

"Not as much as I once did."

Slowly, a smiled bloomed across Adam's face. "Do you think you've saved enough money?"

"That remains to be seen. I have no idea what stores sell for. So for now, say nothing about this to our sisters." Seth locked gazes with his brother. "They can't keep anything secret. And if they tell *Mam*, undoubtedly she'll tell *Dat*."

"I hope this works out. It could be a new beginning for you."

The last thing Seth needed was to get his hopes up too soon. "Here comes our food, and I'm starving. So that's enough about the future, whatever it may be."

After they ate, Seth drove his brother home. Neither said much, which was okay with him. He couldn't wait to get home and check his computer for comparable real estate listings. Over the past few years, he'd discovered he didn't belong in the English world. He might be able to surf the web and he drove a truck instead of a buggy, but he didn't agree with mainstream values. This could be his one chance, his only chance to go back to the fold.

When he reached the Miller farm, Seth pulled up the drive-way and stopped next to the porch. "You've got a heavy load to carry," he teased, pointing at the Howard's sack.

"I want you to know something," said Adam. "*Mam* still sets a place for you every Sunday. And Rachel and Mary both cook extra, just in case you want to drop by sometime. No strings attached."

"I'll keep that in mind." The moment his brother climbed out, Seth threw the truck into reverse and barreled down the driveway, spinning gravel. He couldn't start thinking about dinners with his family again. The road ahead was bumpy and filled with potholes.

Chapter 5

By Monday morning, Hannah couldn't wait to get back to Bluebird. As much as she loved her family, farm life just wasn't for her. She yearned for updating inventory on the computer, waiting on customers, and smelling birdseed the moment she opened the door. But first, she would help can the last of the apples. Hannah put on her most worn-out dress and went downstairs, where she discovered Lydia had already peeled and cored half a bushel. "What time did you wake up?" she asked.

"I wanted a head start, so I got up with *Mam* and *Dat*. They're still out in the milk house." Lydia refilled her mug and poured a cup of coffee for Hannah. "Don't worry. I left some for you to do."

"Wouldn't have it any other way." Hannah took a sip of coffee and lifted a full basket to the counter.

"I almost forgot." Lydia extracted an envelope from her apron pocket. "Somebody stuck this in our mailbox and put up the flag."

Written in perfect cursive was her name, Mrs. Hannah Kline.

No stamp. No postmark. With trembling fingers, Hannah ripped open the envelope, extracted the single sheet, and skimmed the contents. "It's from Martha and Lawrence Howard. They didn't want to disturb our Sabbath yesterday so they left this in our mailbox."

"Well, what does it say? Will they let you buy their store?" Lydia tried to read over her shoulder.

Hannah shrugged. "I don't know. They've invited me to their home at one o'clock for lunch. I guess we'll discuss my offer then."

"One o'clock *today?*"

"Yes, today." Hannah pressed the letter to her chest. "I've never been to their house before. It's a good thing they wrote down the address."

"You'd better start getting ready." Lydia pointed at the stairs.

"I don't need four hours to wash and change clothes. But I will go next door and arrange to be picked up at noon. Save me some apples," she called halfway out the door.

The retired English couple living next to the Troyers insisted on taking Hannah to Bluebird themselves, since they had errands in that direction. When they picked her up several hours later, Hannah had not only peeled, cored, and sliced every apple in the house, but had taken another shower and put on her best dress. After all, potential store buyers shouldn't smell like apple cobbler. She stowed her suitcase in the trunk and handed the neighbor, Mr. Cobb, the address. Just as he programmed the car's GPS, Lydia ran from the house with a Tupperware carrier.

"Here, take them a pie," she said breathlessly. "It might help with negotiations. And your pie will be waiting on your porch, Mr. and Mrs. Cobb."

Thirty minutes later, the Cobbs dropped Hannah off in front of a two-story house with a metal roof and circular driveway. "I can't thank you enough," she said, stepping from the car.

"Call us if you need someone to bring you home," Mrs. Cobb called out the window.

Hopefully, I'll be staying in Bluebird for a long time, Hannah thought, as she waved at the Cobbs. Bravely she marched up the steps and rang the bell.

Martha hugged her the moment she stepped across the threshold. "I'm glad you're early. Let's leave your bag by the door and join Lawrence in the dining room. He's ready to get started."

"Here's a pie baked by my sister." Hannah set her suitcase next to a potted plant and handed Martha the Tupperware. Then she gazed up at the massive chandelier in the two-story foyer. "Your home is beautiful, Mrs. Howard."

"Thank you, but I'm so ready for a ranch on one floor."

Martha led Hannah into a sunny room with a table that could easily seat ten people. Mr. Howard sat at one end with a dark-haired Englisher on his left.

"Ah, Hannah, come join us." Lawrence Howard pulled out the chair on his right. "This is Mr. Miller. Seth, this is Mrs. Kline."

When the man peered up, his strikingly blue eyes looked rather odd with his black hair. "Nice to meet you, Mrs. Kline." He half rose and bobbed his head.

"How do you do," Hannah murmured, taking the seat Mr. Howard indicated. "I didn't know you were having other guests for lunch," she whispered to Martha as the older woman handed her a cup of coffee. "I'd hoped to discuss business today."

"And that's what we're all here to do," boomed Mr. Howard. "You and Seth Miller are in the same boat." He slapped the younger man on the back.

Hannah glanced at Mr. Miller, who looked as confused as she, and then around the table. Martha focused on arranging veggies on a platter. "Exactly what boat am I in?" Hannah asked.

"Don't beat around the bush, dear," said Martha. "Have you forgotten what it's like to be young?"

Lawrence Howard smiled at his wife. "All right then, I'll get to the point. As you both know, last week the corporate head-quarters of Kings Hardware made an offer to buy my store. Then this week I received two more offers—one by mail from Mrs. Kline, and one over the phone from Mr. Miller. I must admit that surprised us and put us in a quandary."

Hannah stared at the black-haired man with the worst English haircut she'd even seen. "*You* wish to buy Howard's?" she asked.

"I do." Seth returned her stare.

"But I've never seen you inside the store, not even once."

"Actually, I visited for the first time last week with my brother, Adam. He's been a regular customer for several years." The man kept his voice soft, his demeanor calm.

Hannah folded her hands on the table. "You stopped in *once* and decided to make an offer?"

"Yes, I fell in love with it." The corners of his mouth lifted into a smile.

Like a peeved schoolteacher, Hannah crossed her arms over her chest. "Are you some kind of eccentric millionaire? Do you even know anything about running a hardware store?"

Mr. and Mrs. Howard's focus bounced from one to the other as if they were watching a tennis match, but they didn't interrupt.

Seth Miller stretched his long legs under the table and leaned back in the chair. "No to both questions, Mrs. Kline. But I'm a fast study."

"Then you should have applied for a job at the store years ago, Mr. Miller. With Mr. and Mrs. Howard moving to Florida, there will be no one here to train you." Unfortunately, Hannah's tone turned harsh, behavior that would have earned her a reprimand from her mother.

Mr. Howard cleared his throat. "Seth, if I might clarify, Hannah has worked with us for years, and has practically run the place since my health began to fail. She's been invaluable to Martha and me." He smiled with the fondness of a father.

"With all due respect, sir, this is the twenty-first century and Mrs. Kline is . . . Amish."

Hannah narrowed her gaze. "My bishop granted permission to take computer classes at the Vo-Ed center. Afterward, Mrs. Howard taught me to use the accounting and inventory software for the store. I don't believe being Amish would hamper my effectiveness."

Seth scratched the stubble on his chin. "I seem to have been bested on all fronts. So I must surrender to my worthy adversary. I wish you well, Mrs. Kline, and I'll pass the news on to my brother." He started to rise from the chair, but Martha placed both hands on his shoulders.

"Not so fast, Seth," she said. "Now we come to the interesting part of our meeting."

Mr. Howard cleared his throat. "It's been our desire to sell to someone Amish, because they would be familiar with that end of the business. We'd even be willing to owner-finance the right buyer." He nodded at Hannah. "However, Mrs. Kline doesn't have the necessary 50 percent down payment for the transaction." He swiveled toward Seth. "Mr. Miller has worked as a roofer and commercial carpenter for five years, giving him expertise in the English building trades. He also has a rudimentary understanding of plumbing, something Mrs. Kline lacks. Unfortunately, his down payment doesn't meet our minimum requirement, either. But if we add the two offers together—"

"I see where you're going with this," interrupted Seth. "But it would never work."

Martha chose this moment to intervene. "Why? Because your male pride couldn't deal with having a female partner?"

"No, ma'am, I've got nothing against females. But I am familiar with the Amish culture. Married women can't go into business with anyone other than their husbands. Mr. Kline would never permit such a partnership."

Hannah felt the bottom fall from her stomach as every bit of her courage vanished. "I'm afraid . . . it won't be Mr. Klein . . . who objects to our partnership."

Martha placed an arm around her shoulder. "Mrs. Klein lost her husband in an accident. She's a recent widow."

Seth scrubbed his face with his hands. "I'm sorry. My brother asked about you while we were in the store. Adam had been unaware of your loss. But I didn't . . . put two and two together." He pushed himself to his feet. "Thank you, Mr. and Mrs. Howard, for inviting me to your home. Again, my sympathy for your loss, Mrs. Klein. I wish you luck with your endeavor."

"Now don't go rushing off all embarrassed, young man." Mr. Howard refused to let the matter rest. "Mrs. Klein doesn't need luck. She needs more money or we'll be forced to sell to the Kings Hardware chain."

Hannah's mouth dropped open. "I'm sure you mean well, sir, but Mr. Miller has made it clear that an Amish woman would make an unacceptable partner. And I don't see myself comfortable working with him, either."

"See, Lawrence?" Martha shook her head. "I told you this was a bad idea. Neither of them wants this store as much as you and I did."

"You two were a married couple, not a pair of strangers," said Seth.

"You think being a pair of *newlyweds* makes it easier to launch a new business? You must never have been married."

"No, ma'am, I haven't." Seth sat down in his chair.

"We ask only one thing. Stay and eat the delicious lunch my wife has prepared. And talk to each other. See if there's *any* way you can see past your preconceived prejudices. Remember, you two don't have to become friends. Only get along well enough to make Howard's Hardware the best store in this part of Pennsylvania."

"Oh, is that *all?*" asked Hannah.

"Yes, dear child, that's all." Martha gave one of her *kapp* ribbons a tug.

"Where are you two going to be?" Seth looked scared. "Aren't we eating lunch together?"

"No, after we make our plates, Lawrence and I will eat in the kitchen. We'll come back in an hour to clear the table and to hear your decision. Agreed?" Martha looked from Hannah to Seth and back again.

"Yes, ma'am." Seth sat straighter in his chair.

"Agreed," said Hannah, reluctantly.

As the Howards shuffled from the room, Hannah and Seth silently admired the framed prints on the wall. Soon the couple bustled back in with two trays, which they unloaded into the center of the table.

"Cauliflower soup." Martha pointed to the tureen and bowls. "Then we have an endive and radish salad." She set small plates in front of them.

Lawrence plopped his platter in the center of the table. "Next there's fried chicken with parsley potatoes and buttered green beans. You'll find a pitcher of iced tea on the buffet in case you're tired of coffee."

Hannah stared at the heaping bowl of chicken. "All this is for us?"

"Maybe Seth will want to take anything extra home."
Martha grinned at him.

Then they left the room, and Hannah and Mr. Calm-and-
Collected were alone.

They locked gazes, but he was the first to speak. "Looks like
we must make polite conversation for sixty minutes. Soup,
Mrs. Kline?" He picked up the ladle.

"Yes, please." Hannah handed him her bowl. "How do you
know so much about the Amish culture?"

His blue eyes almost bored holes through her. "My family is
Old Order. My brother is Adam Miller."

"Oh my, yes." Hannah did a poor job of hiding her surprise.
"He's a very nice man and speaks highly of his wife, Amanda."

"Yes, he is. As I am if you had met me in less combative circumstances." Seth handed her a bowl of cauliflower soup.

"Excuse me if I behaved rudely. I was thrown off-kilter by
the Howards' trickery." She dipped her spoon into the soup.

"You think they planned to serve lunch in this fashion?"

"Absolutely. They're as dear as my own parents and want what
they *think* is best for me." She swallowed a second mouthful.

"Why would a partnership be good for you?" He sampled
the soup and frowned.

"Because I'm a widow with a baby on the way. They know
if I don't buy the store, I'll have to return to my parents' farm."

"Why would that be so bad?" He tried another spoonful
and pushed away the bowl.

"It wouldn't be bad, Mr. Miller. But it's not how I want to
support myself or my child." She placed both hands on her
stomach.

Seth blushed. "I see, but why me?"

"I suppose because you're the only individual who expressed
an interest. I couldn't very well partner with Kings Hardware. I
would only work for them as an employee."

Nodding, he began to eat his salad.

Hannah finished the delicious soup. "Now it's my turn to ask questions."

"Of course." Seth glanced up from slicing his tomato.

"Since your family is Old Order, I gather you were Amish once upon a time?"

"Yes, but I left more than five years ago. I've lived as an Englisher ever since."

"Were you shunned by your district?"

He took his time before answering. "No, but the consequences have been the same. I'm not welcome in my father's home or among members of my former district."

Hannah didn't understand, yet didn't feel comfortable pursuing the topic. "Let's talk about the store. If you bought Howard's, would you expand the selections to attract more English customers?"

Seth pulled over the bowl of chicken, took two pieces, and pushed the bowl to her side of the table. "Quite the contrary. Howard's Hardware could never compete with a big-box store in terms of selection. Its strength lies in uniqueness. I would expand our nonelectric line of products, catering to the Amish and to those Englishers who want to live off the grid."

Hannah laughed in a rather undignified fashion. "They will never give up their dependence on electricity."

"I'm not talking about cutting the lines, but Englishers like self-sufficiency when the power goes down. From what I've been reading, that will happen more frequently in the future. The sale of gasoline generators is at an all-time high. And no wants to be unable to open a can of baked beans or soup if there's a power failure."

Hannah took a chicken breast and pulled over the bowl of potatoes. "That makes sense. My father mentioned the same thing about Englishers."

Seth accepted the bowl from her. "Have you ever been to Wayne County in Ohio?" When Hannah shook her head, he continued. "There's a hardware store that's become a tourist attraction. They have a great selection of products for the Amish and plenty of goods made by Amish hands for the tourists. Busloads of people come from miles away to shop there. I visited that place once and loved it."

"*That's* what you want for Howard's?"

"Sorry, I'm getting way ahead of myself. If I were the new owner, I would pursue that general idea for Howard's over the course of my lifetime. Making the store special, different from the rest—that's how it can survive."

Hannah concentrated on eating for the next several minutes. Then she dabbed her mouth and set down her fork. "Mr. Miller, I would like to see this hardware store in Wayne County, Ohio."

Seth put down his fork, too. "I'd be happy to drive you there someday, Mrs. Kline. In the meantime, what should we tell Mr. and Mrs. Howard when they return to clear the table?"

Hannah closed her eyes, trying to see her husband's dear face. But instead, all she could see was an endless supply of apples in need of peeling and long, lonely hours with nothing but memories of broken dreams. "Would we be equal partners in this business venture?"

"Of course, we would have an attorney draw up proper documents."

"I mean would we share in all decisions?"

Seth hesitated before answering. "You're the one experienced in running a store, not me. You would divide the job responsibilities according to our abilities. We would then each make decisions pertinent to our area, but share in all major decisions."

"That sounds . . . fair and practical. Could you please give me a minute?" Hannah bowed her head and prayed.

When she lifted her head, he asked, "Do we have a deal, Mrs. Kline?"

"You are getting ahead of yourself again. First, we need to see if our combined funds will be sufficient. Then I need to talk with my family and our bishop. But I do like your ideas, so why don't I tell you some of mine after I finish lunch? You're not taking *my* share of food home."

Chapter 6

As soon as Hannah ate her piece of chicken, she outlined her dreams for Howard's Hardware. If she became the owner, she would buy the empty building next door, knock out a wall, and instantly double their square footage. The more space they had, the better they could meet the community's needs. After providing for herself and her child, she would plow any profits back into the store. The Howards had already promised her cheap rent for the next two years as part of the purchase agreement.

Seth liked her ideas, especially her plan to reinvest future profits. If their bid was accepted, he would move from his apartment in Harrisburg and rent a room in Bluebird or one of the outlying farms.

By the time the Howards walked into the dining room, they knew Hannah and Seth's answer with one glance. "Judging by those smiles, I guess your answer is yes?" asked Lawrence.

"It is indeed, sir," said Seth.

"Are you surprised, Mrs. Howard?" asked Hannah.

"Nope," said Martha. "You two are smart enough to get out of your own way. Who's ready for dessert to celebrate?"

Seth raised his hand while Hannah groaned. "Not for me," she said. "But I will have another cup of coffee."

While the three enjoyed a piece of chocolate cake, Mr. Howard explained forming a legal partnership through an attorney and contacting a real estate agent to handle the transaction. He also outlined their timeline for moving to Florida, providing they found a buyer for their home.

"What about the offer from Kings Hardware?" Seth asked.

"I made it clear I wouldn't make a hasty decision and that I would be considering all offers. Should Kings tire of waiting, they're welcome to look at other properties for sale."

"Hopefully far away from Bluebird," added Martha to everyone's amusement.

When Hannah drained her mug, she pushed to her feet. "I'm sorry, everyone, but my head is swimming with all this information. After we do the dishes, I'm calling for a ride back to my apartment."

"Nothing doing, young lady," said Martha, stacking the plates. "We have a dishwasher that's seldom used with two people."

Seth swallowed his last bite of cake and stood. "No need to call anyone, Mrs. Kline. I go right past the store on my way home. I'll drop you off."

Hannah felt helpless. She didn't like leaving Martha's kitchen a mess and liked getting into a stranger's car even less. Yet she'd just gone into business with the same stranger. "All right, then. Thank you, Mr. and Mrs. Howard, for lunch. I'll see you back at the store tomorrow." Walking to the foyer on shaky legs, she couldn't help but think: *What on earth am I doing?*

Seth thanked their host and hostess, carried her suitcase to the truck, and opened the passenger door. Once she'd climbed into the cab, he programmed his GPS with the address. "Soon I'll know my way to the store from every direction."

"That would be helpful, Mr. Miller. That is, if everything goes smoothly with the sale." Hannah cast a quick glance in his direction. "But if we're to go into business together, I'd like to know more as to why you left the Amish church."

"I guess you have a right to know." After a pause, Seth told a sad tale of false accusations, damage done by the rumor mill, and a lack of trust by his father—a story which broke Hannah's heart. "Since I hadn't officially joined the church, I never was shunned. But my father ordered me never to darken his doorstep, and since he was respected in the area, I imagine most of the district believed him." Seth finished just as they pulled up in front of Howard's Hardware.

"I don't know what to say, Mr. Miller, other than I'm sorry you suffered due to that Englisher's accusation."

"So you believe me?" he asked.

"Yes, why wouldn't I?"

He shrugged. "Well, it's water long over the dam." Jumping from his truck, he set her bag on the sidewalk. "But if the deal goes through, do you think you could call me Seth?"

Hannah held her stomach and jumped down from the high step. "*If* we become partners, I will call you *Seth* and you may call me *Hannah*. Thank you for the ride." She grabbed her suitcase and walked toward the steps.

"What are your plans for tomorrow?" he called.

"Why?" she asked.

"I want to learn all I can from the Howards. I can set up an appointment with an attorney from here. If you're at the store, you can help with my training."

"Tomorrow I need to discuss this partnership with my parents. I also have to talk to the bishop."

"Of course. Good night, Mrs. Kline."

"Good night, Mr. Miller."

* * *

Hannah awoke in the metal bed she'd shared with Daniel. For a few seconds she didn't know where she was. Then the incredible sequence of the past week's events came rushing back, leaving her both frightened and sick to her stomach. She took care of the nausea with a quick trip to the bathroom. Then she banished her fear the only way she knew how—by getting busy. Some people could lie in bed for hours, rationally planning a solution for any tough situation. But Hannah only knew how to work through problems, even if her actions took her down one dead-end path after another.

After thoroughly cleaning the four rooms from top to bottom, she packed up her laundry in a black trash bag. If she was going to *Mam's*, she might as well use the propane washer on the porch. Her driver arrived less than thirty minutes later and Hannah arrived at her parents' farm well before noon.

Oddly, her parents didn't seem surprised to see her. "I told your father you'd be back soon. You no longer have a reason to keep saving a big pile of money."

Hannah felt her baby kick. "We'll talk about that later. For now, what can I do to help you?"

"Just set the table. Lydia invited Nathan to lunch, so she's doing the cooking." Sarah Troyer grinned and rolled her eyes. "That young man has no idea what he's getting into."

As Hannah set the table, she kept an eye on the stove. Her sister would rather clean barn stalls, pick fruit, or weed the garden—anything but stand over a hot stove. But today, Lydia did a fine job with pork and sauerkraut and a mixed green salad. And with Lydia doing most of the talking, the meal passed pleasantly enough.

When they finished eating, Nathan stood and reached for his hat. "Thank for lunch, Mrs. Troyer, Lydia. I'd better get back to work." Then the shy young man vanished out the door.

Lydia also jumped up. "I'll clear the table and start the dishes," she said.

But Hannah grabbed her sister's arm. "No, you and I will do them later. Right now I have news to share, and a decision in which I seek my family's approval."

Lydia sat back down, while *Mam* refilled coffee mugs. "What is it, daughter?" asked *Dat*.

Hannah spelled out the details of Mr. and Mrs. Howard's idea of her and Seth Miller forming a partnership. She mentioned Kings Hardware, along with the advantage of having *Plain* owners instead of a corporate chain.

To their credit, her parents stopped to consider what they'd heard, while Lydia looked like an animal caught in a hunter's crosshairs. Finally, her father spoke. "Hannah, no matter what the merits, this partnership comes too soon after your husband's passing. You aren't ready to make such a decision. You have not finished grieving."

That was the exact argument she feared. "I don't disagree with you. I thought the same thing when Mr. Howard made the suggestion. But they cannot wait six months or a year to sell. Mr. Howard's health is failing. He gets tired walking to the store from his car. They wish to spend their remaining time with their family in Florida."

"How does this concern you, daughter?" Her mother's brow furrowed into deep creases.

"If they get half the money as a down payment, they're willing to owner-finance the store for an Amish buyer. If none steps forward, they must go with a chain hardware store that will line up financing through a bank."

Sarah looked to her husband, who also seemed at a loss for words. "It's not seemly for a widow to go into business. The bishop will never agree to such an idea."

"Our bishop understands that *Plain* folks need to form partnerships to remain independent in the world. Remember, I will soon have a child to support."

Her father offered another perfect rebuttal. "They may form partnerships, yes, but not with Englishers."

"His name is Seth Miller and he's not really an Englisher. He had a disagreement with his father and left home to work in construction. But since he never took the kneeling vow, Seth was never shunned by his district."

John Troyer shook his head. "In my book, that still makes this man English. I'll need to discuss your forming a partnership with the bishop. Tell me about this disagreement with his family."

Swallowing hard, Hannah took a gulp of coffee. "Seth got his driver's license and bought a beat-up old truck during his *rumschpringe*. His bishop allowed it, as long as he sold it once he joined the church. Seth drove his family and members of his district on their errands. At the time he worked for pay as a roofer and handyman for Englishers, but he followed the bishop's rules regarding no power tools."

"What did he do with the money he earned?" John Troyer interrupted.

"He gave most of it to his father." Hannah paused a moment, then continued. "Seth was fixing a door that kept sticking in an Englisher's house. She was an elderly widow named Mrs. Robb. All Seth had to do was sand down the bottom of the wooden door and adjust the closure. But when he finished with the door, Mrs. Robb accused Seth of stealing her wedding rings. She said she put them in a little bowl to do the dishes and now the rings were missing."

Her parents exchanged a look. "Didn't the woman stay in the kitchen while Seth was working?" asked Sarah. "Sanding down the door shouldn't have taken too long."

"That's what I asked him, too. Seth said Mrs. Robb went out

to her garden to pick some flowers. She didn't check the bowl on the sink until Seth was ready to leave. That's when she noticed the rings were gone. Seth swears he didn't steal her jewelry," cried Hannah, watching her father's complexion darken. "He turned out his pockets and emptied his toolbox onto the floor. But Mrs. Robb didn't believe him and called the sheriff."

Her mother's opinion became all too apparent. "Oh, daughter. You can't possibly go into business with a thief."

Hannah closed her eyes to steady her nerves. "Aren't we to give people the benefit of the doubt? Even in the English court of law, aren't people presumed innocent until proven guilty?"

"Tell us the rest, daughter," prodded *Dat*.

"When the sheriff arrived, he searched Seth, the toolbox, and his vehicle, even though he hadn't gone out to his car. Then he filed a police report but never charged Seth with a crime. The case is still open."

That piece of information had little effect on her parents.

"So Seth drove home and told his father what had happened. At first, his father believed him. But after Mrs. Robb spread rumors and word got back to their bishop, he changed his mind. His father ordered Seth to give back the jewelry, apologize to the widow, and repent of his sins because *he'd broken a commandment*. He and his father had a terrible argument, and his father ordered him to stay away from the house. Well, you can't give back what you don't have," Hannah concluded as tears filled her eyes. "I believe Seth Miller is telling the truth."

Again, Sarah looked to John for direction, who sat rubbing his chin for a full minute. "That very well may be the case, daughter. If Seth Miller was falsely accused, the good Lord knows the truth. And it's only God's opinion that we need to worry about, not the elder Mr. Miller, or Mrs. Robb, or the local sheriff. Yet in the meantime, Seth Miller isn't Amish, so I doubt our bishop will agree to your forming a partnership." He clucked his tongue, a habit he'd learned from *Mam*. "You're moving too quickly. Daniel just died. Live with us for a year or two. Have your little one here. Perhaps by then your future will be made clear."

Hannah's gaze scanned the table, hoping for someone to take her side. But it was not to be.

"That sounds like a wise idea, John." Sarah smiled at him.

"I agree," said Lydia, jumping to her feet. "I can't wait to be an aunt. In the meantime, let's get this kitchen cleaned up."

Hannah picked up a stack of plates and followed her sister to the sink. For now the matter was settled. There was no point in arguing. But later that night, after Lydia had gone to her room and her parents dozed in the living room, Hannah wrapped a shawl around her shoulders and walked outside. In a yard bright with moonlight, cold stars shone down from an unfathomable distance, as though mocking her insignificance. Closing her eyes, she heard the familiar night sounds of hoot owls, and one lonely coyote. Then Hannah quieted her mind and listened with her heart. Call it intuition; call it God's favorite method of communication, but she knew in an instant she had to find Mrs. Robb's missing rings.

Until someone discovered the thief's true identity, she would never get her hardware store. And one righteous man would never be restored to his family or to his faith.

Chapter 7

The next morning when Hannah announced her intentions to return to Bluebird, her sister looked disappointed and her mother confused.

"I thought you agreed to see what the bishop decides," Sarah said, placing one hand on her ample hip.

"I did. I won't go against the bishop's decision. But until the store is sold, the Howards need my help. I will work until they close their doors."

Sarah nodded. "Do you think Mr. Miller will buy it by himself?"

"No, he can't afford to." Staring out the window, Hannah nibbled a piece of toast.

"Then I will pray he finds a more suitable partner." Sarah picked up a basket of laundry and headed for the clothesline.

Hannah finished her breakfast and headed next door to call for a ride. Her heart ached because the house in which she'd been born felt alien to her. And her heart ached for Daniel and their broken dreams. Only when she immersed herself in work at the store did her pain subside. If she had to stay busy every minute of the day until she fell into bed, that's what she would do.

Around midmorning, Mr. Howard shut his ledger and rubbed his eyes. Martha had already walked across the street to buy them coffee and donuts. "Let's take a break, Hannah," he said. "Tell me about your visit home. What did your parents think about the idea?"

Hannah stopped filling bags with birdseed and approached the front counter. This wasn't a conversation she wanted to have. "They had their . . . reservations due to the newness of my widowhood. But my father will check with our bishop."

Mr. Howard studied her face. "His reservations are justified. Daniel's death came as a terrible shock to you."

"Yes, but Kings Hardware won't wait for a reasonable mourning period." Regretting her harsh tone, she said in a controlled voice, "I do have one possibility, the nature of which I'd rather not discuss at this time. Do you have a phone book?"

Mr. Howard gaped at her. "I do, but it's rather old." He passed a tattered White Pages and his cell phone across the counter. "Make all the calls you want."

Hannah quickly flipped through the pages, then called every B. Robb in the book. Two of the numbers had been disconnected and the others weren't the correct Mrs. Robb.

"Can I help you find someone? You don't have to tell me the reason." Mr. Howard pushed his glasses up his nose.

"Could you Google a Mrs. Bernice Robb who lives here in Lancaster County?" she asked after a moment. "She's a widow lady in her eighties."

He did as she asked. After a few minutes of fruitless searching, he shook his head. "I found no one that could possibly be her. Someone her age might not have any social media presence."

Hannah wasn't sure exactly what that meant, but the gist of it was clear. "Thanks anyway. It was a long shot."

Glancing up, Mr. Howard's face bloomed with a grin. "Seth, I didn't expect you today."

"My foreman gave me the day off," a familiar voice said over her shoulder. "Thought maybe I could get in some training. Good morning, Mrs. Kline."

Hannah wheeled around on her heel. "How long have you been standing there?"

"Long enough to know you're butting your nose into someone's business."

"Who's butting their nose in?" Martha Howard bustled in from the back room. She set three large Styrofoam cups and a bakery bag on the counter.

"Let's let the young folks sort this out, dear." Mr. Howard pulled two donuts from the bag. "Grab your coffee. We'll take ours in the back."

After Martha followed him through the door, Seth crossed his arms and frowned. "Well?"

Hannah picked up her coffee and nodded toward the front. "Let's talk outside."

He trailed after her, but his expression didn't change. "All right, nobody can overhear us. Why are you looking for Mrs. Robb?"

Hannah peered into his stony English face with that bad haircut and blurted. "Because if I don't find her rings or who really stole them, you won't rejoin the Amish church and then you and I can't be partners." She inhaled a quick breath. "And I want to buy this store."

Seth seemed to be holding back a smile. "Why would you want to be partners with a thief?"

"Because I know you aren't one, and nobody else is stepping up to buy Howard's with me." She lifted and dropped her shoulders.

He released a chuckle. "Do you always say exactly what's on your mind, Mrs. Klein?"

"Pretty much. Now will you drive me to the house she once lived in? Maybe she's still there."

"This is pointless. She would have called if she ever found the rings. She might have even passed on by now."

"I have to at least try or I'll regret it the rest of my life."

"What about my training?"

"Your training is pointless if we can't buy the store together. I'll explain to Mr. Howard we need a couple hours off. If this works out, I can train you in the future."

"As you wish." Seth lifted his hands in surrender.

"Here, take these." She handed him her donut and coffee. "If I'm riding in a car, I shouldn't eat anything."

The Howards beamed when Hannah said they were "pursuing an obstacle in the road to their partnership." But to Seth she owed a bit more explanation.

"I'm sorry you overheard my conversation. But I never told Mr. Howard *why* I'm looking for Mrs. Robb. You can wait in the truck while I talk to her. You can even park down the street if you prefer."

"It's all right. I know you mean well, but this really is a lost cause."

"You've never seen a motivated woman." Hannah clutched her stomach around the curves and smiled. But an hour later, she began to understand Seth's negative response.

The house in which he'd fixed the kitchen door now had new owners—owners who had lived there for two years. The young couple had no idea where the elderly widow had gone after she sold and moved out. They might be willing to check with their former realtor, but privacy laws most likely would prevent the realtor from disclosing any information she might have.

Hannah climbed back into the passenger side with a scowl. "This was a dead end."

"I'm sorry. I had driven by a few times out of curiosity and thought she had moved away. But it was sweet of you to try."

"I'm not trying to be sweet, Mr. Miller. I'm trying to be practical. How did you find Mrs. Robb in the first place?"

Seth backed out onto the highway. "What do you mean?"

"You were Amish back then. How did you know that woman needed a carpenter? I'm sure you weren't reading English newspapers."

"I don't know. It was a long time ago."

"Think back. This is important, even if you are getting cold feet about the purchase."

Seth's jaw tightened while a tic appeared in his right cheek. "I'm not getting cold feet."

"In that case, try to remember."

For several minutes, neither spoke while Seth drove around aimlessly. Then he said in a soft voice, "Mrs. Robb had posted an ad on the bulletin board in Beechy's Sweets. She went there all the time. I had stopped in to buy candy for my sisters."

"Beechy's in Bluebird?" she shrieked. "That's practically across the street from the hardware store."

"I know, Mrs. Klein, but it was a long time ago."

"Take me back to town."

"Upon your command, your majesty."

Hannah wasn't sure what he meant, so she concentrated on the scenery to keep down her toast and jam. *Why do Englishers drive so fast? Must they get everywhere in a hurry?*

When they reached Bluebird, Seth dropped her off and then parked behind Howard's. Hannah crossed the street as fast as her legs would carry her.

"Hello, cousin," Rose Bontrager sang out from behind the display of bright candies in big glass jars. "Nice to see you again. How are you feeling?"

"I'm well, thank you. I'm sorry we didn't get much of a chance to talk at Daniel's wake."

"That is understandable, but I'll be staying in Bluebird for a while so our chance will come. Have you stopped in for something sweet?"

"No, thank you. I was wondering if you still had a bulletin board here."

"Yes, right behind you on the wall. Let me know if you need anything." Rose returned to boxing up varieties of fudge.

Hannah hurried to the wall behind a pretty whitewashed table with mismatched chairs and scanned every index card posted. However, none were from a Bernice Robb. "Rose, is Mr. Beechy here?"

A few minutes later, Jacob came limping out from the back. "Hello, Hannah. What can I help you with?" He leaned on his crutches, taking the weight off his recently broken knee.

"Do you remember an Englisher named Mrs. Robb?"

"Of course, I do. She used to stop in three or four times a month. Always bought the same thing—butter pecan fudge. Haven't seen her in years."

"Would you have her current address?"

"No, her purchases were always cash and carry. Why do you ask?"

Hannah felt weak in the knees. "It was just a long shot for a friend. I'd better get back to the hardware store." She staggered to the door.

"Are you all right?" Jacob Beechy circled the counter in one direction while Rose went around the other.

"I'm fine," Hannah assured them. "I was just riding in a truck and got a little carsick." She waved goodbye and crossed the street to where Seth waited on the sidewalk. "Another dead end. You were right—this is hopeless."

"Let's go inside." Seth tried to steady her arm. "You look very pale."

"No, I'm going upstairs. Tell Mr. Howard I need to lie down. Perhaps he can tutor you on the basics." Before Seth could respond, Hannah hurried around the corner of the building and climbed the stairs.

Once inside the safety of her apartment, she parted the curtains with one finger. As expected, Seth was still on the sidewalk, as though waiting for her to return. Now her heart ached for *him* as she let the curtain fall.

For the rest of the day, Hannah remained in bed. A few hours later Martha came to check on her with a container of chicken soup. Although she thanked Martha profusely, she could barely eat the salty broth and overcooked noodles. That night she tossed and turned for hours, thinking that her one opportunity to stand on her own two feet was slipping away. And she couldn't do anything to stop it.

The next morning Hannah opened the store at the usual time despite the fact that she wasn't able to place any new orders. Kings Hardware would have their own idea about the merchandise they would stock. Instead she busied herself tidying and organizing each shelf, rack, and display.

Then around noon, cousin Rose bounded into the store, letting the door slam shut. "Hannah. Hannah Klein, are you here?" she called breathlessly.

Hannah pushed to her feet from a crouched position. "I'm here. What's wrong? Has something happened to Jacob?"

"No, no. He's fine. Are you still looking for that English woman? If so, drop what you're doing and come with me."

Hannah braced one hand on the post. "Mrs. Bernice Robb is inside Beechy's?"

"No, but her daughter is. She stopped in to buy her mother's favorite fudge." Rose took hold of Hannah's hand. "Stop jabbering and go talk to her."

Hannah pulled her dusty apron over her head and ran from the store, flipping the *Open* sign to *Closed* on her way out. She was panting by the time they reached Beechy's cash register, where a well-dressed Englisher was pulling a credit card from her wallet. Rose quietly slipped behind the counter and donned a fresh apron.

"I think I'll add a pound of maple walnut to my order," the woman said. "That's my husband's favorite."

"Nothing for yourself?" asked Rose. "Surely a quarter pound of something wouldn't hurt anyone."

The woman laughed. "You do know how to twist an arm. Okay, give me a quarter pound—no, make that a half pound of salted caramel. If I'm breaking my diet, might as well make it worth my while."

While Rose's helper boxed and bagged the candy, Hannah caught her breath. But when the woman turned to leave, Hannah placed herself exactly in her path. "Excuse me, ma'am. My cousin Rose says you might be Bernice Robb's daughter."

The Englisher smiled politely. "I am. I'm Carrie Morgan. Do you know my mom?"

"No, but my friend does. He stopped in to visit her, but someone else was living in her house now."

"Yes, Mom had to sell her home a few years ago. It all but broke her heart. But when the doctor said she couldn't drive anymore, I hated the idea of her living out there alone. What Mom actually misses the most is not being able to come to Beechy's as often as she used to."

"Does Mrs. Robb live with you and your family now?"

The woman exchanged a quick glance with Rose, who in turn, cleared her throat pointedly. Hannah knew her question was impertinent, if not downright rude, but this was her only chance. She held her breath and waited.

"No, we invited her to move in. We even painted the guest room sunny yellow, her favorite color. But since my husband and I work and our kids are in school, Mom said she preferred to be with people her age. She picked out an independent living facility twenty minutes from our house. She loves it. I'm on my way there with her favorite fudge."

Hannah felt Rose's gaze boring holes in her. "Thanks, Mrs. Morgan. Tell your mom her friends from Bluebird were asking about her."

"I certainly will. Nice meeting you." Carrie Morgan stepped around her. "Thanks, Rose," she called over her shoulder. "See you next month."

Hannah followed her out the door to her car. "Would that be the Lancaster County Assisted Living, south of the city?" she asked.

With one hand on the door handle, the Englisher paused. "No, Mom lives in Sunnybrook Care Center in Ephrata." With a wave, Carrie Morgan drove away.

Hannah released a sigh of relief. She had no idea if the facility she'd named even existed, having pulled the name from the air. But now she knew the real place. And she had one last chance to save her dream.

Chapter 8

For several days Hannah worked in the store and trained Seth when he finished his shift as a carpenter. The Howards rarely stopped by since they were busy with garage sales, showing their home, and packing for their upcoming move. Hannah decided not to tell Seth what she'd learned about Mrs. Robb. Just because she had a current address for the woman didn't mean she was any closer to finding the missing rings.

Seth learned quickly, worked hard, and greeted customers liked an old pro. He would make a great owner, except for the fact he had only half the down payment. She had the other half in the bank, but had no desire to disrespect her parents or disobey the bishop. Their church leader had arrived at the same conclusion as her father—a partnership would be possible only if Seth joined the church and resolved the issue with his family.

Money springing up in the garden next to the cabbages would be just as likely.

Then a week after meeting Carrie Morgan, Hannah got the break she desperately needed. She had barely slipped on her work apron when Rose Bontrager skipped into the store.

"How would you like to spend the day doing a good deed?" she asked with a smile.

"Love to, but I have to work today, same as you."

Rose leaned both elbows on the glass counter. "Isn't there someone who can take your place? It's not every day you get a chance to deliver Valentine candy to senior citizens in a nursing home."

"What are you up to, cousin?" Hannah narrowed her gaze.

"Jacob told me that every year Beechy's delivers free candy to the residents of Sunnybrook Care Center. Doesn't that name ring a bell with you?" Rose's expression turned downright impish.

"It's where Mrs. Robb lives. But what does delivering candy have to do with me?"

"Jacob hired a driver to take me there and pass out the treats. I thought you could come along and help."

"I would love to, but Mr. Miller won't be here until after—" Then like a lightning bolt, Hannah remembered today was Saturday—Seth's day off. "Goodness, he'll be here any minute for his training. You go get the Valentine treats ready and I'll join you as soon as he arrives."

Rose was barely through the front door of Beechy's when Seth's truck parked next to Howard's. A few minutes later the tall, muscular new employee entered the shop.

"Good morning, Mrs. Klein. I hope you're feeling well."

"I feel just fine as long as I'm not riding with a crazy English driver," Hannah teased.

Seth blushed to the roots of his scalp. "What would you like to do first?"

Hannah had no time to waste. "Actually, I have a favor to ask. Could you handle the store while I run an errand?"

"Of course, if you think I'm ready. How long will the errand take?"

She smoothed down the folds in her dress. "Don't rightly know—could be most of the day."

Seth lifted a brow. "I can ring up purchases just fine. But what if the customer asks a question I don't know?"

"Tell them to call Mr. Howard at home. He won't mind and his number is on the scratch pad."

"What kind of errand is this?" Seth sounded a tad suspicious.

"Let's say it's a private matter and hope for a good outcome."

Her implication triggered another blush, but Hannah would rather he thought the errand involved her pregnancy instead of the truth. "If I'm not back by six, turn off the lights, and lock the door when you leave."

Grabbing the broom, Seth started to sweep. "I'll do my best."

Forty minutes later, she and Rose were inside Sunnybrook Care Center, pushing a cart filled with small white boxes of fudge decorated with hand-drawn red hearts and curlicues. Although Rose was a first-timer, too, Mr. Beechy had schooled her on exactly where to go and whom to see. The nurse in charge of assisted living greeted them warmly and thanked them profusely.

Hannah and Rose stopped at every room along both sides of the corridor, presenting the Valentine candy and visiting with each resident. As expected, just about everyone wanted to chat. It was amazing to see how much joy four pieces of fudge brought to lonely senior citizens. Within two and a half hours Hannah and Rose finished their task, yet Hannah hadn't seen "Mrs. Bernice Robb" on any name plate.

As Rose pushed the empty cart out to the van, Hannah approached the nurse who had welcomed them to the facility.

264 / *Mary Ellis*

"Excuse me, ma'am. I had hoped to run into Mrs. Bernice Robb today. Her daughter, Mrs. Morgan, said she lives here."

The middle-aged nurse smiled. "She does, or rather she did. Mrs. Robb was just moved to the Memory Care Unit of Sunnybrook."

Hannah extracted one last box of fudge from her pocket. "I saved this for her. Could you please direct me to her room?"

"Gifts from Beechy's are for independent living only. Residents in Memory Care might have dietary restrictions limiting sugar that they're unaware of."

Hannah's eyes filled with tears, which did not go unnoticed by the floor supervisor.

"Let me check the computer. Mrs. Robb's doctor was recently here to sign the transfer." She tapped the screen of her computer several times. "That's what I thought. Mrs. Robb has no dietary restrictions whatsoever. She's in Building C, room 146. Perhaps a little candy will brighten her day."

Hannah wiped her eyes, thanked the nurse, and hurried out to the parking lot. "Rose, please return to Bluebird without me. You need to work this afternoon. I can call for a driver after I speak to Mrs. Robb."

"I don't know about this." Rose wrung her hands. "That's a lot of unnecessary expense."

"Please, Rose. This is important, so I don't mind the cost."

"What should I tell Seth Miller at the store?"

"Don't tell him anything. I'll talk to him later myself. And I hope to tell you the whole story someday soon."

Rose kissed her cheek lightly. "Good luck, cousin. I hope your long shot pays off."

After the van drove away, Hannah found herself alone in Ephrata, an unfamiliar town. But before she could give the matter much thought—or lose her nerve—she found building C and marched into room 146.

"Good afternoon, Mrs. Robb. I'm Hannah Klein from Bluebird."

"Hello. Do I know you, dear?"

"No, ma'am. But today I'm helping my cousin deliver Valentine's Day candy from Beechy's Sweets. Do you remember Beechy's?"

"My goodness, yes. I love their fudge. I visited almost once a week when I could drive."

Hannah pulled out the small, brightly decorated box. "These are for you. I hope one of the flavors is your favorite."

Mrs. Robb wasted no time opening the box. "There it is—butter pecan!" She held it out for Hannah to see.

"Dear me, maybe I should wait till after lunch." She wrapped her fingers around her left wrist. "But I can't find my watch. Do you have the time?"

"I don't wear a watch."

"Check your cell phone."

"Don't have one of those, either, but I'll find out for you." Hannah stopped the first passerby in the hallway. "It's a little after eleven," she announced upon returning.

"Still a good hour to go." Mrs. Robb took a bite of fudge. "Could you help me look for my watch, Linda? I was wearing it this morning."

"It's Hannah. And I'd be happy to help you." Hannah scanned the table tops and bathroom counter. Then she got down on hands and knees and looked under the bed and dresser. Finally she checked the pockets of each cardigan hanging in the closet. Mrs. Robb remained in her recliner, nibbling fudge.

"Sorry, I can't find it."

"Why don't you check those boxes?" The woman pointed at a stack against the wall. "I just moved here from home and haven't unpacked yet."

Since that statement didn't match what Hannah had learned from the nurse and Carrie Morgan, Hannah grew a bit uncomfortable. Someone might wonder why a total stranger was pawing through an elderly lady's possessions. "Maybe you should ask one of the nurses to help you. Or wait until your daughter gets here."

"*Nurses?* There are no nurses here. This is a senior citizen apartment complex. And I haven't seen my daughter in months. Please find my watch. Otherwise, I'll miss lunch and dinner and I'm hungry already."

The woman sounded so sad, so lonely, Hannah couldn't refuse. "All right, I'll help you look." Hannah carried one box after another to where Mrs. Robb sat and carefully removed the contents for her to see. A complete mishmash of photo albums, scrapbooks, pieces of clothing, and accessories filled the first three boxes, including three pairs of eyeglasses, which Hannah placed on her bedside table. But no watch. In the fourth box, Hannah extracted a set of keys from a mass of knotted scarves.

"My keys! Now I can finally drive my car." Mrs. Robb snatched the set from Hannah's fingers and slipped them into her pocket. "Thank you, Miss . . . what did you say your name was?"

"Hannah. My name is Hannah. Would you like me to hang up your clothes in the closet and put your socks and scarves in a drawer?"

Mrs. Robb looked aghast. "Oh no, some of that stuff isn't even mine."

"Why don't I place the photo albums in one box? I could label each box with what's inside."

"No, dear, I have everything organized how I like it."

As Hannah finally understood what kind of disability the Unit C patients suffered, her heart ached. She carefully returned the items to the box in the same disorder she'd found them. Just as she rose to her feet, she heard a voice from the doorway.

"Hi, Mom. Are you ready to go down to lunch?"

Hannah locked gazes with Carrie Morgan.

"You're the woman I met in the candy shop. I thought you didn't know my mother."

"This is Linda," said Mrs. Robb helpfully. "She dropped by to help me unpack."

"Hello, Mrs. Morgan, Hannah Klein. Today I'm helping Rose from Beechy's deliver candy to the residents." Hannah pointed at the empty fudge box on the floor. "Your mother asked me to help look for her watch in those boxes. We found her missing car keys, but no watch. She put the keys in her pocket."

Carrie sighed. "Mom, I'll be right back to take you to the cafeteria. Could you please join me in the hallway?" she asked Hannah.

"Of course, but before I forget we found three pairs of your mom's eyeglasses."

Carrie carefully closed the door to her mother's room and stared at the ceiling for a long moment. "Hannah, right? First of all, my mother lost her watch years ago and I never replaced it. Secondly, she has never worn glasses in her life. But I will try my best to find their rightful owners."

"I figured out she'd lost her memory halfway through the boxes. I'm so sorry."

"At least she still knows who I am, but that won't always be the case."

Carrie looked much older today than when Hannah had met her in the store. She chose not to mention Mrs. Robb's comment about her daughter not coming for months. "I'm sure they take good care of her here."

"Yes, they do." She leaned against the wall. "Last week you were curious where she lived. I'd like to know why you really came to see her."

"I'll tell you, but it's a long story and your mom said she was hungry."

The woman's nostrils flared. "Fine, you and I will walk her to the dining room. Then we'll talk while she eats." Carrie opened the door and motioned Hannah through, as though not wanting her out of her sight.

On the way to the dining room, Mrs. Robb chatted about some show on TV. Once she was seated with her friends, Carrie motioned to a pair of upholstered chairs in the waiting area. "Now, why don't you tell me what's going on?"

Hannah launched into the convoluted tale of how she worked for the Howards, had lost her husband, and met Seth Miller, along with the Howards' idea about a partnership. Next she described Seth's estrangement from both his church and family due to the missing diamond jewelry. Then she explained her parents' desire that she only go into business with an Amish partner. "I know Seth didn't steal your mother's rings," Hannah concluded.

"Knowing what we know now about Mom's memory loss, that may well be the case. Some cases of Alzheimer's disease progress slowly in the beginning. But from what I understand, Seth was never charged with the theft. So how could this have caused such repercussions in his life?"

"It's true, he wasn't charged. But his father never believed in his innocence. That's what drove Seth away. No one wants to be accused of a crime they didn't commit."

Carrie reflected for a moment. "I understand. But if my mother couldn't remember where she put her rings five years ago, how can you expect her to now?"

Hannah wiped her damp palms down her skirt. "I don't. But I thought if she let *me* look and if I found them, it would prove to his district and especially his father that Seth wasn't a thief. I know it's unlikely but I had to try." Hannah looked up, expecting to see Carrie laughing at her foolishness.

But the woman's face was full of sorrow. "Oh, Hannah. It's been five years. We had to get rid of most of Mom's possessions when she moved here. There's so little space in her room."

"What did you do with her furniture?"

"Let's see. We moved a few pieces to my house. We held a garage sale, donated plenty to charity, and left everything in the basement and garage to the new owners of the house. She only brought those boxes of mementoes, her lamp and table, and her favorite recliner to Sunnybrook. And I checked her recliner when the rings first went missing. Oh, and she told her nieces and nephews to take whatever they wanted. I'm afraid those rings are gone forever."

"I guess it's hopeless, but thanks for your time. I'll keep your mother in my prayers." With a sigh, Hannah pushed to her feet.

"There must be something I can do to help." Carrie scrambled up. "Why don't I go talk to the elder Mr. Miller? I'll explain Mom's memory loss, and that we're sure the rings were lost, not stolen."

"That's very nice of you. But several people in his district already tried talking sense to him with no luck. I'm afraid Mr. Miller is a stubborn man."

"I hope for your sake the younger Mr. Miller won't be as stubborn about rejoining the church."

"I hope so, too. Goodbye, Mrs. Morgan." Hannah smiled weakly and walked from the noisy dining room.

"Wait a minute." Carrie hurried after her. "There are a few

boxes in Sunnybrook's storage area that I could search. If I happen to find the rings, how can I reach you?"

"Sounds like another long shot," said Hannah, but jotted down both the number for Howard's Hardware and Beechy's Sweets. "Call either number. Both know how to get a message to me. And thanks for trying to help."

Chapter 9

For two weeks, Hannah buried herself in work. Since Mr. Howard hadn't accepted the bid from Kings Hardware, everyone operated on the premise she and Seth would buy the store. As promised, Seth turned out to be a fast study. He took prodigious notes while she explained the ins and outs of inventory, pricing, and customer service. Then each night he took home catalogs to familiarize himself with every tool and gadget known to man . . . or woman.

As potential partners, they were well suited. Soft-spoken Seth was patient and slow to anger, even with the most ornery of customers. He treated her with respect and never once presumed some inherent superiority based on gender. Women's rights hadn't gained much foothold in the *Plain* community, yet if Hannah was to thrive in a partnership outside of marriage, she needed someone who valued her knowledge and abilities. Seth Miller was that man.

Each evening while Seth studied catalogs, Hannah prayed for guidance and for God to make her path clear. Yet day after day, she and Seth were no closer to concluding their purchase of Howard's than that day in Martha's fancy dining room. *Was this one of those times God needed a little help?*

On Saturday, a steady stream of people stopped in to shop and wish the Howards good luck in retirement, despite the fact that inventory was rather low. Almost everyone asked who the new owner would be. Whenever Lawrence or Martha explained that Hannah would be one of the two, her cheeks flushed with embarrassment. Amish women weren't used to being the center of attention. Finally she grew tired of answering questions and fled to the back room to help Seth pack the Howards' personal possessions. Later that afternoon Hannah was about to lock the front door when she spotted Rose Bontrager crossing the street.

"Hold up there, Hannah," Rose called, bounding up the front steps.

"You should be more careful, cousin," Hannah scolded. "You barely looked both ways."

"I will next time, but right now Carrie Morgan wants to talk to you. She insisted on waiting, so Jacob sent me to fetch you."

"Mrs. Morgan is on the phone at Beechy's Sweets?"

"Yes, so come quick." Rose grabbed hold of her arm.

"Seth, please watch the store," Hannah called. "I'll be right back." She hated screaming like an English teenager, but Rose wasn't giving her much choice.

"Hello, Clara," she greeted Jacob Beechy's mother a few moments later as she entered the fragrant shop. "I hope you don't mind me tying up the line."

"Not at all, dear. Carrie is one of my favorite customers. Plus, she said it was important." Clara pointed at a phone dangling by the cord.

"Hello, Mrs. Morgan?" Hannah asked with both women watching.

"Yes, it's me. Did I catch you at a bad time?"

"No, I was about to lock up the store. Did you find your

mother's jewelry?" Suddenly, her baby kicked as though he or she sensed anxiety.

"Not yet, but I still have one more place to check. I've got a good feeling about this one."

"It wasn't in the storage unit?"

"No, but don't give up hope. Where will you be tomorrow?"

"At church services with my family. Then I'll have dinner at my parents' house."

"Give me their address. I want to be able to find you if my hunch proves correct. Do you have some way of reaching Seth Miller?"

"He gave me his cell phone number."

"Perfect! Give me that number and then sleep well tonight. Tomorrow I might have good news for you."

Hannah recited both pieces of information, said goodbye, and hung up Clara's phone. *Sleep well?* After that odd conversation, she would be lucky to sleep at all. Hannah thanked her friends and stood outside for several minutes. By the time she crossed the snowy street to the hardware store, she had reached a decision.

"Thanks, Mr. Miller," she called upon entering. "I'll lock up for the evening."

"No problem." Seth scrambled up from the front counter and returned to whatever he'd been doing.

On her way past a display of reading glasses, Hannah caught a glimpse of herself. But she didn't need a full length mirror to know exactly who she was—a widow with her first baby due in six months. She needed to work. And she needed the ability to support her child without depending on her parents . . . or some hasty second marriage to relieve them of the burden.

Marching into the back room, Hannah found Seth shrugging on his winter coat. "What are your plans for the evening?" she demanded.

"I'll probably study seed catalogs over a bowl of leftover mac and cheese," he said. "Then maybe a little basketball on TV. Why?"

"I thought we could eat supper at the diner down the street. Tonight their special is meatloaf with mashed potatoes." When he didn't respond, she added, "They also have a full menu if you don't like meatloaf."

Seth closed the metal locker. "Meatloaf is just fine. You surprised me, that's all."

Hannah wrapped her heavy cape around her shoulders. "We have something important to discuss."

What had been the beginning of a smile on Seth's face faded away. "I think I know what this is about. Lead the way, Mrs. Klein."

She waited to broach the subject until they were seated in a booth with menus and glasses of water. "We have kept Mr. and Mrs. Howard waiting long enough."

"I agree," Seth interrupted. "Let's tell them to accept the offer from Kings Hardware. We've been selfishly hoping for a miracle while Lawrence and Martha have been hung out to dry. Those two need to get on with their life."

It took Hannah a moment to decipher his metaphor. "That's not what I meant at all. Yes, the Howards should move on with their plans. And we should sign the partnership contract and present our offer for the store."

This time Seth needed a moment. "Nothing has changed, Mrs. Klein. I'm not Amish and haven't reconciled with my father."

"But you're looking more *Plain* each day. Are you going to remain stuck between two worlds forever?"

"Hopefully not. Some who leave the Amish happily embrace the English lifestyle. I haven't been able to do that, not completely. I do love wearing jeans and driving my truck, but Amish is who I am. I just realized it the other night. But until I swallow my pride and face my father, I can't take the kneeling vow." He lifted and dropped his shoulders.

"Whether you return to the Amish faith or stay English, I'm willing to form this partnership, even without my parents' approval. I'm a grown woman and I want to do what's best for my child."

"You folks ready to order?" asked the waitress, breaking the tension.

"I'll have the meatloaf special with iced tea," she said.

"I'll have the same, ma'am. Thank you." Seth set his menu on the edge of the table, but he never took his gaze off Hannah. "The fact you're willing to go against the bishop only makes me sad. And I can't let you do it."

"Then you're just being stubborn."

Seth turned redder than a bowl of tomatoes. "You haven't thought this through. I know exactly what it's like to live without a family's love and support. That's not what I want for your son or daughter . . . or you. Besides, your parents are right—this purchase comes too soon after your husband's death. You could regret a hasty decision after you've properly grieved."

Hannah swallowed hard, but the lump in her throat refused to budge.

"I believe God closed one door when he took Daniel home. But maybe he opened another with this partnership."

Seth didn't blink. "Not if all you would have to rely on is a half-Englisher. With a child to raise, you'll need your family and district."

Abruptly, the waitress plopped down their meals. "Here we go, folks, two speedy specials of the day. Either of you want more iced tea?"

"No, thank you," they said simultaneously.

"We seem to have reached a stalemate," Hannah murmured once they were alone. "Why don't we eat before the food gets cold? It looks delicious."

For the next ten minutes they limited conversation to requests for salt, pepper, or the bowl of extra gravy. When they finished the meal, Hannah extracted a twenty-dollar bill from her wallet.

"No, Mrs. Klein, I insist on paying."

"But I invited you, so I should pay."

"But I'm just plain stubborn, remember?" Seth picked up the check and strolled to the cash register.

Hannah left money for the tip and followed him out the door. "Why don't we take the weekend to think things over? If we still can't come to an understanding, we'll tell the Howards *no* Monday morning." With a shiver, she tightened her coat around her throat.

Seth rubbed his chin where a beard had sprouted. "Agreed. Now let's get you home." He took her arm until they reached the shoveled sidewalk. "Good night, Mrs. Klein. Stay warm and I'll see you on Monday."

"Good night, Mr. Miller. Try not to be late for work."

With Mrs. Morgan's carrot dangling before her nose, Hannah couldn't sleep no matter how many sheep she counted. She tossed and turned half the night before uttering a familiar prayer: "I accept your will, whatever that may be," and then finally fell asleep.

Although a last blast of winter was predicted for later on, the morning dawned bright and sunny. With clear roads, Hannah had no trouble getting to services on time with her usual Sunday driver. What proved difficult was sitting through a two-hour service and a long buggy ride home without telling the family her decision.

No sense in worrying them until she and Seth spoke on Monday. And Carrie Morgan's *good feeling* about her final place to check? Hannah put the possibility out of mind. With a far more accepting attitude about things beyond human control, *Plain* folk were less prone to premonitions and hunches.

On the buggy ride home, Lydia filled Hannah in on her wedding plans. The marriage would take place in six weeks, once spring planting was finished. Hannah was grateful, not only that Lydia's beau had popped the question, but because her parents had no chance to ask about the store.

When her father brought the horse to a stop next to the house, Hannah climbed out and hurried indoors. She would help *Mam* set out a cold dinner, while Lydia tended livestock with *Dat*. During the meal, Lydia described Nathan's ambitious plan to build them a house.

"Was that a car in the driveway?" asked *Mam*. "Who would be calling today? Our English friends know we don't sell eggs or chickens on Sunday."

Hannah's chin snapped up. "I'll go see who it is. The person might be looking for me."

"Transact no business on the Sabbath, daughter," cautioned her father.

"I won't." Wrapping a shawl around her shoulders, Hannah ran out the door and down the steps.

"Slow down, Hannah." Carrie Morgan climbed from her SUV. "We don't want you to fall."

"Did you find the rings?" she asked, dispensing with social niceties.

"Yep, come take a look." Carrie pulled a plastic bag from her pocket and poured two rings into her palm—one a plain gold band and the other sparkling with diamonds.

"They're lovely. Where did you find them?"

"In the sofa Mom gave to a niece and her husband. They had fallen in between the frame and the springs, down so deep even the re-upholsterer hadn't found them." Carrie shook her head. "Mom had a bad habit of taking her rings off when arthritis swelled her fingers. I didn't remember the sofa until yesterday. We gave most of the furniture to Goodwill."

"Seth will be so relieved that Mrs. Robb has her rings back."

"He's not the only one who should be relieved." Carrie rocked back on her heels.

"Of course, I am, too. Since I've decided to go ahead and buy the store, my family will be glad Seth will be cleared of any wrongdoing."

"Very true, but *your* family isn't the one I meant." Carrie's grin couldn't get any wider.

"What are you up to, Mrs. Morgan?"

"You and I are going to pick up Mom at the nursing home. Then Mom and I will apologize to Seth in person. These rings have caused so much grief."

Hannah remembered how easily Seth became embarrassed. "Oh, I don't think that's necessary."

Carrie waved off the comment. "It certainly is and it's long overdue. We'll all meet at the home of Seth's parents. They should be home today. Seth's estrangement with his family was a direct result of Mom's forgetfulness. This will give his father a chance to do the right thing."

Hannah felt the blood rush to her face. "I know you mean well, Mrs. Morgan, but this isn't a good idea."

"Why not?" Carrie set both hands on her hips.

"Seth has a stubborn streak. He'll never agree to meet us at his parents' farm."

"A real chip off the old block, eh? What do you suggest, then?"

A bead of sweat formed on Hannah's lip. Since she was one who had involved Carrie in the first place, she'd better think of something. She stared over the snow-covered fields until an idea came to mind. "Seth would go to his sister's if you told him I was there!" she blurted.

"Perfect! Do you know where his sister lives?"

"No. Only that Rachel lives around the corner from their parents."

"Okay, tell me where the parents live." Carrie opened the GPS on her phone.

"I don't know that, either." Hannah pressed a palm to her forehead.

"I need a little help here," Carrie said with a laugh.

Hannah inhaled a deep breath. "All I know is his brother lives at the farm, and Adam has been a regular customer of Howard's Hardware. If you take me back to the store, I can look up the address and then call Uber. In the meantime, you go pick up your mother."

Carrie looked confused. "And then what?"

"Once Uber picks me up, I'll find the Miller farm, then figure out which house his sister lives in. Then I'll call you with Rachel's address."

"But you don't have a phone."

"The Uber driver will. If necessary, I'll pay him to use it." As fast as ideas popped into Hannah's head, they flew from her mouth. "You tell Seth to meet me at Rachel's house and bring your mother there."

"This is a very complicated plan, but with any luck it might work."

"Let me get my heavy coat and tell my parents I'm visiting new friends," Hannah said over her shoulder. Halfway up the steps she felt her baby kick and knew if this crazy plan worked, it would have nothing to do with luck.

Chapter 10

Hannah's daring plan worked well until the Uber driver pulled into the unplowed driveway of a large, rambling house.

"You sure this is the place?" the man asked. "Doesn't look like anybody's home."

"It doesn't, but this is the first house around the corner." Hannah stared at the dark windows with flagging courage.

"If I pull farther up, I might get stuck in the snow."

"That's okay. I've got boots on. I'll walk up and ask, but please don't leave yet."

"I promise. Hey, look. People live here after all." The driver pointed at the front porch where two, then three, and then four children appeared.

Hannah paid the fare, along with a healthy tip, and climbed out. "Those kids are Amish." She ducked her head back into the van. "That's a good sign. I'll be right back."

Before she went twenty paces, a man and woman joined the children at the railing, followed by another couple. A crowd had formed to watch her trudge through the snow. Hannah opened her mouth to shout, but a gust of wind blasted her face with snow. When the wind died down, she cupped her hands around her mouth. "Hello. Are you Rachel Miller—the former Rachel Miller?"

After a bit of discussion the woman yelled back, "*Ya*, I'm Rachel Miller. Can I help you?"

Hannah took a few more steps and nearly fell on a patch of ice.

Suddenly, the second man shouted. "Hannah? Hannah Klein?" Hurrying down the steps, he slipped and slid his way to her side. "It's me, Adam Miller. What on earth are you doing here?"

"It's a long story, but I need a favor before I tell it." Hannah extracted a slip of paper from her pocket.

"Of course, what do you want me to do?"

"Go ask the van driver if we could use his phone one more time. Then call this number and tell whoever answers this address—your sister Rachel's address. Mrs. Morgan is expecting the call."

When Adam stared blankly, Hannah pleaded. "Please, Adam. I'll explain everything inside the house."

Prodded to action, Adam hiked through the snow, while Hannah continued her slow trek toward the house. Soon the other man, presumably Rachel's husband, arrived to help her up the steps and into the house.

Before she knew it, Hannah was sitting before a roaring fire in the family room with a blanket around her legs and feet. The four children, all dressed in Sunday black and white, watched her from positions along the wall.

"Hannah, is it? I'm Rachel Mast." The woman handed her a cup of hot tea.

"Yes, Hannah Klein. My husband was Daniel, my parents are John and Sarah Troyer of northern Lancaster County."

Pulling a chair close to Hannah's, Rachel continued the introductions. "That was my husband, Thomas, who helped you into the house. I won't confuse you with the names of my *kinner.* You already know Adam. And this is his wife, Amanda." A pretty young woman stepped forward to shake hands.

"How can we help you?" asked Adam, returning from his errand. "It must be important to come out in this weather."

Hannah took a sip of tea. "I'm here about your brother, Seth. He and I are about to form a partnership in order to buy Bluebird's hardware store."

"I love Howard's Hardware," exclaimed Amanda. "You must be so excited."

Thomas Mast wrapped an arm around his wife. "Although Rachel and I don't get up that way much, we wish you two the best."

"Thank you, but I'm not here to solicit new customers. Something is about to take place that will allow me to form this partnership."

"Take place *here?*" asked Rachel, bewildered.

"Yes. This was very presumptuous of me, but I didn't know what else to do." Hannah looked from one confused face to the next. "Seth is on his way here, but he knows nothing about this. Mrs. Robb and her daughter are on their way, too."

"Isn't that the English woman who accused my brother of stealing her wedding rings?" Adam asked.

"Yes, her rings have finally been found and her daughter feels terrible about the trouble they caused. She wants to apologize to Seth and his family in person."

"Why the daughter and not Mrs. Robb?" asked Rachel.

"Mrs. Robb suffers from advanced memory loss, which probably accounts for how this all happened five years ago."

"How awful for Mrs. Robb." Rachel pressed a hand to her heart. "What can we do?"

"I know one thing." Adam jumped to his feet. "Thomas and I need to shovel that driveway before more company arrives." Without another word, the two men and four children vanished into the back hall.

With only Rachel and Amanda left in the room, Hannah relaxed a bit. "Seth might resent my meddling. I know he's a private man who has lived on his own for a long time." She focused her gaze on Rachel.

"Don't worry about my brother. Seth is lucky to have a friend willing to mend fences like this." Rachel rose to throw more wood on the fire.

"Sounds to me like that Englisher did most of the meddling. We'll stand with you." Amanda patted Hannah's shoulder.

"You rest, while Amanda and I prepare a snack and brew more tea." Rachel patted her other shoulder as she left the room.

The women hadn't been gone five minutes when Hannah heard the unmistakable sound of a truck in the driveway, followed by heavy boots stomping snow in the back hall. She pushed herself up from the chair just as a big, snow-covered bear lumbered into the room.

"What's going on, Mrs. Klein? Some woman called and told me to go to my sister Rachel's house. She said *you* would be here." Seth shrugged off his jacket and tossed it across a chair. "Are you all right?"

Hannah didn't know whether to laugh or cry. "I'm fine. In fact, I've never felt better. You're the one who should sit down." She pointed at the opposite chair. "And you might want to start calling me by my first name now."

When Seth sat, Hannah returned to her chair by the fire. "Soon the woman who called you, Carrie Morgan, will arrive with her mother. Her mother's name is Mrs. Robb." Hannah paused until the significance became clear.

284 / *Mary Ellis*

"Mrs. Robb had the door that needed sanding. I take it you finally found her?" Seth dropped his head into his hands as Rachel and Amanda slipped back into the room.

"Yes, I not only found her, but her daughter found the missing rings. They had fallen between the frame and springs of her sofa. Even a re-upholsterer hadn't seen them. But Mrs. Morgan remembered the sofa had been given to a niece. When they practically tore it apart, they found the rings. She insisted on apologizing in person for the heartache her mother caused. Poor Mrs. Robb suffers from dementia."

As Seth lifted his face, his eyes glistened with tears.

"Are you angry because I butted my nose into your business?" she asked.

"*Angry?* No, Hannah. My pride caused this heartache, far more than Mrs. Robb's forgetfulness. I'm just amazed you went to all this trouble for a stubborn man like me."

In the shadows Rachel and Amanda released a collective breath.

"*We* really want to buy that store." Hannah placed both hands on her belly.

"And so the three of us shall. I'll present myself for the Sunday morning baptism classes and take the vows before the next communion service. Tell your parents your business partner will be Amish."

Rachel slipped her arm around Seth's waist. "I can't wait to tell the bishop, brother."

"You should tell him of my decision, but since I need to live close to Bluebird, I'm hoping Hannah's district will have me."

"We'd better iron out the details later," said Amanda Miller at the window. "I just saw someone pull into the driveway. It'll take a lot more shovels to get Mrs. Morgan's car up to the house."

Hannah jumped up to join the Millers and Masts.

"No, Hannah. You stay by the fire," said Seth. "You've done enough for one day. Now it's up to me and my family."

August

Seth stepped onto his front porch with his first cup of coffee of the day. His old-fashioned drip pot might not work fast, but the coffee tasted just as good. His coffee maker, along with his laptop, electric clock, microwave oven, toaster, and George Foreman grill had been sold at a garage sale, along with his power tools, cell phone, and every other piece of technology. He contributed the proceeds from the sale to the medical fund for his new district. His old Levi's, leather belts, flannel shirts, and Carhartt jackets went into the Goodwill collection box at the grocery store.

His mother and sisters sewed new shirts, trousers, and jackets, while his brothers supplied him with suspenders and hats for every season and occasion. All the hand tools he used to repair an unused *dawdi haus* on the outskirts of Bluebird came from his store, Howard's Hardware. He and Hannah decided to leave the name alone, as a tribute to their friends and mentors, Lawrence and Martha Howard. He bought a used buggy and a five-year-old Standardbred straight from the trotter auction and named the quick little gelding, Bob. The two of them got along fine. Of his former English life, only his Ford F-150 remained, and that truck should be gone within a few days. He'd found a buyer weeks ago, but the young man had had trouble lining up financing. Seth could afford to be patient with him.

Ever since that snowy day in early March when Mrs. Robb and Mrs. Morgan stepped out of the cold into his sister's warm house, Seth had gained far more than he'd given up. Now he had a little house in the country with a view of cornfields, a job he looked forward to every morning, and the prettiest, most intelligent business partner in the world. Someday, when the time was right, he would ask Hannah Kline to become his wife. But until that day, he would thank God every night she'd never lost patience with a stubborn half-Englisher.

Throwing the last of his coffee into the flowerbed, Seth finished dressing for church. Today he would take the vows of the Amish faith and be baptized by the bishop, along with the other young men and women ready to leave *rumschpringe* behind. Then he would join Hannah, her family, and members of his new district for the communion service, followed by a potluck lunch.

"Let's go." The booming voice of Adam Miller rattled through the house. "You sure don't want to be late today, brother."

"I'll be right there," Seth said, grabbing his hat from the hook. "Hold your horses."

"I doubled my horse power for today." Grinning, Adam shook the reins over a matched pair of mares in harness. "Climb up here with us."

"Nope, I'm good in the back." Seth squeezed into the rear-facing bench with his nephews and nieces, allowing Thomas, Rachel, Adam, and Amanda a more comfortable ride. Although the Miller family district was fifteen miles away, his siblings insisted on attending the baptism. And for his family's support, Seth was grateful. He was also grateful the family hosting today's service didn't live too far away.

After they parked the buggy at the end of the row, Seth spotted Hannah standing with her parents, along with Lydia, and her new husband, Nathan. Jacob Beechy and his new bride, Hannah's cousin Rose, were there, too. Seth cordially greeted those he hoped would also be his family someday, then entered the house where the baptism would take place.

"Hold up there, son. Grant me a minute or two."

Seth recognized the voice of his father but couldn't believe his eyes when he turned around. Joseph Miller stood with his sweet-faced mother and his former bishop next to a hired van. Seth closed the distance between them in a few long strides. "Thank you for coming, *Dat, Mam,* Bishop. I am grateful, but I need to go inside now."

"Please, son. Let me say my piece." Joseph Miller gazed up with watery eyes. "I sinned grievously against you. I was wrong and it has weighed heavily on me. Can you ever forgive me?"

"I forgave you last March when I begged God to forgive me. Send your driver on his way and stay for the communion service. Afterward, I'd like you to meet Hannah Klein and her family."

"We've heard good things about her," said his mother.

"If that's your wish, we will stay." Joseph Miller held out his hand.

But instead of shaking, Seth pulled his father into a tight embrace. "Today is a new day for us all," he whispered in his ear. "And we'll speak no more of the past."

Seth had one more surprise waiting for him after the baptism portion of the service. While district members filed in for communion, Lydia grabbed hold of his arm.

"My sister needs to get to the birthing center. A new little Kline is on the way. Hannah says you bought a quick little gelding." Lydia dragged him out the door and down the steps.

"I'd be happy to take Hannah, providing you and both my sisters ride along. If that new little Kline refuses to wait, I want plenty of women around who can take over."

"I have a better idea," said his new bishop. "Let's not take any chances. Since the new owner hasn't picked up your truck yet, I believe we can let you use it one more time. The women will keep Hannah comfortable until you come back for her."

Seth ran to the fenced paddock and mounted the only saddled horse he saw for the short jaunt home. He might not win any more barrel races, but he still knew how to ride. And as Hannah would later attest, he still knew how to drive like an Englisher.

Please turn the page for a
taste of more holiday-themed
Amish romance from Kensington . . .

A MOTHER'S GIFT

by Charlotte Hubbard

Chapter 1

As Lenore Otto sat on the bed with Leah, wistfully watching the dusk of late November fill her daughter's room, her heart was torn. The two of them had shared this evening ritual of talking and praying since Lenore's husband, Raymond, had died last year. It had always brought her a comforting sense of peace, along with the certainty that she and her daughter would move forward with the plans God had for them. After all the cleaning they'd done and the preparations they'd made to host Leah's wedding festivities the next day, she was ready to relax— but she needed to speak the words that weighed so heavily on her heart.

Tomorrow, when Leah got married, their lives would follow separate paths. Lenore knew she would be fine remaining on the small farm alone, making and selling her specialty quilts. She supposed some of her qualms about her daughter's marriage plagued every mother. . . .

Lord, I wish I could believe my Leah's reaching toward happiness rather than heartache.

Before God's still, small voice could respond to Lenore,

Leah let out an ecstatic sigh. "Oh, Mama, it's a dream come true," she whispered. "Starting tomorrow, when I marry Jude, my life will finally be the way I've always wanted it. My waiting is over!"

Not for the first time, Lenore sighed inwardly at her daughter's fantasy. As she returned Leah's hug, savoring these precious moments in the room where her little girl had matured into a woman of twenty-eight, she didn't have it in her to shatter Leah's dreams. No mother wanted her daughter to forever remain a *maidel,* yet during these final hours before the wedding, Lenore thought she should try once again to point out the realities of marrying Jude Shetler. Jude was a fine, upstanding man any parent would be pleased to welcome as a son-in-law, but as a widower he carried a certain amount of . . . baggage.

"Leah, your life will change in ways you can't anticipate when you marry," Lenore began softly. She rested her head against the headboard, grasping her daughter's hand. "When you move into a man's home—"

"Oh, Mama, you've already told me what to expect in the bedroom," Leah interrupted with a nervous giggle. "It's not as though I haven't seen the cows and the horses mating."

Lenore closed her eyes, praying for words that would gently pierce the balloon of maidenly naïveté in which Leah seemed to live. "There's more to marriage than mating," she whispered earnestly. "You'll be moving into a home where Jude and his kids have established their routine. We've both heard the rumors about how Alice and Adeline might be behaving inappropriately during their *rumspringa*—"

"They're sixteen, and they're very pretty," Leah quickly pointed out. "Twins are inclined to get into double trouble as part of their nature at that age. *I* certainly found mischief during my running-around years."

Lenore sighed again. She wished Raymond were here to help her with this difficult discussion. "Sweetheart, I doubt you were ever out of your *dat*'s or my sight for more than an hour at a time. The pranks you used to pull at sale barns when you were helping Dat with the livestock were nothing compared to the way I've heard the Shetler twins run the roads with English boys in their cars."

"I rode in a few cars—and pickups—you didn't know about," Leah shot back. "It's not as though I spent my time hanging around with *girls* at the auction barns, you know."

Squeezing Leah's fingers so she'd focus on the matters at hand, Lenore held her daughter's gaze in the dimness. "I probably should've insisted that you learn to cook and sew and keep house instead of tending the animals with your *dat*," she said with a sigh. "But you were a tremendous help to him—and you were the only child God blessed us with. More than anything, I've wanted you to spend your life doing what makes you happy."

"And I *am* happy, Mama!" Leah said blissfully. "I make a *gut* income selling my dressed chickens and ducks, my goat's milk, and raising crossbred cows—the same way Dat did. If I hadn't spent so much time in the sale barns around Jude, he would never have come to know me—or love me."

Lenore paused, searching for another conversational path. She had no doubt that her daughter's love for Jude was sincere, and that Jude loved Leah, too, but it took more than shared affection to make a marriage work and to keep a household running smoothly.

"And Mama, if your quilts don't sell—or if you want to stop working so hard on them," Leah said tenderly, "you know I'll help you out with money so you can stay here at home. I know how much you and Dat have always loved this place."

Tears sprang to Lenore's eyes. Once again, her daughter spoke with utmost sincerity, unaware that Jude might have different ideas about Leah's income—or that he might insist she give up raising and selling her chickens, ducks, and goats. He might also be reluctant for his wife to raise cattle, which required so much time and energy, even if he admired Leah's way with those animals.

"*Denki* for thinking of me, dear, but we're talking about you now," Lenore insisted gently. "I'm concerned because Jude's *mamm*, Margaret, also lives with Jude and the twins—not to mention Stevie, who seems rather immature for five. Margaret will have her way of doing things, because she took charge after Frieda died. And with Stevie still missing his *mamm*, you'll have a lot of little-boy emotions to deal with as you prepare him to start school next year. Most new brides only have a husband to get used to until the babies start coming."

"*Jah*, but with Margaret running the household and tending the three kids—especially Stevie—their routine can remain uninterrupted," Leah pointed out. "That will give Jude and me time to adjust to being husband and wife, and it'll mean that meals are put on the table and the laundry and cleaning will still get done. From what I know of Margaret, she'll have instructed Alice and Adeline about doing their part in the process, too."

From what I know of Margaret, Lenore thought sadly, *she'll be snipping at you every chance she gets, calling you a slacker—or worse—because you're not assuming the traditional role of an Amish wife.*

Lenore stared at the far wall, sensing whatever she said would go unheard. "Just be ready for your plans to be changed, Leah," she warned gently. "Spending most of your time with Jude at auctions, or in the barnyard tending your animals, might not work out the way you've imagined. Margaret will be a woman with a plan, too, you know."

Leah rested her head against the wooden headboard, closing her eyes. "I'll cross that bridge when—or if—I get to it, Mama. Tomorrow's my big day, and I know it'll be just perfect because Jude's sharing it with me. The light in his eyes when he looks at me is all I need to see to believe he'll love me forever and ever."

Lenore looked out the window at the half moon, which shone brilliantly in the night sky. *Bless your heart, Leah, I wonder if you still believe the moon's made of green cheese, as Dat and I teased you about when you were a child,* she thought with a sinking heart. *We probably should have done a lot of things differently as we were raising you . . . but it's too late to change your way of looking at the world.*

"I wish you all the best as you start your new life, Leah," she said softly. With a final squeeze to her daughter's hand, Lenore rose from the bed. "You'll always be in my thoughts and prayers—and I'll always love you. *Gut* night and sleep tight."

"You can sleep for me, Mama. I'm too excited to close my eyes."

Lenore paused in the doorway of the unlit room for a last glance at her giddy daughter. *Bless her, Lord, and hold her in Your hand,* she prayed. *At this point, only You can keep Leah's happiness from turning into a disaster.*

Connect with Us

Visit us online at
KensingtonBooks.com
to read more from your favorite authors, see books
by series, view reading group guides, and more.

Join us on social media

for sneak peeks, chances to win books and prize packs,
and to share your thoughts with other readers.

facebook.com/kensingtonpublishing
twitter.com/kensingtonbooks

Tell us what you think!

To share your thoughts, submit a review,
or sign up for our eNewsletters, please visit:
KensingtonBooks.com/TellUs.